In A World Of Our Own

Chasing Dreams and Love

A. Goswami

A GOSWAMI

Free Lesbian Romance Novel by A Goswami

Hello Dear Readers,

Please don't forget to download your **free 300-page** Lesbian Romance Novel worth $3.99 by me, A. Goswami, that I would like to present to you as a thank you for reading and enjoying this book.

Download it right now by clicking here

For paperback readers, copy, and paste this link in your browser : mailchi.mp/8f0f411551ce/a-goswami

Chapter One

(Sophia)

I play absentmindedly with the now cold chicken meatballs on my plate, my fork dancing around the food as my mind drifts to the people around me. The restaurant buzzes with laughter and clinking glasses, but the absence of one particular person starts to eat at my patience.

Chris. Always late, always unpredictable. I shoot a quick text to him, my annoyance clear even through the screen. But no reply. Typical.

My thoughts are interrupted by a sudden commotion at the door. I look up to see Chris barging in, almost knocking over a couple of people in his haste. He's disheveled and out of breath, but the sight of him only fuels my anger.

"There you are!" I snap, unable to mask the irritation in my voice. "You know, some of us actually value punctuality."

"And some of us value making millions of dollars for their company," Chris says, running a hand through his wavy blonde hair.

I roll my eyes.

Chris is handsome, in an Abercrombie and Fitch sort of way, but still not handsome enough for me to switch sides.

"How many millions did you make today?" I ask, my tone

dripping with sarcasm.

"Not enough to keep my old man satisfied," Chris says with a light chuckle.

"How much does he want you to make?" I prod, genuinely curious.

"I don't know. He's not happy with any numbers I throw at him. I grated my balls to help us break even in the North, but that's not enough for him; he wants to see profits."

I wave my hand dismissively. "Okay, I'm already bored with your business talk. How have you been? And when you answer, remember I don't want to hear words like 'Excel sheet,' 'corporate meeting,' 'stocks,' or 'share price.' Okay?"

Chris grins at me, his eyes twinkling with mischief. "Speaking of boring, have I told you about my new apartment? It's a killer spot in Manhattan, but what's even more killer is the guy I've started seeing."

I raise an eyebrow. "Oh really? Do tell."

He leans in, lowering his voice. "He's this Wall Street guy. Picture this: We're on a date, and he starts comparing his daily routine to a stock market chart. I mean, if that doesn't scream 'excitement,' what does?"

I can't help but laugh. "That sounds...thrilling. No wonder you're so smitten."

Chris chuckles, nodding. "Oh, you have no idea. He's the kind of guy who thinks a wild night is rearranging his investment portfolio."

"I see your dating life is as fascinating as ever," I say, smirking.

"At least I'm dating, Miss 'I can't stand even the thought of it,'" he retorts, playfully poking me in the ribs.

I swat his hand away. "Hey, I have my standards. And they

include not listening to someone drone on about stock options over dinner."

Chris laughs, shaking his head. "Fair enough, fair enough. But seriously, Soph, when's the last time you went on a date?"

I sigh, avoiding his gaze. "I don't know, Chris. It's just not something I'm interested in right now."

"And that's because… you're a hideous ogre, who smells like the New York Subway?"

"Yeah, that's the reason. I'm a wrinkling old ogre who managed to become a supermodel. I must be the luckiest ogre alive," I say, ignoring how a part of that sentence is true. "Anyway, you know the reason."

"Firstly, Shrek is the luckiest ogre alive, and second, I think it's a shitty reason."

"Did you pull me out of the comfort of my house to make me feel bad about my dating life?" I ask, taking a bite out of my meatballs.

Chris's smile fades, and his eyes start darting around the room, avoiding mine. I can see him fidgeting with the napkin on the table.

"Sophia," he begins, his voice cracking a little. "There's something I need to ask you. And before you jump to conclusions, it's up to you if you want to help me or not, but I really, really hope you will."

I raise an eyebrow, intrigued by his sudden shift in demeanor. "You're acting all mysterious. Spill it, Chris. I'll decide if I want to help once I hear what you have to say."

He takes a deep breath, clearly struggling to find the right words. "It's about my family… and… and the upcoming reunion. I need you to pretend to be my girlfriend."

I nearly choke on my meatball, eyes widening at his

request. For a moment, all I can do is stare at him, trying to comprehend what he's just asked of me.

"What?" I manage to mutter.

"See, you're making that face again. That tells me you don't like the idea already."

I scrunch my nose, looking at him incredulously. "Duh! You're gay, and I'm also gay. The thought of holding your hand makes me wanna puke."

Chris leans forward, his blue eyes twinkling. "But wait till you hear what's up for grabs!"

"What? A date with Kendall Jenner? Because that's the only way I'm doing this."

Chris shakes his head, a mischievous grin on his face. "Even better. A shot at me becoming the CEO of Anderson Group of Departmental Stores, and you... becoming the official face of the brand. The brand ambassador, baby!"

I blink, stunned. My mind races, processing his words. "The brand ambassador? For Anderson Group?"

"Bingo!"

"What's the catch, Blondie? This sounds too good to be true."

He spreads his hands, still smiling. "There's no catch. You know how my father is a staunch conservative? So, that fact has made it a little difficult for me to come out to him. And now, he's looking to hand the company over to someone else, and he is too proud to give it to an outsider. That leaves either me," he points dramatically at himself, "or my younger sister, Alissa, who heads the Southern division."

"And you want to win over your father by showing him you're on your way to becoming a family man yourself, right?" I ask, understanding his plan.

"Yeah, that, and also he... kinda... told me directly that he'll only give me the position if I do something to kill the rumors around my sexuality."

"He knows?!" I exclaim, my eyes widening.

"No, but the corporate world is evil, babe," Chris sighs. "Our enemies have been doing a good job trying to embarrass him by... using these rumors."

"So, this family reunion..." I begin, narrowing my eyes.

"Is where he will decide and let people know," Chris interjects. "I need to make a strong impression on him. Like really strong, Soph."

I nod, letting his words sink in before asking, "What about your sister? Does she have a shot?"

"She might. She's doing great down south," Chris explains, pride mixed with concern in his voice. "The revenues are through the roof, unlike anything we have seen before. But it will be tough for her. Dad being a traditionalist and all, he won't give it to a woman, even if she is his own daughter."

"I don't really like your dad too much. What age is he living in?" I mutter, annoyance bubbling up.

"Don't get me started," Chris groans. "But that's beyond the point. Look, I know I deserve it, and not because I am a man. I have worked hard all these years. I was the one that expanded our company into the northern states. I know I can do it. I just... need you to be my beautiful girlfriend for a month."

"A month?" I gape at Chris, shock written all over my face. "Bro, that's a long time to fake anything, let alone an entire relationship."

"It will work, Soph. Trust me," Chris pleads, his eyes sincere.

I take a deep breath, considering the opportunity in front of me.

"You've done a lot for me, Chris," I begin, capturing his blue eyes with a look of seriousness. "You came to my rescue when my career was done. And I can't even imagine how difficult it must be for you to hide who you are, for the sake of your ambitions and career. I'll do it, blondie. But…" I pause, my brows furrowing, "I will need intel on your family members, and we will need to come up with a plan, or some kind of a blueprint."

"Oh my god, you have no idea how relieved I am to hear that! You are a true friend, Soph!" Chris exclaims, his face lighting up.

"Yeah, yeah, just don't get me shot by your gun-slinging Texan father once he finds out it was all a lie." I smile, a playful glint in my eyes.

Chris chuckles and waves over a waitress, ordering a bottle of red wine. "Okay, so we leave in three days."

"Great, why didn't you tell me the day before, you idiot?" I quip, rolling my eyes.

"I am two years older than you. Show some respect," Chris retorts, his tone mock serious.

"Shut up, and tell me where we are going, and how many Andersons I will have to tolerate," I demand, leaning back in my chair and eyeing him with playful defiance.

Chris smirks, leaning in to whisper the details, but I can tell he's still on cloud nine after my agreement.

Chris leans in, his eyes bright with excitement. "Okay, Soph, let's get down to business. You're going to meet seven Andersons in total. Brace yourself."

I tilt my head, feigning shock, "Seven? Only? I was hoping for a dozen at least. Break it down for me."

He grins. "First, there's my father, Henry. Shrewd

businessman, self-made billionaire, and the hardest nut to crack."

"Sounds delightful," I interject, raising an eyebrow. "Where does he keep his billions? In the study with him?"

"Most likely," Chris laughs, "He's usually locked up in his study, so you'll be safe. Just don't challenge him to a game of chess. My mother, Mary, she's an angel. You'll love her; she adores me, so she'll love you too."

"How could anyone not?" I tease. "Alright, who else?"

"Next up, Uncle Daniel and Aunt Martha. They run the ranch we'll be staying at. He acts all tough but turns into a puddle around my father. Martha is his shadow, religious and conservative."

I pull a face. "Oh boy, I'm going to need a drink or two around them."

"You and I both," Chris agrees. "And then there's their daughter, Susie. A real religious zealot. Think anti-modernism, strict upbringing, the whole package."

"So, no fun talks about the latest fashion trends with her, then?" I quip, smirking.

Chris shakes his head. "Definitely not. Last but not least, my dear sister Alissa. Bright, clever, liberal, but she's Daddy's girl. She's the only one standing in my way for the CEO position."

I lean in, my eyes narrowing. "So we've got to charm her without letting her get suspicious?"

"Exactly," Chris nods, his eyes serious.

I sigh, leaning back. "Sounds like a walk in the park. Tell me about the ranch, though. I need to know where I'll be pretending to be madly in love with you."

Chris's eyes twinkle. "It's a vast place, horses, cattle, a real Texan ranch. Think barn dances, open fields, and sunsets. You'll love it."

I shudder dramatically. "I'll have to take your word on that. But seriously, Chris, a barn dance?"

He chuckles, "You'll fit right in, cowgirl."

I roll my eyes. "I'll have to get boots, won't I?"

"Absolutely," he confirms, grinning. "But don't worry, we'll have fun. We'll make this work."

I look at Chris with wide eyes. "Horses could be a problem, though. Please tell me you're not expecting me to ride one. I have nightmares about being trampled to death by those things!"

Chris laughs, his eyes dancing with amusement. "Don't worry, my love. The only thing you need to focus on is taking care of your devoted boyfriend." He flutters his eyes at me, and I can't help but laugh.

"Imagine if your macho friends could see you now," I tease, smirking.

"I'll have you know I'm in touch with my feminine side," he retorts, feigning offense.

I can't resist pushing further. "So, is your sister hot?"

Chris's eyes widen. "Ew! How am I supposed to answer that?"

I grin. "Okay, is she good-looking? Is that better, you son of a conservative?"

He almost chokes on his wine. "Yes, she is. Takes after her dashing brother."

"Blonde?" I ask, leaning forward.

"Very blonde," he confirms, a playful glint in his eye.

I narrow my eyes, trying to rile him up. "Will she be a distraction for me?"

"She's straight, Soph, and even if she wasn't, you're not messing up our plan by hitting on my sister," he warns, but I can see the smile threatening to break through.

"Don't worry, my corporate automaton. I've sworn off all romantic feelings and distractions," I assure him, raising my glass.

"That makes you more robotic than me," he quips, clinking his glass with mine.

"Happy to be one," I reply, laughing. "I'm a robot with style."

∞∞∞

I pick up the phone, seeing Mom's name on the screen. "Hey Mom! How's everything? Still in London?" I chirp, trying to mask the disappointment that's already creeping in.

"Oh, darling, yes," she says, sounding distracted. "You know, these press tours can be so exhausting. Bella's just been marvelous, though. How are you, sweetie?"

"I'm good, Mom." I force a smile even though she can't see it. "Looking forward to seeing you this weekend. How's the new album going?"

There's a pause, and I can already feel the letdown coming. "About that, Soph..." she trails off, "We have this thing that came up. Bella's got an interview with BBC, and then there's a charity event. I don't think I'll be able to make it this weekend."

The sting hits me, and I try to laugh it off. "Again? Mom, you promised."

"I know, darling, I know," she says, her voice filled with false cheerfulness. "It's just one of those things. You know how it is. Bella's career is really taking off."

"Bella, Bella, Bella," I mutter under my breath, biting back the jealousy. "Yeah, I know, Mom. Bella's the best."

"Sophia, don't be like that," she chides, picking up on my tone.

"I'm not being anything, Mom. I get it. It's business." I fight back the tears, not wanting her to hear them in my voice. "We'll catch up another time."

"Sophia, I love you. We'll make plans soon. I promise."

"Yeah, love you too, Mom," I say, ending the call and staring at the screen, feeling that familiar ache of being second best.

It's always about Bella these days. She's more successful, more everything. And now, she's even closer to my mom than I am. I shove the phone away, angry at myself for feeling this way, but unable to shake the jealousy that's gnawing at me.

I flop down on the couch, the phone call with Mom still buzzing in my ears. The loft used to be filled with so much life, so much energy. Laughter, banter, late-night conversations—it's all a memory now.

Bella's voice would fill the space with her soulful singing. Kaylee, my ex, always joking around, pulling pranks. We'd spend hours in this very room, arguing about movies, music, or anything else that caught our fancy.

And now? It's just me.

The emptiness echoes, bouncing off the walls, reverberating in the silence. The memories play like a movie in my mind, so vivid and yet so distant.

Bella, my once roommate, now a globe-trotting superstar, lighting up stages around the world. And loving my mom. Who could've seen that coming? I blessed their relationship, really, I did. But lately, it's just been grating on me. It's like they're in their own bubble, and I'm on the outside looking in.

And Kaylee? We broke up. It was mutual, but it still stings. The massive bed in my room feels so cold without her, so I've taken to sleeping on this very couch.

I wrap myself in a blanket, feeling the chill in the room. I tuck myself in, looking around at the emptiness, the shadows that stretch and dance. I can almost hear the laughter, the banter, the love that once filled this space.

But it's gone now. All changed. All moved on.

I close my eyes, fighting the tears. Life moves fast, and sometimes, it's hard to keep up. The people I once considered my closest companions have their own lives, their own journeys, and I'm left behind, trying to figure out where I fit in this new reality.

I drift off to sleep, the thoughts swirling, the loneliness aching. I'll wake up to a new day, a new challenge. But tonight, I allow myself to feel the loss, the longing, the nostalgia for what once was.

∞∞∞

The sound of hooves pounding fills my ears, my heart racing in time. Horses, galloping at me, wild-eyed and ferocious. Kaylee's hand in mine, warm and reassuring. But something's wrong. I can feel it in the pit of my stomach.

The horses come closer, their eyes gleaming, and suddenly Kaylee's hand slips from mine. She's gone, deserting me. The terror grips me, clawing at my insides.

The horses charge, their nostrils flaring, their hooves thundering. I can't move, can't run. I'm trapped, helpless, fear washing over me in waves.

I wake up with a start, sweating and scared, the remnants

of the nightmare clinging to me. My breath comes in gasps, my body trembling.

I look around, disoriented, the loft quiet and still. The dream was so real, so vivid, so terrifying. I wipe the sweat from my brow, trying to shake off the fear, but it lingers, haunting me.

It was just a dream, I tell myself. Just a dream.

I try to sleep, but the memories, the longing, the desire, they won't leave me alone. My mind drifts back to Kaylee, to her touch, her smile, her love.

I know it's toxic, know it's wrong, but I can't help myself. I close my eyes, and she's there, with me, beside me. I can feel her body against mine, hear her whispered words of love, taste her lips on mine.

I can't resist it anymore, the pull of the past, the need to feel something, anything. The memory of Kaylee's touch is too strong, too real. My mind drifts to a time when we were together, happy, alive.

I close my eyes, and she's there with me. I can see her smile, hear her laugh, feel her body pressed against mine. The memory is so vivid, so intense, it's like she's really here.

My breath catches as I imagine her hand in mine, guiding me, encouraging me. Her fingers trace the lines of my body, her touch gentle and loving, knowing exactly what I need.

I give in to the fantasy, my own hand taking over where my mind's Kaylee left off. I know it's wrong, know it's just a figment of my imagination, but it feels so right, so real.

My body responds, my heart aching with longing, my soul craving connection. The pleasure builds, slow and steady, each stroke a reminder of what I once had, what I've lost.

I can hear her voice, soft and sweet, whispering words of love and encouragement. Her touch grows more insistent, more demanding, pushing me closer and closer to the edge.

I lose myself in the fantasy, the pleasure, the love. It's all-consuming, all-encompassing, filling me with warmth and connection.

My body trembles, the pleasure peaking, crashing over me in waves. I cry out, a mix of joy and sorrow, pleasure and pain.

I'm left breathless, spent, the fantasy fading, the emptiness returning.

The wheels touch down, and here I am: Dallas, Texas. Stepping into the arrivals gate, I scan the crowd, feeling like a fish out of water. Chris is busy on his phone, coordinating the cavalry that's supposed to rescue us from the hustle and bustle of the airport. "Where is that ride?" he mutters, scrolling through his contacts.

The Texan sun is blazing down on us, and it's only April. A far cry from the unpredictable mood swings of New York weather. I soak it in, wondering, Maybe I'll finally get that sun-kissed glow. Heck, by the end of the month, I'll be a walking advertisement for sunscreen.

Then Chris spots her. "There's Alissa," he says, pointing.

My eyes follow his finger, landing on a vision that practically demands a double-take. She's sauntering toward us in a power suit that could rival Wall Street's finest—tailored to accentuate every curve of her southern charm. I'm struck by her uncanny resemblance to Alissa Violet, a vision in blonde ambition. But Alissa Anderson? She's a spectacle all on her own.

As she gets closer, one of her suited security personnel springs an umbrella to shield her from the sun. With a wave of her hand, she dismisses the offer. But then she does something unexpected. She grabs the umbrella and opens it over the security guy himself, laughing as he squirms in mock humiliation.

Well, she's definitely not one for following the script, I think, already captivated.

As I take a closer look at Alissa, it's like a punch to my aesthetic senses. She's the epitome of southern elegance but with the modernity of a New York influencer. She's got those wide, deep blue eyes framed by long, lush lashes. Her straight blonde hair flows down her back, contrasting sharply against her dark business suit. Her lips? Painted the perfect shade of nude-pink, like they were begging to make a statement without uttering a word.

Just as I'm piecing together this walking, talking piece of art, I'm jolted back to Earth by her embrace. A soft scent, something like vanilla mixed with exotic spices, fills the air around her. It's intoxicating, paralyzing even. For a few seconds, I'm lost. When I finally regain my senses, her voice snaps me back to reality.

"Welcome to Texas, Sophia. It's so lovely to meet you," she says, releasing me from her hug but not from her spell.

"You really are a sight for sore eyes, aren't you? I saw you from afar, and I was sure you couldn't be my brother's girlfriend. Surely, he couldn't have snagged someone like you!"

I smile and do a very awkward job of receiving her compliments.

"It took a lot of begging on his part, I'll admit, and I couldn't say no to those sad, blue eyes," I say, my gaze lingering on the blue in Alissa's eyes.

"Brother, I am impressed!" Alissa and Chris do a fist bump, and I feel myself sinking into the quicksand of even more embarrassment.

"I saw you walking toward us as well, and I was also

mesmerized. I thought Chris was the best-looking one in the family, but clearly, I was wrong," I say, trying to keep my voice casual, not letting the hopeless, desperate sigh of wonderment creep into it.

"Babe, you are in Texas. You'll find curvaceous blondes walking down the streets every two seconds, but you... you look exotic. You will stand out here. Especially with that mole on your face; it's like an exclamation mark for your beauty, like it's telling us, 'There she is, Sophia, ladies and gentlemen!'"

Wow, how did she come up with that so quickly?

Chris rolls his eyes but joins in the laughter. "A month of this banter and we'll all need a vacation from our vacation."

"So how was your flight, Sophia?" Alissa asks, diverting the topic.

"Long and boring. But the in-flight movie was 'The Nun,' so I got to hide behind the complimentary airline blanket," I say.

"Ah, that's one way to start a trip," Alissa nods. "I usually just sleep and hope to wake up in another dimension—ideally, one where I'm sunbathing in Bora Bora."

I picture my fake boyfriend's sister in a skimpy bikini, laying down on a white sand beach, and berate myself mentally for being a sucker for blondes in skimpy bikinis.

"I guess we all have our coping mechanisms," I say.

"So when was the last time you guys saw each other?" I ask, turning the focus back on them.

"Feels like ages," Alissa sighs. "I've been drowning in work. It's a jungle out there in the department store world. You turn your back for one second, and you're neck-deep in Black Friday planning."

"A whole month here might be your much-needed break then," I say, smiling at her.

"You're not wrong, but I will still be working. I stay in Dallas, which is like an hour away from the ranch, so...work won't really leave me," Alissa replies, a thoughtful look crossing her face. "A month can be a lifetime if you make it interesting though."

At that moment, I can't help but think, Why do the most captivating women I meet always have to be the forbidden fruit?

I barely have time to get my bearings when two men burst onto the scene, giving Chris a firm smack on the back of his head.

"Chris, dude! Thought you could slide into town without telling us?" the first one, tall with messy curls, blurts out.

"Mark, Jared, what the—? How'd you guys know I was back?" Chris rubs the spot where he was smacked, but he's grinning like a Cheshire cat.

"We've got our ways, man," says Jared, who's built like a tank but has this mischievous look that makes you want to join whatever scheme he's planning.

"Meet Sophia, everyone," Chris says, nodding toward me, "And you've already met the family diva, Alissa."

I'm doing my best to keep up with the quick-fire introduction. "Hi, I'm Sophia," I muster a greeting.

"Wow, Chris, keeping secrets now? You didn't tell us you were dating a supermodel," Mark says, openly checking me out.

I see Alissa's eyes narrow for a moment. "Classy, as always, Mark," she comments, her tone a mixture of annoyance and jest.

"Come on, she's really something, Alissa. Even you can't deny it," Jared adds, shooting a quick glance from Alissa to me.

"Let's keep it respectful, shall we? Sophia isn't an exhibit," Alissa replies, her voice holding an edge of warning but she keeps her smile on.

"We're just joking, Alissa, don't be the spoilsport you've

always been," Mark shoots back.

"I haven't been the spoilsport, from what I remember, Melancholy Mark!"

"Wow, still stuck on that?" Mark retorts.

"Guys, chill out! Stop acting like we're still kids," Chris jumps in. Alissa and Mark glare at each other for a few seconds, then divert their eyes to us, the new couple in town.

"Man, I'm really happy for you," Jared tries to ease the tension, giving Chris a hug. "And I can't wait to mess around for a month at the ranch, like old times, eh?"

"Yeah, like old times," Chris agrees, pulling me in for a side hug.

I lean into Chris, playing my part perfectly.

"So, how are you guys getting to the ranch?" Mark asks.

"Me being present here should explain that, genius," Alissa mutters.

"Well, from this moment onwards, you're off duty. We'll take it from here. Sophia, if you'd like to ride in a proper Texan vehicle and have a little fun, follow us. Or if you'd like to be holed up in a boring old Mercedes, follow the spoilsport," Mark gestures at Alissa, who rolls her eyes.

I look at Chris, hoping he will save me from this situation, but he stays quiet, apparently enjoying my dilemma.

"I think I'd pick the Merc. I've had a long flight, and I don't think I have the energy to keep up with you boys right now. How about you drive Chris, and I follow with Alissa?"

Marks looks disappointed, but relents, "Okay, we'll make you one of the boys soon enough. Alright Chris, the monster awaits. Give us your bags."

∞∞∞

"You can leave us here, I'm in the mood to drive," Alissa tells the man in the suit, trailing behind us. "Us girls can have fun too, right?" She winks at me.

I return her grin, my heart doing a silly somersault. "Lead the way."

Security Man—yep, I'm just going to call him that in my head—nods and hands over the keys to Alissa before stashing our luggage into the trunk. He's all efficiency, this one.

"Thank you," Alissa pipes up, gripping the keys like a queen holding her scepter. I echo the sentiment, and he saunters off, probably to hail a cab or something.

Then, as if it's the most natural thing in the world, Alissa walks around to the passenger side and holds the door open for me. My heart, already doing gymnastics, now feels like it's on a trampoline.

I slide into the car, quipping, "Who needs Prince Charming when you've got a Texan bombshell opening the door for you?" I can't help but let a goofy smile stretch across my face.

Alissa's British twang dances through the car as she quips, "I also only open doors for Persian Princesses, darling."

I retort, "Oxford or Cambridge?"

She smirks. "Both. Undergrad at Oxford, Masters at Cambridge."

God, Mom would worship this woman.

"A Texan with a British education... sounds rare."

She floors the gas pedal, making the Mercedes leap forward. "I'm a rarity. Had to fight tooth and nail to even get involved in the family business. Dad's not too keen on women in power, you see."

"Yeah, I've heard," I say, my eyes darting to her Prada shades as she deftly maneuvers the car.

Damn, she's like a Fast and Furious character.

"He'll change. He's just got those claws of traditionality dug in deep," she adds.

"Let's hope," I say, still entranced by her driving skills. This woman is something else.

Then, she blindsides me with, "So, how did you end up with my brother?"

"He gave me a chance when no one else would. Helped me out with the Anderson Launch Campaign in New York."

"So, a charity case?" she teases, her blazer now tossed aside to reveal a white button-up that clings to her like a second skin.

I clear my dry throat. "No. I fell for him. He's hard-working, kind, and knows how to treat a woman."

Her smirk turns mysterious. "You really believe that, don't you?"

"Why? Don't you?" I ask, reading skepticism in her eyes.

"Let's just say, I haven't seen him in a while. I guess he must have changed," she muses.

The tension sits there for a moment, like an uninvited guest. Then, she throws me another curveball, "Do you want to go the scenic route or the quick way?"

"What's the scenic route?" I ask.

Alissa's mischievous grin widens. "The scenic route? Oh, that's just the same route, but with me gradually losing articles of clothing until I'm driving in lingerie."

I feel my eyes go saucer-wide. Is she serious? But then she

bursts into laughter, shattering the bubble of absurdity.

"I'm kidding, I'm kidding! The scenic route goes through the heartland of Texas. The short route is the freeway. Your choice."

A sigh of relief escapes me. Seeing Alissa in lingerie might just short-circuit my tired brain. "I think the shorter route. I'm beat."

Alissa considers this, her fingers drumming on the steering wheel. "How about we leave it to fate? Heads, we go scenic. Tails, freeway. Deal?"

Do I really want to flip a coin with a woman who suggested driving in lingerie as the scenic route? Eh, why not. "Deal," I say, not wanting to be a buzzkill.

She produces a coin from somewhere—honestly, I don't even want to know where—and flips it. It clatters on the dashboard: heads.

My heart sinks a little, but Alissa catches the look on my face and chuckles. "Don't worry, darlin'. You're the guest, and Southern hospitality is still a thing. We'll go your way. But next time, I won't go easy on you."

She winks and, honestly, I don't know if I'm relieved or just a tiny bit disappointed. But hey, there's always a 'next time,' right?

"So, what do you do, Sophia? I only got the cliff notes from Chris."

"Well, I was a model for several years. Had a good run, too. Walked for some big names, you know? But these days, it's mostly social media influencing."

"Really? That's a pretty eclectic career shift. Why'd you make the move?"

I sigh, twirling a strand of hair around my finger. "To be

honest, work in modeling sort of dried up. Seems like I've aged out of the industry. Can you believe it?"

Alissa glances at me, eyes wide. "Aged out? How old are you?"

"Twenty-six."

She chuckles. "Geez, ancient, really. All jokes aside, you're probably the hottest 26-year-old I've ever met."

I laugh but can't help feeling bittersweet. "Just last month, I lost a modeling gig to an 18-year-old. They said they were looking for a 'fresh face.' I guess 26 is ancient in dog years or something."

"Ah, the whimsical world of fashion." She rolls her eyes. "Well, if Chris ever stops giving you work for some reason, you're always welcome to work at the Southern Division of Anderson Corp. Our marketing team could use someone with your experience."

I'm touched by her offer. "Really? You'd do that for me?"

"You're basically family now, so yeah, why not? Besides, you'd be a...shall we say, seasoned addition to our campaigns."

I chuckle. "Seasoned? Wow, you sure know how to flatter a woman."

She winks. "Well, what are future sisters-in-law for?"

To hook up with while no one is watching? Geez, I am turning into a wild woman in Texas.

She takes a turn, and we find ourselves merging onto the freeway. "You comfy? Want some music or something?"

"Yeah, that would be nice. Anything in particular you're in the mood for?" I ask.

"How about some classic country? When in Rome—or Texas, in this case." She grins.

"Sounds good to me."

As the strumming guitars and soulful lyrics fill the car, I find myself getting lost in thought, staring out the window at the sprawling landscapes whizzing by.

"You're really quiet all of a sudden," Alissa says, breaking the silence. "Something on your mind?"

"Oh, just thinking about how different Texas is from New York," I reply.

She smiles. "You mean how we actually have space between buildings and don't live in sardine cans?"

I chuckle. "Yeah, something like that."

"Well, get used to it, darling. By the time you leave Texas, you'll be a converted cowgirl," Alissa says with a wink.

The thought makes me laugh. "I can't imagine myself in cowboy boots and a Stetson."

"Why not? You'd look great. Plus, we can Instagram it. 'Sophia's Southern Makeover,' or something like that," she suggests, tapping her fingers on the steering wheel in rhythm with the music.

I consider it for a moment. "Well, if it involves a fun day out with you, then I'm in."

She glances over with a smile that could light up a room. "Deal. But remember, I won't be going easy on you. I told you, Southern hospitality has its limits."

I grin back. "I'd expect nothing less."

Just as the atmosphere reaches a tantalizing high, Alissa's phone buzzes loudly with a message notification. "Ah, work stuff. I've got to take this, excuse me for a second," she apologizes, her eyes darting to the phone as she puts on her AirPods.

I nod, watching her pull up the work call. "No worries, take your time."

As Alissa starts talking, her tone switches to a more professional but equally charming one. I can hear her negotiating with someone on the other end, handling what sounds like a full-blown emergency at one of their departmental stores in Austin.

"I understand, Tim, but you need to get security on that right away. And yes, inform me as soon as the police arrive," she instructs, her voice firm but not harsh.

It's entrancing to watch her juggle it all so effortlessly, to see this different side of her. She's not just a pretty face with a teasing smile; she's a competent, confident woman who knows how to manage a crisis.

Alissa takes another call, her eyes narrowing a bit as she listens. "No, no, no. I've told you before, you can't just do markdowns without clearing it through corporate. It messes up our whole pricing strategy," she says, still remarkably calm, yet assertive.

In contrast, I think of Chris in a work emergency—his face flushed, fists clenched. He tends to snap and growl, the stress transforming him into a different beast entirely. Alissa's cool demeanor is a stark contrast, one that has me even more intrigued.

"Now, listen," Alissa continues, "I need you to reverse the changes. Yes, I understand it'll take time, but it needs to be done. I'll discuss this with you in detail once I'm back. Just fix it for now."

My gaze drifts from her to the passing scenery. It's funny, how emergencies bring out the core of a person, how they handle pressure revealing a glimpse into their inner world. Alissa is grace under fire, a captain steering her ship smoothly even in turbulent waters.

Alissa mutes her mic for a moment and looks over at me. "I'm really sorry about this, Sophia. I promise we'll catch up properly soon."

"I totally get it," I assure her, even though the electric vibe from earlier seems to have diffused a bit.

She smiles, grateful, and unmutes herself to dive into another call. "Hi, Emily. Update me on the Dallas situation, please."

I leave Alissa to be the powerhouse that she clearly is, and I glance out of the window.

Another woman who's killing it. An addition to the roster of successful women in my life. Exactly what I need to kick me while I am down.

I take a deep breath, and try to drown out the soft, yet assertive voice of Alissa, belting out instructions, while efficiently driving us to her home.

The Merc turns onto a gravel road, and suddenly I'm in awe. Forget Pinterest-worthy; this place needs a freaking magazine feature. Acres of untouched land stretch as far as my eyes can see, like some kind of emerald tapestry stitched by Mother Nature herself. Horses graze peacefully in expansive paddocks, their tails swishing lazily in the Texas heat.

"You ever been to a ranch?" Alissa asks, sensing my wide-eyed wonder.

"No, this is my first rodeo," I quip, unable to resist the pun.

Alissa chuckles. "Well, you picked the right place for your initiation."

The car rolls up a long driveway, and my eyes are drawn to a colossal mansion in the middle of the ranch, built from rugged stone. It's like old-world architecture took a time machine to the modern day.

"Damn, it's like the Downton Abbey of Texas!" I blurt out.

"That's one way to put it," Alissa says, a hint of pride tingeing her voice. "This ranch belonged to the O'Sullivan family before we bought it."

"The O'Sullivans? As in..."

"As in one of the oldest Texan cattle baron families. They say some of the stones in the house are as old as Texas itself."

The car glides past a picturesque lake that shimmers under the Texan sun. "Do you guys fish in there?" I ask, eyes widening at the possibility.

"Oh, Chris and Jared have tried, but I think the fish are too smart for them."

She steers the car towards the mansion. "So what else do I need to know about this paradise?"

"That it's not always paradise. Ranching is hard work, but it's a part of us. We're born and bred into it," Alissa explains.

We finally pull up to the entrance of the mansion, where a couple of staff members are waiting. They rush over and open our doors before unloading our luggage from the trunk.

"Thank you," I nod to the help, still trying to absorb the grandeur surrounding me.

"See? Even our southern hospitality is grand," Alissa winks, and I realize that one of these winks will be the death of me in the coming days.

"Ready to meet the Andersons?" Alissa poses the question like she's offering me a ticket to an exclusive show.

"Yeah, but can't we wait for Chris?"

Her eyes lock onto mine. "Why do you need Chris when you have the prettier Anderson to keep you company?"

A reluctant smile spreads across my face. "Fine, you'll do for moral support."

As we stand there, the Texas wind tousles Alissa's golden locks. "Listen, don't take anything too personally. And for the love of God, don't bring up the Democrats around Dad. If there are two things he can't stand, it's Bloomingdales and the Democratic Party."

I can't help but laugh. "Well, my entire family votes blue."

"Try to forget the color blue for a bit then, and you'll be fine," Alissa reassures, patting me lightly on the back.

"Come, Princess of Persia. The Andersons await!" Alissa's words ring in my ears as she leads me through a grand doorway. As we step into the expansive foyer, I'm immediately struck by its blend of old-world charm and modern sophistication. Dark marble floors stretch in every direction. Antique chandeliers hang from high ceilings, casting a golden glow. Persian rugs accent the space, and a grand piano sits elegantly in a corner. Mounted heads of various animals and antique guns adorn the walls, punctuated by a massive family portrait that draws the eye.

"Alissa! You're back!" A voice echoes from an opulent staircase. Descending is a woman almost ethereal in her grace—Mary, Alissa's mom and Chris's mother. She's wearing a classy summer dress, floral prints making her look even more inviting.

Mary embraces Alissa and then turns to me, her eyes softening. "Oh, you must be Sophia. You're even more beautiful than Christopher said."

I extend a handshake, but she pulls me into a warm hug instead. "Nice to meet you, Sophia," she says, stepping back but still holding my hands as if afraid to completely let go.

A heavyset man walks in from an adjoining room. Wearing casual jeans and a button-down, he has the robust aura of someone who's worked the land. "Daniel, this is Sophia," Mary introduces.

Daniel steps forward, extending a rough hand for a firm handshake. "Good to meet you, Sophia. How was your trip?"

"Very comfortable, thank you," I reply, appreciating the small talk.

"Nice of you to visit us. The ranch could use some new faces," he chuckles, his demeanor softening, if only for a moment.

That's when Martha, Daniel's wife, joins the circle. She's in a modest floral dress, her eyes appraising me with curiosity more than judgment. "I trust you've been well looked after?"

"Absolutely," I confirm with a smile.

Finally, a younger woman steps in—Susie, their daughter. She's beautiful, like a young Emma Watson, but dressed conservatively in a long skirt and a top that barely shows any skin. "You're Sophia, then?" she asks, her eyes wide with what could be seen as genuine interest.

"Yep, that's me," I reply, offering a smile.

Just as the atmosphere starts to feel a tad more comfortable, Daniel drops the bomb. "You're the model, aren't you? Not much work in that line these days, I hear."

Martha picks up the cue, her smile still in place. "Competitive but not very... wholesome, you know? Not like working on a ranch."

Susie jumps in next. "You know, I once wanted to be a model. But Mama helped get those sinful thoughts out of my head."

Mary finally intervenes, trying to douse the growing flames. "Well, she is beautiful, isn't she? You've got that going for you, dear."

I force a chuckle, "Well, different strokes for different folks."

Alissa, looking to divert attention, checks her phone. "It's Chris. They're stopping for burgers. Do either of you want anything?"

I shake my head. "No, thanks. Have to maintain my figure, you know."

Martha rolls her eyes, but Alissa fires back a quick reply. "Neither of us wants any. I'm watching my weight, too."

I can literally feel the walls closing in on me. I knew the Andersons were going to be difficult, but not 'modeling is not wholesome' difficult.

"Sophia, dear, you must be tired after all the traveling," Mary says, her eyes as kind as ever.

"Yeah," I whisper.

"Alissa, would you mind showing Sophia her room, or do you want me to ask one of the housekeepers?"

"I'll gladly do it, Mom."

"I hope they won't be sharing the room…seeing they aren't married and all," Martha's curt voice slices the air, and for a minute, I think I have heard her wrong.

"I'll be sleeping alone?" I look around in confusion.

"Umm…for a while. Until Daniel and Henry are certain that you and Chris are serious about each other," Mary says.

FML.

"Okay, Alissa, can you take me to my room, where I'll be sleeping alone?" I say, unable to hide the irritation in my voice.

Alissa throws me an apologetic look, grabs me by my elbow, and leads me away. "I'll try and talk to Dad. This is outrageous," she says, as I feel the stares from the Andersons drilling a hole in my back.

∞ ∞ ∞

The pounding hooves reverberate in my ears, a deafening crescendo that almost drowns out my own heartbeat. A herd of horses gallops toward me through a suffocating fog. This time, my mom—Ava—is holding my hand, her fingers interlocked with mine. For a fleeting moment, I feel a sense of safety, until she loosens her grip and lets go just as the horses close in. "Mom!" My voice breaks, and I wake up, gasping for air.

I sit upright, frantically looking around to ground myself. I'm alone in this massive ranch room. It's an uncanny mix of ancient and modern—a four-poster bed with plush bedding, oak tables with antique trinkets, towering bookshelves filled with everything from ancient history to contemporary novels. Mounted heads of deer and bison loom from the walls, keeping company with some ornate mirrors. A plush, deep-red armchair sits near a fireplace that probably has stories of its own.

Big windows frame the back of the ranch and its sprawling grounds, extending all the way to the stables. The curtains are like specters in the wind, flapping wildly as they let in gusts of the brewing storm outside. Thunder cracks. Lightning illuminates the room in eerie flashes. Even from here, I can hear the horses in the stables neighing like mad. Perfect. From dream horses to real ones, all in the span of a second.

Just when I think I might have to pop a Xanax, a knock on the door jolts me. "Sophia, can I come in?" It's Alissa's voice, laced with a hint of concern.

"Sure, come on in," I call out.

The door swings open, and Alissa walks in, wrapped in a light pink silk nightdress. My God, she's a vision. The fabric clings to her, highlighting every curve, stopping just short enough to leave a lot to the imagination. For a moment, the howling wind and the panicked horses fade into the background.

"Chris is finally home," she announces, taking a seat on the edge of my bed.

"What time is it?" I ask, trying not to sound as unsettled as I feel.

"It's midnight. You've been sleeping for hours. Hungry?"

I shake my head. "Not hungry, just a little...scared, I guess."

Alissa's eyes soften. "Storms can be unnerving, can't they? But sometimes, they're just nature's way of clearing the air."

"It's not the storm, actually. It's the horses," I blurt out before I can stop myself.

"Horses?" Alissa arches an eyebrow, looking genuinely puzzled. "Why?"

"I wish I knew," I say, exhaling. "I see them in my dreams, always galloping towards me. It's terrifying."

"Horses do the opposite for me," Alissa says, her voice softening. "I find it therapeutic, especially groundwork. You know, basic tasks that help establish a bond between you and the horse. Lunging, lead changes, stuff like that. Calms my anxiety right down."

"Wow, I wish they could do the same for me," I sigh.

"Tell you what," Alissa begins tentatively, "why don't you sleep in my room? It's just next door, and maybe a change of space will do you good."

"Yes!" The word escapes my lips with a little too much enthusiasm. "I mean, yeah, sure, that sounds great."

Alissa chuckles, standing up and offering her hand. "Well, let's not waste any more time. The night's young, and so are we."

I take her hand, feeling the warmth spread through me like a splash of bourbon on a cold night. As we walk out of my room, it hits me. It's funny how fate works—forcing me into situations I dread, but then throwing in a lifeline just when I need it most. And as far as lifelines go, Alissa is definitely a glamorous one.

But the horses are still in my head, both the dream and the real ones, galloping through the chambers of my mind. As Alissa closes her bedroom door behind us, I can't help but wonder: Can a change of room really calm a storm? Well, if it can't, maybe Alissa can.

I step into Alissa's room and immediately feel like I've walked into a completely different era. It's lit by candles perched in ornate holders, casting warm, flickering light across the room. Forget modern chic or rustic charm, this is straight-up Victorian English. There's intricate woodwork on the furniture, elegant floral wallpaper, and a collection of porcelain figurines on an antique dressing table. Even the bed is a four-poster one, draped with sheer, flowy fabric that matches the silk of her nightdress. It's like the whole room is paying homage to her English sensibilities, from the vintage teapot on a wooden stand to framed silhouettes that give off a Jane Austen vibe.

"Wow, this room is—"

"Very English, I know," Alissa says, cutting me off, but grinning as she does. "Hope you don't mind the candlelight. I find it cozier than electrical lighting."

"It's beautiful," I manage to say, still taking in the sheer attention to detail.

"If you're comfortable sharing a bed with me," she starts, then catches herself as her cheeks color slightly, "I mean, if you're okay sharing the room with me, we can have your things moved here."

I chuckle at her sudden awkwardness. "I'd love to, actually.

Your room feels like a sanctuary."

She beams, looking relieved. "Great! I'll tell the staff to move your things here first thing in the morning."As I sit down on the edge of the bed, the scent of lavender from the candles fills the air. The horses and my haunting dreams seem far away now. Alissa's room, with its English elegance and candlelit ambiance, is like a haven, an escape from the impending storms—both outside and within me.

The sound of rolling thunder is distant, as Alissa and I stare at each other awkwardly for a few seconds.

Why does every conversation with her feel so sexually charged?

"Is it okay if I change into something a little more comfortable?" she asks.

"Yeah," I say, wondering what could be more comfortable than the sexy piece of silk clinging to her body.

"I'll be back, make yourself comfortable." She beams her thousand watt smile at me and saunters into the adjoining bathroom.

I pull the covers to my face, and peer around the room. Everything in the room screams Alissa, and being in the room feels like being inside Alissa herself, however corny that sounds.

Just as I am about to drift back to sleep, Alissa walks out of the bathroom.

Now, It's already been a year since I dabbled into some lovemaking, and watching Alissa in a simple business suit was enough for me to develop an unhealthy and potentially dangerous crush on her, but throw in bright red panties, and a torturously short crop top, with nipple pokies, and Alissa has gone from an unhealthy crush to being the reason my pussy starts pulsating with desire.

I can't help but stare.

God, I feel overdressed in my hoodie and socks.

She moves around the room, blowing out candles, and I'm ensnared. My eyes follow the curve of her hips, the sexy little dimples at the small of her back, and hell, how her lips come together as she blows out each flame. Everything seems to slow down when she bends to reach the lower candles, her hips lining up directly in front of me. The moonlight catches a twinkle in her eye, a secret she's not sharing.

Her hair dangles in loose curls, just brushing her shoulders as she moves. I feel this pull, this yearning I can't quite shake off. It's as if all the ghosts haunting me just faded into the background. Only Alissa exists in this moment.

"Done," she finally says, smiling at me as she straightens up. "Now we can really relax."

Yeah, relax. As if every nerve in my body isn't screaming, 'pay attention, Sophia, this is important.' But why?

Why does this feel so pivotal?

I take a deep breath. "Yeah, relaxation sounds great right about now."

"Feel free to make yourself at home," Alissa's eyes soften, meeting mine. "This room is your room now, too."

"I'm as comfortable as I need to be," I assure her.

"You look tense, babe," she observes.

"I'm fine, Alissa."

"Missing my brother?"

"Yeah," I fib.

Alissa crawls into bed on all fours, like she's determined to make me dissolve right there on her luxurious mattress.

"Did you guys talk?"

"Yeah, he called me. Said he'd be late and told me not to wait up."

Chris had actually apologized for leaving me alone. Jared and Mark weren't letting him off the hook so easily, he said.

"How can he be out with the guys when he has a supermodel waiting for him in bed?" Alissa chuckles, reclining against the enormous pillows, casting a sidelong glance at me.

"It's fine. I don't mind. Plus, you forget that we won't be sharing a room. So, this supermodel will be sleeping alone for the foreseeable future."

"Alone... or with me?"

Fuck my life. Twice over and then multiply it by a gazillion.

"Yeah, I mean with you. I haven't shared a bed with a girl for over a year. My old roommate and I used to sometimes."

"Oh, really? I thought you stayed with my brother?"

Oops.

"Well, it was a back-and-forth thing. I liked having my own space sometimes. Gave me a sense of security."

"I get it. It's more comforting to have your own place and then live with your boyfriend than always fearing you'll be tossed out onto the streets."

I nod. The conversation stalls. Mostly because Alissa has decided to lay on her side, facing me. Her breasts are pushed together, and my brain decides this is its cue to short-circuit.

Was I ever this horny in the past year?

"I think you should sleep now." Her voice practically oozes seduction. She's got to be doing this on purpose.

"Yeah. Thanks for rescuing me tonight," I manage to say.

"No problem." Alissa smiles. "I hope you dream of something sexy tonight, instead of horses trying to kill you."

Can I dream of you? Get a grip, Sophia!

"I'll try," I stammer, my voice barely above a whisper.

Alissa reaches over to her nightstand and picks up a slim volume. "It's Emily Brontë. Her poetry helps me wind down."

She opens the book and her eyes dance over the lines. The sight feels like some soft spell, drawing the chaos out of me.

"Goodnight, Sophia," she whispers without looking up.

"Goodnight," I murmur.

As I close my eyes, the tension slips away. No more stampeding horses, no more vanishing mothers, no more haunting exes. For the first time in forever, sleep welcomes me like an old friend, and I plunge into its peaceful abyss.

But not for long.

I am woken for the second time in one night, but this time, not by the sound of horses, but by…Alissa moaning?

My eyes flutter open, and I hear her.

I sense movement beside me, and the soft, whimpery moans of the blonde.

My heart starts to race.

I am facing away from Alissa, but every fiber in my body wants to turn and see what's going on.

"Ah…aaah."

She is doing her best not to cry out, and to be as still as possible, but it is not working, or…maybe she isn't putting enough effort?

"Fuck…" she moans, "oh yes!"

I squeeze my eyes shut, trying to drown out her voice by the voices in my head, but the voices in my head are asking me to take a look, to see how the gorgeous beauty is writhing in pleasure on the same bed as me, merely inches away…inches away from my touch, inches away from my lips.

A long sigh, a little grunt, and she is done.

The room falls silent, and I imagine her beside me, fingers still inside her, wet, slimy, dripping, begging to be tasted.

My own wetness dampens my panties, and I insert a hand inside my panties.

I know I can do a better job of being silent.

I don't waste time. My finger slips inside, and I bury my face in my pillow, the covers providing the veil of secrecy I need.

I cum within seconds, and for the first time in months, I don't have to resort to imagining Kaylee to reach an orgasm.

Alissa does the job perfectly.

Who knew Alissa and I shared a common trait? Pleasuring ourselves for a dreamless slumber. Maybe we could help each other out someday, or maybe I could lose my friendship with Chris, my chance at being the brand ambassador of a billion dollar company, and my peace of mind.

Chapter Two

(Alissa)

We've got the whole Anderson clan gathered under this massive oak tree for breakfast. The table's sprawling with all kinds of gourmet stuff, but honestly, no one's paying attention. Even the morning sun and chirping birds aren't doing much to lighten the mood. Daniel, Mom, and Martha, are at the head of the table, doing their best to look relaxed, but it's like they've both swallowed a lemon whole.

Susie, my younger cousin, is here too, barely looking up from her phone. Chris, my older brother, seems to be deep in thought, probably about some business deal or another. Sophia's here, visibly out of her element but doing her best to blend in. Oh, and let's not forget the staff, fluttering around us like they've got wings.

The elephant not in the room? Henry Anderson. My dad, the patriarch, the head honcho of Anderson Corp. Everyone's trying to act casual, but let's be real: the moment Henry walks in, that's when the real breakfast meeting starts.

I'm wedged between Sophia and Mom at the breakfast table, the atmosphere so thick you could slice it. Out of the corner of my eye, I catch Chris sliding his hand into Sophia's and giving it a gentle squeeze. They've been quite into public displays of affection this morning—well, Chris has been, at least. Sophia, on the other hand, seems a little hesitant.

In just one day, Sophia has turned into a revelation in my life, intriguing and teasing me in equal measures. Sure, she's my brother's girlfriend, and fantasizing about your future sister-in-law probably borders on the sinful.

But hey, it's all in my head, right?

I've felt pangs of jealousy toward Chris before, but that's mostly been about his male privilege. Never thought I'd envy him for the woman he's with. What a world.

My gaze meets Sophia's. She looks like she's bracing for an orc attack from The Lord of the Rings. When our eyes lock, she offers me a sweet smile. Ah, those full, lush lips that I can never—should never—kiss.

I've always had a soft spot for exotic women, and Sophia fits that bill to a T. From her Persian features to her long, jet-black hair, her deep, coal-like eyes, the mole, bold eyebrows, and the most tempting feature of them all—thick thighs—she's a smorgasbord of temptation. And the fact that I can't have her only fuels my desire.

But it's not just her physical allure that captivates me; it's also the lingering sadness behind her smile, the depths she's hiding. Sophia is like a mirage, an illusion concealing something she might have forgotten herself. I sense it in her words—self-doubt, a reluctance to unleash what I believe is a latent fierceness. I want to discover what dimmed her inner fire.

Just as I'm about to delve deeper into my Sophia-centric musings, a sudden commotion snaps me back to reality. Henry Anderson, the patriarch himself, is making his grand entrance, hustling toward the breakfast table flanked by his trusty secretary, Joanna, and Timothy, the sales honcho at Anderson Corp.

Henry Anderson finally graces us with his presence, swaggering over like he owns the place—well, he does, but you get what I mean. With a thick white beard that looks like it's been manicured to perfection, a stout frame that's more bear than man, and eyes that could make a hyena rethink its life choices, he's the epitome of intimidating. You'd think Logan Roy from "Succession" was based on him or something. "Good morning, everyone," he booms, his voice laced with a cocktail of authority and casual indifference.

His entourage tries to hover around him, but he swats them away like pesky flies. "Not now, Joanna. Timothy, I don't need you here. Shoo," he dismisses, and they scuttle away faster than cockroaches when you flip the light switch.

"So, Christopher, Alissa, how's the southeast division project?" Henry sets his scrutinizing gaze on us.

Chris, forever the golden boy, recites his answer like it's a rehearsed line from a Shakespeare play. "Everything's on track, Father. We should be wrapping up the initial stages by next week."

I can't let Chris steal all the thunder. "We're ahead of schedule, actually. Also, we've found a way to cut operational costs by 15%," I quip, reveling in the brief flicker of surprise that dances across my father's eyes.

"Very well," Dad grumbles, but I can tell he's pleased. For him, money talks louder than anything else.

Then, like a hawk spotting a mouse in a field, he turns his eyes toward Sophia. "And who do we have here? Sophia, isn't it?"

Ah, this should be good. Sophia's been holding her own pretty well, but Henry Anderson is a different kind of beast. I lean back in my chair, crossing my legs. Popcorn, anyone?

So, what's it going to be, Sophia? A stammer or a statement?

"Hello, Mr. Anderson, it's great to finally meet you," Sophia says, her voice exuding confidence.

"You bet. Meeting a billionaire is always great," Henry

retorts, prompting laughter around the table. The joke is lame, but his aura commands it.

"Do you like the ranch?" he inquires.

"It's wonderful."

"And I've heard you're quite fond of my son as well?"

"A lot." Sophia beams.

Easy there, girl. Pops doesn't dig the perma-grin.

"Enough to marry him before year's end?"

Sophia's smile wavers but rebounds, weaker this time. "I'm waiting for him to pop the question." She glances nervously at Chris, who suddenly resembles a deer in headlights.

"What's the hold-up?" Dad barks at my brother.

"I... I, uh..."

"He's probably waiting for her to quit her modeling gig," interjects Daniel Anderson, a heavier, older clone of Dad.

"You model?" Henry asks, eyebrows arched.

"Yeah, but not as much these days. I'm more of an influencer now."

"Influence? To do what?"

"Change people's buying behavior," she replies, quick on the draw.

"By revealing a bit too much skin, I assume?" Martha, Daniel's wife, takes a potshot. I can feel my blood simmer.

"Most of our recent sales surge has been through beauty and fashion influencers. Sophia is one of them," Chris finally pipes up, gaining a point in my book.

"Sales are sales, it doesn't matter how you get them, as long as you get them," Dad declares, diving into his bacon. "And once Sophia joins the family, she won't need to work."

"What if she wants to?" I blurt out, unable to hold back.

Dad fixes me with a gaze that could petrify a charging bull. "Then she would have to forfeit becoming an Anderson. But she wouldn't want to miss that, would she?" His voice softens.

Sophia doesn't smile.

"Anyway, she's here for a month. That should give her enough time to get a feel for us, as a family. For now, let's focus on breakfast," he redirects.

"Of course," chimes in Mary, the ever-compliant wife.

The rest of the meal proceeds with subdued murmurs; everyone seems hesitant to raise their voice.

I find myself itching to talk to Sophia, who's engrossed in a deep conversation with Chris. Why that irks me, I can't quite place.

"You handled that well," I say to Sophia when I finally get her attention.

"Did I? Chris seems to think I was a bit standoffish near the end." She leans in, her lips dangerously close.

"What? No, you were fine."

Sophia smiles and takes my hand. "Thanks for having my back, babe."

How could I not? Your back is as juicy as your lips.

"Anytime," I reply, managing to keep my wayward thoughts on a leash.

"Alissa," Mom whispers, her voice barely registering over Daniel's thunderous laughter, "would you mind showing Sophia around? A little tour of the ranch?"

"Absolutely, I'd be delighted," I say, putting on my best gracious-hostess face.

"Are you sure? You look like you're swamped," Sophia says, her eyes widening innocently.

Oh, I'm swamped alright. I've got a conference call in about 30 minutes that I should be prepping for. But the pull of Sophia, this Arabian goddess incarnate, is too strong to resist. Why am I doing this? Couldn't tell ya, but it's happening.

∞ ∞ ∞

As I trail behind Sophia, I can't help but admire how the soft curves of her body fit into that blue summer dress. Damn, it's as if the fabric itself is hugging her, reluctant to let go—kind of like how I'm feeling. My thoughts veer dangerously toward the indecent; I envision my hands exploring that curvature. Yeah, I'd call that ass a work of art, right up there with the classics gracing the walls of this library.

"So, who's the artist behind this one?" Sophia interrupts my lascivious musings, pointing to a painting that captures a dark, brooding landscape illuminated by bursts of intense oranges and reds.

Caught red-handed, or rather, red-minded, I force my eyes to meet hers. "Ah, that's an original by Margaret Keane. You know, the one known for the big-eyed children? This is part of her lesser-known landscape series. The vivid colors are supposed to represent the chaos of the human soul, or so the art snobs claim."

Sophia looks impressed, and maybe, just maybe, a little intrigued. "You seem to know your art."

"Oh, you have no idea," I say, matching her intrigued look with a sly one of my own. "Art isn't the only thing I'm good at appreciating."

Smooth, Alissa. Real smooth.

I lead Sophia out of the library and into the courtyard, where the sunlight dapples through the leaves of towering oaks, casting a soft glow on the cobblestone pathway. "This is where Mom hosts her garden parties," I say, sweeping my arm across the manicured lawns, blooming flower beds, and ornate fountains.

"It's beautiful," Sophia observes, her eyes taking in the colors around her.

"Yeah, it's the kind of beautiful that looks great on Instagram but is a nightmare to maintain," I joke, chuckling when she laughs softly. "So, tell me more about your influencing world. Make people buy stuff with a snap of your fingers, eh?"

Sophia smiles, that smile again—magnetic but with a touch of sadness. "Something like that. It's not as easy as it looks, you know. You have to genuinely believe in what you're promoting, or at least, that's how I do it."

"Ah, a conscientious influencer. That's a breath of fresh air," I say, watching her expression change, curious but still a bit guarded.

"As opposed to?" she teases.

"As opposed to the sell-your-soul-for-a-free-product types," I shoot back.

We laugh, and there's a comfortable pause, a moment of stillness where I catch her looking at me with...what exactly? Interest? Curiosity?

"Well, enough about the corporate mumbo-jumbo," I say, eager to steer the conversation into safer—but tantalizing—waters. "Let's move to the indoor pool area. You'll love it."

We make our way through the stone arches leading to a Romanesque indoor pool, complete with mosaics and marble statues. The air is thick with the smell of chlorine and lavender, and the water glimmers under the recessed lighting.

"Wow, this is incredible," Sophia breathes, her eyes wide with amazement.

"Incredible but impractical," I counter. "Nobody ever uses it, except for Dad's occasional business contacts who are more interested in bragging rights than actual swimming."

Sophia leans closer, and her scent fills the air—some exotic blend of spices and flowers that makes my head swim a little. "What about you? Do you ever swim here?"

A loaded question, or maybe I'm reading too much into it. "Not often, but I'm more of an ocean girl. I like my water like I like my relationships—unpredictable and not confined within four walls."

Sophia's eyes flicker with something unspoken, and I can't help but wonder what's going on in that mysterious head of hers. Is she feeling this low-key tension too, or am I just projecting?

"Sounds adventurous," she finally says, breaking the silence.

"Life's too short to play it safe, don't you think?" I ask, my voice dipping lower than I intend it to.

She holds my gaze for a moment longer than necessary. "I couldn't agree more," she replies softly.

"Come on," I say, pulling myself out of the moment before I say or do something I might regret. "Let me show you the horse stables; they're my favorite part of this ranch."

"As long as it's not another beautifully impractical spot," she teases.

"Trust me, the stables are as real as it gets," I say, leading her toward the far end of the estate.

"Yes, and the horses that haunt my nightmares also appear

as real as it gets," Sophia jokes as she follows me out of the pool area.

∞∞∞

The moment we step into the stables, it's like walking into another world—a comforting bubble that keeps the complexities of life at bay. The smell of hay and horse mingled with the subtle undertones of saddle soap feels like a bear hug to my senses. But then, I sneak a glance at Sophia, and the knot in my stomach tightens. Horses are not exactly her idea of a peaceful Sunday, given they're the starring creatures in her nightmares.

"So, welcome to the sanctuary for all the four-legged Andersons," I say with a flourish, trying to lighten the mood. "These stables are state-of-the-art, air-conditioned with built-in misters, 'cause in Texas, even horses get a five-star treatment. Say hello to Buttercup and Thunder; they're like the Beyoncé and Jay-Z of this place."

But as I list off the creature comforts, I notice her eyes—those spellbinding eyes that have captured more than my casual attention—aren't leaving the horses. She's locked in a silent face-off with them, and I don't think she's winning.

"You okay?" I finally ask, unable to hide my concern.

"These horses remind me of my nightmares," she admits, her voice tinged with a vulnerability that suddenly makes me want to shield her from everything bad in this world.

In a somewhat daring move, I walk over and take her hand, our eyes locking. "Can you trust me for just two minutes?"

She hesitates, probably contemplating if trust is something she can dish out right now. Finally, she nods.

"Okay, come with me," I say as I guide her towards Sugarplum, the sweetest mare in the stable. She's docile and wouldn't hurt a fly, the total opposite of Thunder, who's been known to have, let's say, an 'assertive personality.'

With her hand in mine, I slowly extend our linked hands towards the mare's soft neck. "Just let your hand glide over her coat. She's a sweetheart, really."

Sophia's hand meets the horse's skin and Sugarplum nuzzles closer, as if sensing the deep well of emotion flowing between us. For a second, I see Sophia's eyes lighten—a subtle lift, but enough to know that something good just happened here.

Gently positioning myself behind Sophia, my chest almost flush against her back, I lean in closer. "Let's get a bit more acquainted with Sugarplum, shall we?" Guiding her hand across the mare's strong but elegant back, I'm nearly undone by how close I am to her. Sophia's luscious black hair tickles my nose, sending whiffs of her intoxicating scent my way.

"Would you believe this beauty used to be a racehorse?" I murmur, my voice a whisper next to her ear. "Rescued her from a life of ruthless competition and endless stress. I guess we both needed saving, in a way."

As I speak, I feel Sophia growing braver, her body inching closer to the horse. And God help me, I inch closer to Sophia, my fingers weaving through hers. I'm so close I can feel her heartbeat, or maybe that's mine—hard to tell when you're drowning in a pool of desire and untamed horses.

In this charged moment, her hips almost graze my crotch. And let me tell you, if she weren't technically about to become my sister-in-law, I would've pulled her back against me and kissed the living daylights out of that delicate neck of hers.

But just when I'm about to dive headfirst into a daydream

47

of recklessness, Sugarplum decides she's had enough of this romantic tension and neighs loudly, whipping her head around like some daytime soap opera actress making an entrance.

Startled, Sophia jerks back, losing her footing. Time goes into slo-mo as I lunge to catch her from taking a tumble. My hands wrap around her torso, steadying her, and for a wild second, we're a bundle of tangled limbs and unspoken words.

Caught in my arms, her chest rises and falls rapidly. I could let go, but why would I? We're both suspended in this electric moment, and girl, if I could bottle this up, I'd be richer than all the Anderson department stores combined.

"Are you okay?" My voice is thick with concern and a tinge of regret—perhaps pushing Sophia towards Sugarplum was a bit too ambitious. But looking into her eyes, I can see her initial fear has faded, replaced by a grateful glimmer.

"Yeah," she breathes out, "thanks to my knight in shining Wranglers."

Ah, there it is, a wry comment. I smirk. "Well, this cowgirl's always ready for a dramatic rescue."

Gently releasing her from my arms—more's the pity—I take a step back. "You sure you're okay to continue? The paddock's up next."

Sophia steadies herself and gives a small, determined nod. "Lead the way, cowgirl."

The paddock, my next destination, is where some of our younger and more energetic horses spend their time frolicking or doing whatever it is horses do when they're not being watched. As we make our way over, I can't help but steal glances at Sophia. She looks like she's readjusting, her eyes taking in the landscape, perhaps noticing the striking sunrise that's beginning to paint the Texas sky.

We reach the fenced-off area where several horses are

grazing, their tails flicking lazily at flies. There's a tranquility here that never fails to calm me, but it's tinged with the rush of my own heartbeat this time.

"I usually come here when I need to think," I admit, more candidly than I intended. "There's something about seeing them so free, unburdened by the complexities we humans love to drown in."

"How often are you able to do that? I'm guessing your work doesn't allow you much time to just come here and think," Sophia says, standing next to me and watching the horses with an eye of wonderment.

"You hit a nerve there," I respond. "I try to carve out some time, but more often than not, I find myself fighting a losing battle."

"If I had a dollar for every time my mother said that," Sophia muses, her smile tinged with sadness.

"Mommy issues?" I turn around and watch Sophia with an unflinching gaze.

She looks as pretty as the skies above us, or the horses in front of us.

"Sort of," Sophia replies.

"I get it. I've got daddy issues."

"That's sexier. Mommy issues for a girl is just... sad," Sophia chuckles, and I notice the two dimples that grace her cheeks as she laughs.

"You know what's even sexier?" I ask, turning my gaze back to the horses. "A hot girl riding a majestic horse. Want to give it a try?"

"Are you saying I'm hot?"

"I'm just calling my horses majestic."

"Oh, thanks for nothing, I guess," Sophia banters.

"Babe, you're the hottest woman to step into these stables, and it would be a pity if you don't ride one of our horses."

"Can I . . . take a rain check?" Sophia asks, her expression tinged with guilt, playing with the hem of her skirt and biting the corners of her lips.

You're not biting them properly, love. Give me a chance to show you how I'd do it.

"Why?"

"Touching a horse is enough for one day. Let me take baby steps?"

I smile. "Again, I'm letting you off the leash, but my patience is thinning."

"I don't like to be on leashes."

"Not a fan of bondage?"

"Only with the right person," Sophia says, meeting my gaze with her own and sending my heart to outer space.

"Ew! And that person is my brother. I gotta take a rain check from this subject!" I moan in displeasure, and a little bit of jealousy.

Okay, a lot of jealousy.

Okay, 100% of jealousy.

Just as I'm considering whether or not to unpack my jealousy with Sophia, I see my brother Chris sauntering toward us. Oh great, as if I needed a reminder.

"Hey, ladies," Chris greets us, planting a quick kiss on Sophia's cheek.

Seriously? A kiss on the cheek? You're slipping, man,
"How's the tour going?" he asks, shooting me a knowing

look as if asking, Did you ruin it yet?

"It's been amazing! Alissa showed me the stables, the horses, and that really cool tree swing!" Sophia gushes, her enthusiasm radiating off her like a beam of sunlight. "She's taking really good care of me, Chris, maybe even better than you."

Chris chuckles. "Yeah, Alissa's always been the overachiever in the family."

"And don't you forget it," I retort. "Someone's gotta make up for your lack of attention to detail, whether it's the business or your girlfriend."

He smirks. "Touche, sis."

"Anyway, the boys and I are heading to the court to shoot some hoops, it's about a half-hour away. You'll be alright, Sophia?" Chris asks, the tone of his voice suggesting he's a bit worried to leave her alone, especially with me.

I catch Sophia's eye and wink. "Don't worry about her, Chris. I'll take good care of her."

Chris raises an eyebrow. "Don't steal my girl, Alissa."

"Too late," I say, pulling Sophia closer to me, "already stolen."

∞∞∞

The sun is shining, birds are chirping, and Sophia looks like a celestial goddess sitting beside me. She's swapped her earlier outfit for a flowy black skirt and a tight, full-sleeved T-shirt, and I can't help but drool a little.

Compose yourself, Alissa. You're in mixed company.

We're all gathered under the old oak tree, where a ladies'

picnic is unfolding. Plush blankets cover the ground, and wicker baskets filled with all sorts of delicacies are scattered about. There are finger sandwiches with cucumber and cream cheese, homemade quiches, fruit skewers, a variety of cheeses, and for dessert, apple pie and chocolate mousse.

"So, Sophia, how's your first day going?" Mary, my sweet-natured mother, asks.

"It's been truly amazing. I've seen so much already—the stables, the horses, even that wonderful tree swing," Sophia begins, shooting me a grateful glance. "Alissa's been a fantastic host. I haven't had a moment of boredom."

Martha, Daniel's rather conservative wife, chimes in. "And what would you usually be doing on a day like this back in New York?"

Sophia leans back, thoughtful. "Well, I'd typically start my day with some high-intensity workouts, maybe journal a bit, go for a morning run sometimes. Then it's a whole lot of replying to emails, prepping for lunch, maybe attending a shoot or two, and winding down with a drink in the evening."

"Don't you think that's a bit... indulgent?" Martha asks, raising her eyebrows.

Sophia furrows her brow, clearly puzzled. "I'm sorry, I didn't catch what you mean?"

"What do you do in a day that's not for yourself? What do you do to give back to the community, your family?" Martha continues her probing.

"I pay my taxes, Martha. I also try to be a kind and empathetic person, a good citizen. I believe just being kind to people around you can be a significant service to the community. Being religious and being kind are two completely different things," Sophia responds.

"All religious people are kind," Martha retorts, narrowing

her eyes.

"If you genuinely believe that, Aunt Martha, then you're deluded," I interject, no longer able to hold back my own thoughts.

"People who turn to atheism are deluded; people who do drugs are deluded. Girls marrying other girls, and boys marrying other boys are deluded," Martha snaps back, her words so ludicrous that I have to stifle a laugh.

Martha's jabs and outdated viewpoints stopped riling me up a long time ago. Now, they just make me pity her.

"How can you say that? Are you aware of the struggles the LGBTQ+ community faces daily?" Sophia jumps in, surprising me with her vehemence.

"What struggles? They'd be rid of all their struggles if they just turned to God," Martha scoffs, her eyes like embers.

"You really think it's that simple?" Sophia presses.

"Yes, I do. The youth today have been brainwashed by all this 'love is love' nonsense."

I catch Sophia's eye, and I see the fire burning there. I grasp her hand and give her a look that silently communicates, 'It's not worth it.'

Sophia compresses her lips and regards Martha with a look that's a cocktail of pity and disgust. "I'm not in the mood for lunch anymore. Can I take a rain check?"

"But you've hardly eaten anything," Mom chimes in, visibly concerned.

"Have a sandwich with me, and then we can go for a little walk, okay?" I suggest, rubbing Sophia's thigh reassuringly as I smile at her.

Sophia relents, taking small bites of her sandwich as if each one helps her regain her composure.

Mary suggests playing cards to lighten the mood. "How about some friendly competition?"

"I don't know how to play," Sophia admits.

"Let me teach you," I offer. I shuffle the deck and explain the rules of 'Crazy Eights' to her, sneaking in glances to relish her adorable concentration face.

God, she's cute.

As we play, Martha makes a comment about how card-playing isn't the most virtuous of activities. I almost roll my eyes. Just then, Sophia, who's gotten the hang of the game, places an eight on the pile.

"Switch the suit to hearts," she declares, giving me a wink. I feel my heart skip a beat. Even in a game, she knows how to steal the moment.

Then, out of nowhere, Susie says, "You know, Sophia, it's not too late to change your lifestyle and find some solid ground, morally speaking."

I'm about to burst, but Sophia handles it with grace. "Different grounds make for different gardens, Susie. Your blooms are beautiful, but so are mine."

And just like that, the atmosphere changes. Sophia has an uncanny ability to shift energies, a magic I find endlessly fascinating.

Damn, I think I'm falling for this woman.

As the card game wraps up, Susie accidentally knocks over a glass of lemonade. It spills, but only toward her side of the blanket.

Martha starts to scold her, but Sophia interrupts, "No worries, Susie. Accidents happen to all of us."

I find Sophie's strategy of 'killing em with kindness' enduring, but knowing the Andersons, I know it won't work.

But Sophia's intent has surely got me seeing her with newfound respect.

Slowly, and steadily, Sophia keeps making inroads to my heart, and now, I am in a state of panic.

I can't fall for my brother's future wife, but then again, I am just the person who would do something outrageously stupid like that.

∞∞∞

Ah, a walk in the setting sun, a moment to pause and reflect on life, love, and whatever the hell that picnic was about. Sophia and I leave the heavy air behind, each step distancing us from a tangle of judgments and outdated beliefs. I steal a glance at Sophia, who's back to her Brooklyn cool, with her black skirt billowing around her like she's some urban sorceress. A sorceress who's cast a bloody spell on me, by the look of it.

"So, picnic under the oak tree, a staple of the Anderson family tradition," I start, attempting to slice through the awkward silence.

Sophia chuckles, "Yeah, complete with a serving of judgment and a dash of homophobia on the side."

"Wouldn't be an Anderson gathering without a few unnecessary opinions, eh?"

"Preaching to the choir, darling," she says, her eyes on the horizon, where the sun dips low, kissing the world goodnight.

We walk a bit farther until we reach the overlook, a cliff that offers a panoramic view of the ranch—miles of fences, rolling fields, and just a whiff of endless possibilities.

"How'd you manage to be so different from your family?"

Sophia's curiosity tugs at the words as we navigate a narrow path that leads to the lake.

"I guess I've always been the black sheep, the questioner, the skeptic. When people told me to jump, I didn't ask 'how high,' I asked 'why jump at all?'"

A squirrel dashes across the trail, its tail flicking as it disappears into the underbrush. Sophia's eyes trace its path momentarily.

"So you're not, you know, homophobic or anything?" she asks cautiously.

"Me? Nah, I'm as far from homophobic as you can get."

Sophia grins mischievously. "So you're gay?"

I stumble over a stone, momentarily losing my balance. "Wait, what?"

"Well, that's the opposite of being homophobic, isn't it?"

I exhale a sigh of relief. For a second there, I thought Sophia was catching on. "What I mean is, I champion freedom—freedom to be whoever the hell you want to be."

"But how do you square that belief with living among people who are basically its antithesis?" She poses the question just as the lake appears before us, glinting in the waning sunlight.

"That's the rub, isn't it? My ambitions box me in. On one hand, I despise the regressive mindset I'm surrounded by. On the other, my ambitions keep me tethered to it all. It's a bit of a cognitive dissonance, you could say. I have my eyes on the CEO seat, even if that means competing with Chris, my own brother."

"And what if Chris gets it?" Sophia asks as a gust of wind sweeps across the lake, whipping her hair around her face.

"Then I'd be thrilled for him, but gutted for myself," I confess.

"Maybe losing would free you to finally be yourself," she suggests, and damn, she's got a point.

"It's a costly freedom, though," I say. "One that comes with a broken heart."

Sophia nods thoughtfully. "Chris feels the same pull—torn between family expectations and a desire to be free. He might not show it, but it's there."

"Really? I think we should talk then," I say, my eyes lowering to the ground, "Maybe he and I share more things in common than just our last names."

"Yeah, including me, now that I spending more time with you than him," Sophia jokes, but the effect it has on me is pretty serious.

Sophia gives me a sidelong glance, a playful sparkle in her eyes. "So, you and Chris—you've been 'together' for a while?"

I detect a layer of caution in her tone. "Yeah, 'together' is one way to put it. Chris and I share something special, but you know how it is—complicated doesn't even begin to cover it."

"Complicated? Because of the whole family dynamic?"

"Exactly. There are a lot of expectations, and you can't talk about breaking free without shaking the foundation. And neither of us wants that."

She's playing her cards close to her chest, and who can blame her? Family entanglements can unravel the best-laid plans.

Sophia's gaze wanders to the lake, focusing on another building on the opposite shore. "What's that? Another mansion?"

Following her gaze, I see the smaller mansion across the lake. "Yes, that's also part of the estate but a bit of a different world. It's available for rent, generally for those who prefer to steer clear of the Andersons. It's under renovation now. We're sprucing it up—some modern flair but keeping its old-world aesthetics."

"It looks inviting, even from this distance," she says.

"It is. Interested in a closer look someday?"

Her eyes meet mine. "Very much."

"I sometimes dream of a different life over there—one far removed from family judgments and expectations."

"A tempting thought," Sophia muses, "running away from it all. But running away from the world doesn't mean you've escaped yourself."

"True. Perhaps what we're seeking isn't a new place, but a new mindset—or maybe even someone who changes how we see the world."

She smiles, and my heart sings a quiet note of agreement. The sun sinks lower, casting golden hues on the lake, yet what glows brighter is this unspoken connection, still undefined but impossible to ignore.

"Mind if I get a little personal?" Sophia queries as we reach the water's edge, the lake's gentle waves barely brushing our feet.

"Ah, diving into the juicy stuff? Lap dances, pole dancing, and sonnets that make you weep," I quip.

Sophia looks at me, perplexed. "What are you talking about?"

"I thought you were about to inquire about my guilty pleasures?"

Her laughter unfurls like a melody, imbuing the sinking sun and tranquil lake with a unique, irreplaceable beauty. "No, but for the record, I also have a thing for lap dances and know the world's best pole dancer. We'll table that for later. What

I want to know is—have you ever been in true love? The all-consuming kind?"

"I've loved the way people touch, the way they kiss, and the way they make me feel, but not the people themselves," I confess.

"Why not?"

"Because." I pause, wrestling momentarily with emotions I'd rather keep chained. "I'm a busy woman with no room for romantic detours."

"I think if you wanted to, you'd make time," she prods.

"I don't want to."

"And why's that?" She's really digging in now, isn't she?

"Because my love is reserved for equestrian pursuits, spreadsheets that add up, and steamy encounters that don't promise forever, not for sunset walks with someone who'll turn mundane."

Sophia smirks, her eyes twinkling. "So, what you're saying is that I'm on the cusp of becoming yesterday's news after this picturesque walk?"

"As my guest, it's my job to be interested in you," I reply, offering a sly smile.

"I hope your 'job' extends for a while. Wouldn't want to roam these expansive fields alone," she quips back.

"Don't worry, you've got my attention—today, tomorrow, and possibly long beyond that."

∞∞∞

We wrap up our lake-side chat, talking about everything from our most embarrassing moments to our dream vacations. I have to say, Persian Princess here has more layers than a damn onion. As we walk back, I can't help but feel a twinge of something. It ain't boredom, that's for sure.

When we're almost at the ranch, Janice, one of the housemaids, comes running up. She's panting like she just finished a marathon. "Miss, your father wants to see you. He's in his study."

Ah, shit. Dad summoning you is like being called to the principal's office, but worse. "Any idea what it's about?" I ask Janice.

She shakes her head, "No, Miss. He just asked for you."

Sophia chimes in, "You go ahead. I should probably find Chris. He must be back, and I have almost forgotten what he looks like."

Right, the boyfriend, who is my brother, who is dating the woman who I might be crushing on.

"Yeah, go cuddle up with my bro. I'll deal with Daddy Dearest."

I make my way to Dad's study, already feeling the heaviness of the air as I approach. When I open the door, there he is: Henry Anderson, sitting like a king in his oversized leather chair. The study is all mahogany and leather, smelling like cigars and aged scotch. The walls are lined with books that probably cost more than most people's cars. He's got Forbes open on his desk next to a half-empty glass of whiskey and a lit cigar in hand.

"Well, well, look who it is," he says without looking up. "Close the door."

I do as told. Man's got a vibe that commands obedience, even from a non-conformist like me. And here we go; whatever this is about, it ain't gonna be small talk.

"Sit down, Alissa." Dad motions to the chair opposite his desk. I take a seat, reminding myself that I'm in the lion's den now.

"What've you been up to today?" he asks, finally looking up from his magazine.

"Oh, you know, just showing our guest around the ranch, having some meaningful conversations, and taking in the local scenery," I say, trying to sound casual.

"Mmm," he mutters, taking a puff of his cigar. "And why weren't you on the conference call this morning?"

My stomach drops. Shit, the conference call. I totally forgot.

He raises an eyebrow. "Cat got your tongue?"

"No, I just...forgot," I admit.

He chuckles, but there's no warmth in it. "If you're serious about moving up in this family, in this company, you'll have to do better than that."

I clench my fists, holding back an eye roll. "Dad, I've been running the South Division and boosting our profits for the last three years. If that doesn't scream 'serious,' I don't know what does."

He ignores me, swirling his whiskey glass. "So, what do you think of Sophia?"

Uh, careful now, Alissa. "She's fantastic—intelligent, hard-working, quite the looker, and super kind. Why?"

He mulls over my words, then says, "She talked down to Martha today. Your uncle didn't appreciate it."

"Yeah, well, Martha was disrespecting people from the LGBT community, so—"

Dad laughs. "That's hardly a valid reason to talk down to your family."

I grit my teeth. Old man's as stubborn as a mule.

"And do you think she's in love with Chris?" he inquires, looking me straight in the eye.

My mind races through the moments Sophia and I shared today, her hesitation when talking about Chris, their body language—nothing adds up to head-over-heels love.

"I'll need more time to figure that one out," I say, choosing my words wisely.

He leans back in his chair, exhaling a puff of smoke. "Well, you take your time. I'd like to know just how serious this young woman is. We don't want Chris making a mistake now, do we?"

I force a smile. "Of course not."

"Before you go," Dad interjects as I start to rise, "there's something else we need to discuss. Some, uh, rumors about Chris in New York."

My brows shoot up. "Rumors? What rumors?"

Dad struggles with the next words, clearing his throat before he finally says, "That he's, you know, not interested in women."

"You mean he's gay?" The words come out of my mouth before I can stop them.

Dad flinches at the straightforwardness. "Well, yes, that's what the chatter is. It could jeopardize our family's standing and the business. I need you to look into it."

I'm shocked. Chris being gay? That's news to me.

"And while you're at it," Dad continues, "I want you to dig up some info on Sophia. Find out who she is, who her mother is. Hire the best private investigator in the country if you have to."

I sit back, stunned. "Dad, I can't do that. It's a complete breach of their privacy."

He sets his whiskey glass down with a clatter. "Alissa, let me tell you something. When I envisioned building this billion-dollar empire, I knew I wouldn't always be playing by the book.

Do you know how I got my first big contract? I had dirt on a competing businessman—evidence of tax evasion. I gave him an ultimatum; he pulled out, and I got the contract."

"You blackmailed someone?"

He waves a dismissive hand. "Call it what you will, but that's what it took. I knew I had to be ruthless, even aggressive, to get to the top. And if you're going to sit in this chair someday," he gestures grandly to his leather seat, "you'll need to be the same."

"But that's—"

He cuts me off, "Ethics are a luxury we can't always afford. If you're committed to this family and to your future here, you need to show you're willing to do whatever it takes."

My heart's racing, but I look into his eyes. There's no warmth, no love—just a steel-cold resolve. For a moment, I see my life flash before my eyes: a relentless cycle of moral compromises to keep climbing the corporate ladder, to meet Dad's insurmountable expectations, to secure a future that's looking grimmer by the minute.

I open my mouth, but no words come out. Instead, I nod.

Dad seems satisfied. "Good. Now go take care of it. And remember, the best private investigator. Spare no expense."

As I walk out of the room, I wonder if I've just made a deal with the devil. But one thing's for certain: the walls of this opulent study feel like they're closing in on me, and I've never felt more suffocated.

∞∞∞

Saddling up one of my favorite mares, I ride out into the field, letting the cool wind hit my face. It's an instant relief after the pressure cooker situation with Dad. As I guide the horse through the open land, my mind inevitably drifts to Chris and the rumors. Did he ever show signs of being gay? I think back to our high school years; Chris was always sort of a nerd. The time he tried to impress girls by performing a dramatic reading of Einstein's theory of relativity at the talent show comes to mind. That was so hilarious that I still chuckle thinking about it. Not exactly a lady killer.

And what if Chris is gay? God, what a twist that would be—two queer kids from a conservative, empire-building family. Then my thoughts slide toward Sophia. Is she available? I don't want to go there, but I can't ignore the charged moments between us, the fleeting glances, and the subtle hints of flirtatious banter.

After galloping through the fields, I tie up my mare and make my way to the ranch's library. It's the ideal place to catch up on work and make that missed conference call. The high wooden shelves filled with everything from classic literature to business manuals offer a comforting backdrop as I open my laptop. The call is a quick one, mostly centered on quarterly projections, but even while discussing numbers, my mind drifts back to Sophia and Chris.

Finally done, I'm eager to get back to my room and just unwind. My heart feels heavy with all the thoughts I've been juggling—Chris's sexuality, Sophia's potential availability, Dad's expectations, and whatever the hell is going on between Sophia and me.

I reach my room's door and find it locked. God, seriously? I knock, trying to mask my impatience.

"Just a sec," Sophia's voice calls from inside. She sounds...busy?

"Yeah, we're just getting dressed," Chris chimes in, cheeky as ever.

The door swings open, and Chris walks out, while Sophia hangs near the door.

"Sorry, we got a little, um, handsy," Chris grins like the cat who got the cream, tossing a sly look over at Sophia, who's blushing hard.

I roll my eyes, as one does. "Handsiness aside, do I need to get these sheets dry-cleaned or something?"

Chris chuckles, "Come on, it's your room, Alissa. That'd be all kinds of weird."

Sophia jumps in, "Yeah, we're not that bad."

"You sure about that?" I shoot back, trying to keep the vibe light, though my mind's swimming in a weird mix of jealousy and irritation.

"I'm beat," I sigh exaggeratedly, and Chris takes his cue to exit.

"Gotcha. I'm worn out too, y'know. The boys are really taking it out on me," he says, and, knowing the rumors about him, I nearly snort out loud.

"Goodnight, bro."

Before he leaves, Chris plants a sloppy, overly passionate kiss on Sophia and palms her ass. It's kinda gross, kinda jealousy-inducing, and I'm absolutely over it.

"Sorry, again," Sophia mumbles as I finally get to step into my own room.

"Hey, you guys are a young couple made to sleep in different rooms. Shit happens."

Sophia tries to clarify, "But we didn't really—"

I cut her off, "Babe, it's cool. You don't have to explain."

"No, I feel like—"

"Why are you getting so defensive? If you knew the number of girls I've had in here—" I catch myself.

Sophia's eyebrows jump to her hairline. "Girls?"

Crap. Think fast, Alissa.

"Boys, okay? Boys. Dad busted out the good whiskey. You don't say no to Henry Anderson."

I move over to the vanity and sit down. I can feel Sophia watching me, probably analyzing my every word and movement.

"I would've been just as okay if you said girls, you know." Sophia's voice drops an octave, silky and sultry and, God, it gets to me.

I lock eyes with her in the vanity mirror. "They were boys, Sophia. End of story."

Sophia flips her hair and takes a deep breath. "Would you mind holding my phone while I give a quick tour of this fabulous room? My followers are dying to see where I'm staying."

"Sure, but make it look good. This room has my name written all over it," I say, grabbing her phone.

"Hey, before we start filming, do you mind if I borrow that pink silk night dress?" Sophia asks, her eyes twinkling mischievously. "I didn't pack anything too...eye-catching, thanks to Chris's request for 'conservative attire.'"

I smirk. "You're asking to borrow my lingerie before we've even had a proper drink? Bold move, Sophia. But yeah, go for it."

A few minutes later, Sophia is back in the room, now wearing my silk night dress. She looks absolutely divine, and I wonder if I've ever managed to look half as good in it. My phone is ready to record, and so is she.

"And action," I say.

Sophia's face instantly transforms from casual to captivating. "Hello, lovely people. I'm currently staying in this magnificent ranch, rich in history and culture. It's a testament to the legacy of the Anderson family."

She starts the tour with the bed. "As you can see, the sheets are a silky blend, inspired by 18th-century French luxury. Everything here speaks of elegance, doesn't it, Alissa?"

I zoom in on Sophia. "Absolutely. My mother loved everything French. The room's a tribute to her taste."

Sophia takes the camera and pans it over to me. "Let me introduce you to Alissa Anderson, the brains behind the Anderson Corp, a businesswoman extraordinaire, lover of horses and everything British, while also being the most beautiful woman I know," she finishes, recording me looking like an absolute fool.

"Thanks for that, Sophia, but let me take that phone from you. You are the star of this video," I say, and Sophia hands me the phone with a smile as her words float around in my head.

Most beautiful woman she knows. I'd take that.

Sophia brings the focus back to herself. I notice the nightdress is still tied up at the front. "Untie it. Trust me, it'll kick the hotness factor up several notches."

Sophia hesitates for a moment. "You think?"

"Don't worry, I got you," I say, reaching over to untie the knot for her. The silk falls open, revealing a pair of heavenly breasts, pushed together by a lacy, black bra.

My eyes drop to Sophia's cleavage, and I feel a sudden stab of arousal between my legs. They are the perfect shape, the perfect size, complementing her tall frame, and the thick, thunderous thighs that I have come to term as the most seductive feature of this Arabian beauty.

"That *is* better," Sophia exclaims, as I try hard not to keep ogling her breasts.

"Much better," I whisper, and hope there isn't saliva dripping off my lips.

We move towards the French windows. Sophia pulls back the curtain dramatically. "And finally, the view. It's serene. It's like stepping into a painting. Nature in all its grandeur. Isn't it breathtaking?"

She twirls around, and I catch a glimpse of her panties. Black as well, clinging to her ass for dear life.

Heavens have mercy on me and my heart…and pussy.

"Okay, I think this should be it for now. Tomorrow, I'll record a tour of the ranch" Sophia says, walking over to me, and taking the phone from my hand, lightly grazing it as she does so.

"I might not be there to help you tomorrow."

"Why?" She frowns.

"Got a little scolding from Mr. Henry Anderson. Might have to go into the city for work," I say.

"No! What will I do without you?"

"Hang out with Susie, I guess?" I laugh.

"I'd rather be locked in the stables with the horses," she says, gently slipping out of the night dress, and handing it to me. "Thanks for this."

"You should try sleeping in that tonight," I say, thrusting the dress back into her hands, "You will have the sleep of your life."

"Are you sure?" Sophia asks tentatively.

"Positive," I say, "and don't worry, I'll try to finish up early so I can be back at the ranch by evening."

"Please do, because I know Chris will desert me again tomorrow, and then, I'll be stuck with my least favorite Andersons, no offense."

"None taken, babe. I won't desert you like my brother. I am better than him," I wink at Sophia, and I swear I see a little spot of crimson appear on her chiseled supermodel face.

∞∞∞

Lying in bed, I can't seem to find that elusive thing called sleep. The room is dark, but my thoughts are ablaze. Sophia, in that pink silk nightdress, is an image I can't shake. It's not just an image; it's an aura. Her scent lingers in the room, a blend of vanilla and mystery that's disturbingly enticing.

I feel the warmth emanating from her body on the other side of the bed. It's like an invisible force field, pulling me into thoughts I shouldn't entertain. I'm acutely aware of my own body, of the heat accumulating in the space between us, and it's driving me crazy.

I shift, trying to find a comfortable spot that will lull me into unconsciousness. No luck. Every position just heightens my awareness of her proximity. Sophia's peaceful, rhythmic breathing tells me she's lost in slumber, unaware of the turmoil she's stirred in me. I envy her that serenity.

Weeks have gone by without any form of intimacy in my life, and it's catching up with me at the worst possible moment. The temptation to surrender to this magnetism is palpable. I clench my fists, digging my nails into my palms as if the pain could ground me.

I turn my back toward her, thinking distance could provide some form of relief. Maybe if I can't see her, I can escape this relentless pull. As I close my eyes, my mind paints an even more vivid image of her. Sophia, standing there with her nightdress untied at my suggestion, radiant in her newfound freedom. The vision is too intense; it's like she's imprinted on the inside of my eyelids.

I take a deep breath, filling my lungs with air as if I could also draw in self-control. Exhaling slowly, I try to release the tension building up inside me, to drive away the thoughts fueling my imagination. I mentally count sheep, try to think about mundane things—account balances, board meetings, conference calls—but they morph into exhilarating scenarios involving Sophia and that pink silk nightdress.

Finally, I concede to the only option left: getting out of bed. Maybe a glass of water or a walk down the hallway will serve as a cold shower for my overheated mind. I carefully slide out from under the sheets, making sure not to disturb Sophia, and head toward the kitchen.

As I walk away from the bedroom, I realize that the magnetism isn't contained within those four walls. It follows me, embedded now in my thoughts, in the very air I breathe.

As I descend the staircase leading to the bar below, my footsteps grow quieter, almost respectful of the silence that envelopes the ranch at this hour. The bar is as I remember it—grand, a touch rustic, with bottles of varying shades of liquid gold, amber, and clear spirits lined up neatly. I bypass my dad's favorite whiskeys and settle for a simple glass of water. A drink won't solve my current situation; it might even fuel the fire.

Taking a sip, I stand there for a moment, contemplating. This unexpected attraction to Sophia feels like a betrayal on multiple levels. I can't help but grimace at the complexity of my thoughts. Downing the rest of the water, I place the glass back on the counter and head back upstairs.

Walking into the room, I'm immediately captivated by the ethereal sight before me. Sophia has kicked off the covers in her sleep, revealing her body in the pink silk nightdress. She's lying on her side, one leg straight, the other bent at the knee, creating a tableau that could inspire a Renaissance painter. Her hair falls across her face, partially shielding her features, but enhancing her allure.

Moonlight filters through the curtains, casting a soft glow that accentuates the curves of her body. It's as if some cosmic artist decided to play with light and shadow, using Sophia as the canvas. I'm caught in a reverie, stuck between the beauty of the scene and the reality of my feelings.

I tread softly across the room and ease myself into the armchair in the corner, deciding that this is the closest I can get without overstepping boundaries—either hers or my own. From here, I can appreciate the almost celestial vision she makes without getting ensnared by it.

What the hell am I doing? I ask myself, while my eyes refuse to obey my mind, and stay fixed on Sophia, and her long, ludicrously delicious legs.

I should have had that drink.

I reach for the dresser, pull open a lower drawer, and extract a bottle of wine from the depths.

My emergency stash.

I uncork the bottle and touch the mouth to my lips.

The wine rushes down my throat as my eyes roam all over my brother's girlfriend's body.

You need to stop, Alissa. This is not healthy. This is vile. Pathetic!

I don't get up. Instead, my hand snakes down my body, gently grabbing a feel of my own tits on the way down between my legs.

A sigh escapes my lips, as my hand dips into my panties.

"Aaah."

It's her legs I am focussing on and how they would feel on my tongue.

I have accepted defeat.

"Sophia…" I whisper, as my fingers start tracing patterns on my clit.

"Sophiaaa…"

I arch my back, and rub myself close to an orgasm.

"Sophiaaaahhh!" I squirm, kick my feet in the air, and lay panting in the armchair, feeling the soft caresses of the wind on my sweaty face.

Suddenly, my heart fills with panic and dread, as I realize what I have done, and how deep in trouble I am.

Lust is easy to handle, to conquer, as I just did.

But even after my little act of depravity, I continue to feel things for Sophia — the need to cuddle with her, to know what goes on inside her head, to drown into late night conversations until the sky is ablaze with the red and gold of the morning sun.

Lust is easy to conquer, but love isn't, and the thought shakes me to my very core.

Chapter Three

(Sophia)

I eye Chris, my arms crossed, lips set in a frown. "So, you're heading off to play basketball with the boys again?" The question hangs heavy between us like a storm cloud on the verge of bursting.

"Yeah, Soph. I told you, I promised them. We'd be a guy short if I bailed now," Chris says, already lacing up his sneakers.

I roll my eyes. "Oh, heaven forbid you break a promise to the 'boys.' What about me, huh? Alissa is out today, you're off gallivanting, and here I am, stuck on a ranch with the Andersons and their 'Family Values: The Retro Edition.'"

He halts, his gaze locking onto mine. "Sophia, c'mon. You knew this wasn't going to be a walk in the park."

I throw my hands up. "Honestly, Chris? Playing your faux-girlfriend is getting more challenging than trying to get through a Tolstoy novel. Your uncle and aunt? They make me wanna peel my skin off."

"Sophia, this is important. Plus, I am not complaining about you getting a little too cozy with my sister, who is potentially the only one who could sabotage our plans," he says, emphasizing each word as if it would make the situation easier to digest.

"So, I should steer clear of bonding with Alissa because she's in your way?" I retort, my voice tinged with disbelief.

"No, it's just—"

"It's just that Alissa is the only one keeping me sane in this place," I cut him off. "Honestly, you could learn a thing or two from her."

He sighs, his shoulders dropping as if the weight of our charade has finally caught up to him too. "Okay, okay, you're right. I'll make sure I'm around more. But for today, and maybe a couple more days, you're gonna have to fend for yourself. You could shoot some ranch content for your profile or follow up on those collabs you had lined up in Dallas."

I eye him skeptically but then relent. "Fine. But this had better be worth it, Chris. Seriously worth it."

He grins, that signature Chris smile that somehow makes all the trouble seem less bothersome. "It will be, Sophia. I promise."

And with that, he's out the door, and I'm left to contemplate the bittersweet symphony that is my life at the Anderson Ranch. Oh, the things I do for friendship—and the secret, unbidden thoughts about Alissa that are making it all so complicated.

So, I take Chris's advice and decide to shoot some content for my page. I mean, who wouldn't want to see this lush, Texan ranch backdrop, right? With phone in hand and my best influencer smile, I start touring the ranch, recording all the picturesque spots. However, I'm not alone in this adventure. Uncle Daniel and Aunt Martha tail me like a couple of CIA agents on a stakeout.

"Ah, Sophia, dear, are you sure it's wise to be exposing our humble ranch to millions?" Uncle Daniel asks, his words dipped in a vat of condescension.

"Don't worry, Uncle Daniel," I say, flashing a smile. "In the digital age, if you're not seen, you don't exist."

Aunt Martha huffs, "I prefer existing without the entire

world having a look through my window, thank you very much."

I try to survive on my own for the next few days, with only the nights providing some sort of relief when Chris and Alissa come back to the ranch.

The afternoons are the worst, especially the compulsory 'all ladies must eat together like it's the 1700s' lunch. If mealtime was an Olympic sport, I'd be failing the qualifying heats, let alone going for gold.

I've to sit there and pretend to be this Stepford Wife prototype for Chris, who, by the way, isn't even here. I practically have to recite the Book of Martha Stewart to keep up the act. It's exhausting!

Finally, today I venture into the lair of Susie, which feels like someone threw a Bible, a convent, and a teenage girl into a blender and hit 'puree.'

And then, as I walk around marveling at the cross count —honestly, I lost count at 37—something else catches my eye. Tucked beneath the altar of piety, I see the edge of a Vogue magazine peeping out like a socialite at a gala.

"Wait a minute, what's this?" I tease, pulling the stash from its hiding spot. "From the Gospel according to Anna Wintour? My, my, Susie, you wild thing, you."

Susie goes crimson, matching the wine from the last supper hanging on her wall. "Oh, those aren't mine! Alissa asked me to stash them."

Now, it's my turn to raise an eyebrow. "Alissa? Why would she ask you to stash her magazines? She has her own room, with a thousand books on fashion lining the bookshelf."

"She gave them to me, hoping I would take some inspiration from them, but I didn't like them at all."

"Is that why you have marked this article on 'dressing for a first date' as 'maybe one day'?" I tease.

Susie lunges at me, snatching the magazine from my hand, and stowing it away. "I didn't write that."

"It said 'Susie' at the bottom of the page, followed by a heart and what looked like a doodle of a girl sitting by herself at a table, probably waiting for her date?"

"I am telling you, they are not mine. They belong to Alissa, she reads them for fashion tips."

"Of course," I say, smirking. "Just like I watch cooking shows for the plot. Speaking of plots, what's the story of your love life?"

Susie's eyes suddenly look like they're asking the heavens for guidance. "Well, my love for Jesus is unmatched," she begins, which honestly, considering her room decor, isn't too surprising. Then she hesitates, casting a glance at a poster of shirtless Jesus doing carpentry. "But between you and me? There's no one to talk to for miles."

"Ahh, the isolation of pastoral life," I say, sympathetically, but also with a hint of "I've-got-my-eye-on-you" sass. "Maybe someday a shepherd boy will wander onto this hallowed ranch and you two will Instagram your holy union, Vogue magazines in tow."

"I am not on Instagram," Susie says.

"Not much of a surprise, girl."

Needless to say, I decide to keep my eyes on Susie for the remainder of this charade. The thought of exposing her to her 'wholesome' mother seems too good to let go.

After three days of barely surviving, Alissa finally decides to take a break from work, much to Chris' satisfaction, and we decide to venture into the city for a little girl's day out.

∞∞∞

Ah, Dallas, here we come.

Alissa looks stunning behind the wheel, even if she's swapped out her power suits for a casual get-up. She's wearing ripped jeans that fit her like a second skin and a simple white tank top that reveals just a hint of her toned arms. Topped off with aviator sunglasses and her hair pulled into a messy bun, she could easily pass for a cool, indie musician—or the subject of my latest fantasy.

"So, you survived three days with the clan. How was it? As riveting as a telenovela?" Alissa asks, smirking as she navigates through the countryside.

"You have no idea. I felt like I was stuck in an episode of 'Desperate Housewives,' except replace the gossip and drama with passive-aggressive jabs about morality and class."

She laughs, a sound that's way too good to my ears. "Ah, the Anderson brand of love. You get used to it."

"You really don't mind spending your days navigating between Uncle Daniel's sermons and Aunt Martha's judgmental stares?"

"I've mastered the art of zoning out while maintaining a socially acceptable smile. It's a skill. Plus, my work keeps me sane. Also, I spent most of my days in the city. I have rented an apartment there, my own little secret and place of solitude. When the Anderson love gets too much for me, I just slip away to Dallas. Speaking of which, how was your collab hunting in Dallas?"

"Ah, you know, the usual. Had a couple of meetings, scheduled some shoots, and nearly lost my cool explaining to one brand that yes, authenticity does sell better than forced narratives. Is it cool if we make a quick stop at a hotel? I've got a collaboration in the works and need to finalize details with the General Manager."

"Sure, which hotel?"

"The Jewel. It's fairly new, and word on the street is it has an awesome rooftop bar."

"Looks like you've got our day's itinerary all planned, babe," Alissa says, punctuating her words with that signature wink of hers. "And here I was, thinking you'd be missing all the madness at the ranch." Her words drip with sarcasm, but the genuine smile that accompanies them makes me momentarily forget we're talking about my relationship sham.

"Speaking of madness, what's with Chris and his basketball obsession? I've seen teen dramas with less emotional investment," I comment, keen to learn more about this hidden side of my friend.

"Oh, basketball is practically a religion to him. If he's not at the court, he's sulking or plotting his next game. He's a decent player, but for him, it's therapy."

"Can't imagine needing therapy if I were on the verge of becoming a CEO of a multi-million dollar company," I retort.

She casts a brief, contemplative glance my way. "What makes you so sure he'd be the next CEO?"

The air between us turns a bit tense, but I swiftly diffuse it. "It was just a joke. Honestly, I have no idea who's going to be CEO, and frankly, I couldn't care less. So, what's on the agenda for our girls' day out?" I divert the topic.

"Shopping, food, and hopefully, no deep dives into either business or morality," she declares, grinning.

"Sounds perfect to me."

∞∞∞

As Alissa parks the car in the hotel's extravagant lot—think a stretch of pavement worthy of a Hollywood premiere—I can't help but admire how she's managed to pull off casual attire that's somehow drop-dead sexy. She's in ripped jeans and a loose-fitting white tee, but lord, she could've strutted down a Paris runway in those.

The elevator dings, doors slide open, and we step into the rooftop bar. This place is dripping with opulence—marble countertops, plush purple seating, fairy lights entwined around ornamental trees, and a view that could *almost* rival the Manhattan skyline.

I find the General Manager, shake hands, and exchange some light banter before diving into the business. We tour the newly renovated pool, a sparkling oasis of turquoise that's begging for a feature in a luxury lifestyle magazine. "Let's do a poolside shoot," I suggest, envisioning the glam shots. He agrees, and we pencil in some dates, nothing set in stone, but enough to seal an understanding.

I head back to the bar where Alissa's already claimed a table and has ordered cocktails. A brilliant concoction of gin and fruit—I forget the name, but with one sip, I know I'll remember the taste. "Missed me?" she quips, raising her glass for a toast.

"Like a cat misses yarn," I fire back. We clink our glasses, sealing the pact of our perfect girls' day.

And then, as if cued by some ironic twist of fate, a group of gorgeous women swans into the bar. My supermodel friends from Brooklyn, hair like waterfalls and legs for days, spot me and head our way. "Sophia! What are you doing in Texas?" squeals Natasha, her voice a decibel too high for comfort.

Alissa shoots me a curious glance. My worlds are colliding, and I'm bracing for impact.

"Ladies, meet Alissa," I say, trying to play it cool, "My

wonderful tour guide for the day."

Oh boy, the drama dial just got turned up a notch. What was supposed to be a simple girls' day out is quickly shaping up to be a masterclass in juggling different facets of my life.

"Tour guide, huh? Is she showing you all the Texas hot spots?" Natasha winks, and I sense the loaded question. Alissa chuckles, mercifully unaware of the double entendre.

I drain my cocktail, hoping the alcohol will provide some much-needed courage. "Something like that," I reply, locking eyes with Alissa.

I introduce the girls to Alissa, who eyes them from head to toe. Can't blame her; all of them look like they have stepped off the pages of a Victoria's Secret magazine.

"I hope we're not interrupting a hot date or anything," Katty quips, her eyes narrowing playfully as they scan from me to Alissa.

"What? No, no hot date here," I stammer, feeling my face heat up, "Just two friends catching up."

"Uh-huh, because two 'just friends' definitely pick The Jewel's rooftop bar for casual drinks," Layla chimes in, her grin revealing more than a hint of skepticism.

"Okay, but seriously, we should hang out soon in Brooklyn, alright?" I steer the conversation away, itching for them to take the hint.

"Will you actually show up this time?" Layla fires back, her eyes darting between Alissa and me. "You've been flakier than a croissant lately."

"I promise I won't cancel this time," I assure them, eager for them to move on so I can breathe again.

"Cool, maybe bring her along too. She seems like a riot," Natasha says, throwing Alissa a flirtatious glance.

Alissa doesn't miss a beat. "I don't know about being a riot, but I'd love a tour of Brooklyn by you ladies whenever I'm in New York."

Is she really flirting with them? Or is this just Alissa being her naturally charming self?

Natasha smirks. "We'd be more than happy to, as long as Sophia here doesn't keep you all to herself."

"Just business, not pleasure," Alissa retorts, making it sound like an innuendo even when it isn't. She's just that good.

"All right, ladies, we'll let you get back to your 'business' then." Natasha winks as they start to leave. "Sophia, consider your social calendar booked for our Brooklyn adventures."

As they disappear into the crowd, I finally let out the breath I've been holding. Turning back to Alissa, the air between us is different—more charged, if that's possible.

"Wow, you really draw a crowd, don't you?" Alissa observes, arching an eyebrow as she sips her cocktail, watching as my model friends vanish into the Dallas nightlife.

"I guess. Small world, though. Didn't expect to run into them here," I mutter, savoring a sip of my own cocktail. The alcohol suddenly seems more potent.

"So, you and the Brooklyn beauties—always this glamorous?"

"Most of the time, the glam is just for the 'Gram," I confess, relieved that my model friends are gone.

"Ah, the 'Gram—everyone's personal highlight reel," Alissa replies, her eyes still on me.

"Exactly, it's a filtered reality. Honestly, most of my friends nowadays just want to meet up for content."

"That's the world we live in—closer yet more distant than

ever," Alissa says. "So, how'd the chat with the GM go?"

"It's all set. We're doing a poolside shoot soon, and I could use your help sneaking away from the ranch. I promise I'll make it worth your while."

She grins. "Do I get to watch the shoot?"

"Sure, if you'd like."

"Watching you in a bikini? That's an offer too good to refuse."

Is this how friends usually talk to each other?

"So, more cocktails to celebrate?" I ask, hoping to steer away from the whole 'date' mishap.

"Absolutely. But first, what's the deal with your friends thinking we're on a date? Especially a date with a woman?"

Caught off guard again. "Um, they're just used to seeing me stumble romantically. They thought it'd be 'on-brand.'"

"On-brand?" Alissa seems puzzled.

"Yeah, I've done some provocative shoots with female models before, and since then, people joke about me being into girls."

I can't believe I just lied that smoothly.

"Where can I find these shoots?" Alissa finishes her cocktail, setting down her straw a bit too sensually.

"The Internet?" I shrug.

"What do I search for? 'Sophia Miller's sexy pictures'?"

"Something like that. But let's not go there right now, it'd be awkward."

"Don't worry," she says, leaning in, "I'll make sure I'm alone when I check you out."

Okay, this isn't how two new friends, or potential sister-in-laws for that matter, usually converse.

"Enough about your 'brand.' What about you? What's life like in New York?" Alissa asks, looking genuinely interested.

"New York is... an adrenaline rush," I start, choosing my words carefully. "There's never a dull moment, you know? Always something happening—a new gallery opening, a fashion show, or some underground party."

She seems captivated. "Sounds exciting and exhausting at the same time."

"Exactly. It's exhilarating, but it can wear you down if you're not careful."

"And your family?" Alissa ventures, her eyes searching mine.

Ah, family. The tangled web of complicated relationships and buried secrets. My mom and her very public relationship with Bella, my ex-roommate and best friend, is not something I want to dive into right now. "I'd rather not talk about family; it's a sensitive subject for me."

Alissa senses the hesitation in my voice. "I get it, family can be complicated."

"Yeah. I live alone and only talk to my mom once in a while. We don't have the kind of relationship where we chat every day."

She nods. "Distance can be both a blessing and a curse."

I take a sip of my cocktail, contemplating whether to share more. Finally, I do. "When I was younger, my mom wanted me to focus on academics. She had this vision of me in a white lab coat or arguing cases in a courtroom. But I had other plans; I wanted to model."

"And?"

"We had a falling out. A big one. I ran away from home. It took years for us to even talk again, let alone reconcile. Things were good for a while, but they've gotten strained again. That's why I prefer not to discuss it."

Alissa's eyes soften. "Life really doesn't come with a manual, does it? We all make choices, some good, some bad, but in the end, we have to live with them."

"Yeah, but I don't regret my decisions. They made me who I am today."

"And who you are today is someone I find incredibly interesting," she says, her gaze holding mine.

My cheeks warm, but before I can say anything, our cocktails arrive. I take a sip, grateful for the temporary distraction.

"The feeling's mutual, Alissa. You're incredibly interesting too. With the massive empire you manage, it must be overwhelming at times. Does it fulfill you?" I ask, my eyes meeting hers as I put down my glass.

Alissa takes a deep breath before answering. "In a way, yes. But it's become more about proving myself than about genuine fulfillment."

"Proving yourself to whom?"

"My family, mostly. I was always told what a woman should and shouldn't do. My father, especially, underestimated what a woman can achieve in the business world. So, every step I take is sort of a 'take that' to his old-fashioned notions."

"What's your relationship with your father like?"

"Complicated. He's a brilliant man, a genius when it comes to business. But he's also stubborn and full of himself. I love him, but it's become my mission to get him to change, to open his mind to more modern ideas."

I nod, thinking of Chris and his similar complexities. "Chris doesn't have that urge for change. He's content hiding who he is, living a life designed to impress his father."

"I've noticed that about him," Alissa says softly.

"Can I ask you something personal?" she continues, shifting in her chair as though preparing for something momentous.

"Of course," I reply, suddenly feeling tense.

"I've heard rumors about Chris," she starts, "and my father has asked me to find out how much truth there is to them. He wants to know if you genuinely love Chris."

The weight of her words settle in my stomach, heavier than any meal or drink. I have the opportunity to clear the air, but doing so feels like a betrayal to my own heart, which yearns for something else entirely.

"I love Chris," I say, the words feeling like shards of glass on my tongue, "and the rumors are false. He's very much straight. Please tell your father that."

Alissa nods, taking in my words. "I will. I'm glad to hear you're in love."

"Thank you," I say, though my heart is breaking into a million pieces. I want to shout out, to tell Alissa that I'm falling for her, but I can't. I've made a promise, and so, I put on a brave face, drink the remaining sip of my cocktail, and swallow down my feelings with it.

∞∞∞

The rest of the day is like a breeze—light, refreshing, and infinitely pleasant. Alissa and I delve into an array of subjects, from our favorite movies to the latest trends in fashion. We find common ground easily; it's like we're tuned into the same frequency. Our tastes even align when it comes to food, each of us secretly thrilled to find another lover of spicy Asian cuisine.

However, we find our first real point of contention when we start discussing the most iconic supermodels. For me, it's the new generation that takes the crown. "Come on, Kendall Jenner and Bella Hadid are redefining the game," I argue. "They bring a fresh, contemporary spin to modeling. Plus, they have this immense social media influence."

Alissa chuckles, "I won't discredit their influence, but iconic? They still have a long way to go to reach the likes of Kate Moss or Cindy Crawford. Those women defined an era. They broke barriers in a way that's still being felt today."

We each make solid points, but neither of us are convinced to switch sides. It's a good argument, one that leaves us both grinning at its conclusion.

As the sun starts to dip lower in the sky, we decide it's time for a change of scenery. "How about a drive around Dallas?" Alissa suggests.

"Sounds perfect," I reply.

We hop into her car, and Alissa queues up some of her favorite English bands. As we drive, a comfortable silence falls between us. I notice a subtle change in her demeanor—she seems a bit sadder, more distant than before. But I don't press her on it. We spend the next hour exploring—passing by the historic Deep Ellum neighborhood, admiring the Dallas skyline as the city lights begin to flicker on, and even making a quick stop at the iconic Pioneer Plaza to see the bronze cattle drive.

Eventually, we make our way back to the ranch. Upon arrival, I spot Chris and immediately pull him aside. "Listen, Henry told Alissa about the rumors. She was asking me if I genuinely love you."

Chris's eyes widen in panic. "How did you handle it?"

"I saved our asses," I assure him. "I told her I love you, and she seemed convinced. I asked her to report back to your father."

Chris exhales, visibly relieved but still looking concerned. "We need to up the ante, Sophia. We should spend a night together, show everyone that we're so in love we can't stand to be apart."

The proposition leaves me uneasy, but given the precarious situation, I don't see another way out. "Alright," I agree, the words tinged with a hint of regret. But what choice do I have?

As I walk back toward the main area, I catch a glimpse of Alissa. She's laughing at something someone said, but her eyes don't meet mine. In that moment, a quiet sense of loss washes over me, a poignant reminder of the love that could have been but now seems more unreachable than ever.

Dinner with the Andersons is always an event, but tonight it's especially charged. Chris decides to use the occasion to put on a display of our "burning love," announcing that we can't bear to sleep apart any longer. "Sophia will be staying in my room tonight. We are adults, and we're in a committed relationship," he proclaims with a flourish, as if delivering lines in some theatric performance.

Daniel, ever the conservative, balks at the idea. "You can't be serious," he snorts, clearly disapproving.

It's Henry who has the final say, as usual. With a voice that leaves no room for argument, he chides Daniel, "Remember, you may take care of the ranch, but I own it. Let them be." Henry's authority hangs heavy in the room, leaving Daniel unable to counter. He nods, albeit reluctantly, granting us his approval.

Throughout this whole ordeal, I find myself stealing glances at Alissa, who doesn't look up from her plate. She seems lost in her food, or perhaps in thought. Either way, her refusal to meet my eyes feels like a cut, sharp and swift. Tonight, it seems, there will be no friendly banter or whispered secrets between us. Instead, I'll be sleeping next to Chris, and that thought is surprisingly disheartening.

After dinner, Chris and I retreat to his room. He unrolls a mattress on the floor, opting to give me the bed. "I'll take the floor," he assures me, trying to keep the mood light. "And don't worry, I don't snore much."

Chris seems unusually tense tonight. "I'm a bit nervous, Sophia. Dad seems to be digging deeper into our relationship."

I put my hand on his shoulder, trying to assuage his fears. "Chris, we'll get through this. Don't worry." My words seem to comfort him, and soon he's snuggled up on his makeshift bed, drifting into sleep.

But sleep doesn't come as easy for me. The bed might as well be a plank of wood for all the comfort it offers. I toss and turn, staring at the ceiling, then at the empty space next to me, then back at the ceiling again. The emptiness is palpable. It's a large bed, but it feels too big without Alissa. I remember how we would talk late into the night, how her laughter was the last thing I heard before sleep claimed me, and how the sight of her peacefully sleeping face was my morning sunrise.

Here, in this room, the quiet is deafening, the absence consuming. I feel distanced, not just from Alissa, but from myself, as if leaving her side has robbed me of some essential part of who I am—or who I could be. With every tick of the clock, the walls seem to close in a little more, marking not just the passage of time, but the growing distance between me and the woman who has, in so little time, come to affect me so much.

Chris's breathing deepens, steady and even, a reminder of the life I've agreed to lead for the sake of appearances. And yet, despite the man lying just a few feet away, I've never felt more alone.

My phone lights up the room, dragging me out of my loneliness. It's a text from Alissa. For a moment, my heart lifts. But then I see the photo attached: Kaylee and me, lips touching, hands wrapped around each other, framed by the setting sun over Manhattan.

"Do you know who she is?" reads Alissa's text.

A surge of panic replaces the brief uplift in my mood. How the hell did Alissa stumble upon this?

With shaky fingers, I type out a reply. "How did you find this?"

Her response comes almost instantly. "Was searching for some of your campaigns. This popped up among the photoshoots. There was a link to an article about you and Kaylee. Said you two were modern LGBTQ icons, along with your mother, Ava Miller."

I feel my chest tighten and my breathing go shallow. This is overwhelming, too much too soon. I wasn't prepared for my past to ambush me like this. "Can we meet? Right now? I'd like to discuss this face to face," I manage to text back, keeping my composure hanging by a thread.

"Sure. Meet me in the cigar room," she replies.

Careful not to wake Chris, who's sound asleep and blissfully ignorant of the emotional whirlwind inside me, I tiptoe out of the room. My mind races as I close the door softly behind me. I'm entering an emotional minefield; one wrong move could detonate everything.

The cigar room's dim lighting only amplifies the tension I feel. Alissa stands by the window, her back to me, seemingly engrossed in her own thoughts.

"Alissa," I begin, taking a deep breath to steady myself. "I owe you an explanation."

She turns around, her expression unreadable. "I think that would be good, yes."

She looks surreal in a white see through robe, and inside, I can see the outline of her white lingerie.

The moonlight illuminates her frame, and even with a thumping heart, I am briefly reminded of this woman's powerful hold over me.

"Can we sit down?"

"Sure."

Alissa and I sit on the massive leather arm chairs, facing each other.

"Truth is, I did date a girl before Chris," I finally say, figuring half a truth is better than a full lie. "The girl in the picture is Kaylee, my ex and also a former roommate."

"So, you're into girls?" Alissa asks, lighting a cigar.

"Yes," I confirm, watching as she takes a slow puff.

"Why did you lie to us?"

"Why do you think we lied?" I retort, refusing to feel cornered by this captivating woman sitting cross-legged before me.

"Chris feared your past would be too controversial for the Andersons. Either that or it would jeopardize his shot at becoming the next CEO."

"You're right."

"Which one is it?"

"Both."

"And you're insisting you're in love and Chris isn't gay?"

"A hundred percent."

"You can be honest with me, Sophia. I won't betray you two. I'm not like my father."

I pause. The temptation to spill the whole truth is enormous. But I can't. I can't betray Chris.

"I know how this looks, but you have to trust me," I finally say.

Alissa scrutinizes me, as if she's deciding my fate right then and there. Taking another puff from her cigar, she leans in. "Your mother—she's dating Bella Foster, right? The singer and producer?"

"The gay singer and producer, yes."

"And you've dated a girl, while there are rumors about my brother being gay. Do you realize what this would mean for Chris's chances of becoming the CEO if my father finds out?"

I say nothing. The gravity of the situation begins to sink in—I may have just ruined Chris's dreams and handed Alissa the ammunition she needs to snag the CEO position for herself.

"I won't say anything to my father," Alissa declares, confidence tingeing her voice. "I want to earn that position fair and square. But, Sophia, I think you're lying to me, and you don't have to."

"I know, I know I can trust you, but you're fishing where you shouldn't," I retort.

Alissa takes a deep breath and averts her gaze. A dog's distant bark slices through the air, while candles flicker in their antique bronze holders.

"Are you still into women?" she questions.

"It's not a switch, Alissa. But since Chris, let's just say the focus has shifted."

"Do you still find them tempting?"

"I'm not comfortable answering that."

"You owe me some truth; I've caught you in lies."

I exhale deeply. The distance between Alissa and me feels astronomical, as though she's a fading star on the edge of my universe.

"I'm committed to Chris, okay?"

Alissa snorts. "Could have fooled me. You've been checking me out."

"That's absurd. You're my boyfriend's sister; I'm not ogling you."

"Do you watch porn?" she asks, startling me as the chandelier above sways in an odd draft.

"Uh, occasionally."

"Gay or straight?"

"Alissa, this has nothing to do—"

"Just answer."

"Straight. Satisfied?"

"Search history. Now."

I chuckle. "What are you, my mom?"

"No, a concerned sister. Show me."

"I can't. It's personal."

"Fine, but Henry Anderson won't be as understanding. Tell me the truth if you want my help with this family."

My eyes linger on Alissa, a blend of Aphrodite and a mafia queen, puffing on her cigar. She extends her hand for my phone.

Screw it, I think, unlocking my phone and passing it to her.

"Good girl," she says, flipping through my history.

A cocktail of fear and arousal stirs within me as she clears her throat. "Well, well—'Horny Bride-to-Be Fucks Her Sister-in-Law,' 'Two Sister-in-Laws Go At It in the Barn,' 'Shy Girl Is Seduced by a Butch Lesbian Businesswoman.'"

My heart thunders; sweat trickles down my temples.

"I see a theme." She smiles, handing back my phone.

"Alissa—"

"Sophia," Alissa speaks over me, "I want you to go back to my brother's room, have a drink, listen to some music, and then when you lay down in your bed, I want you to really think about what you want to do, and then tomorrow, we will have another conversation, and I hope you will play fair then. Okay?"

"I will do as I please," I say sternly, "and if you want to blackmail me, go ahead. I don't care after a certain point." I rise up. "Good night, Alissa Anderson."

∞∞∞

I race back to my room, my heels clicking on the marble floors of the labyrinthine hallways. Shadow and light duel on the walls as I pass sconces that sporadically punctuate the dark corridors. Finally, I reach the room, quietly unlocking the door and stepping inside.

Chris sleeps on, oblivious to the emotional storm that's brewing. His face is calm, a picture of innocence and trust—traits I'm now doubting within myself. My heart pounds as I consider waking him up, spilling the tangled threads of my secrets and letting him decide what we do next. But I stop. This is not the moment. Besides, would my confessions only make things worse?

I neglect Alissa's advice. No drink. No music. Just the pressing weight of my own thoughts as I lay in the bed.

Alissa's not one to let things go. The woman practically radiates authority, with connections sprawling like hidden roots of a colossal tree. If she decides to dig into my life, how can I hope to keep my secrets buried? Alissa's a siren in stilettos, and I'm caught in her allure, yet I don't know if she'll slice me open with the truth.

Coming clean poses its risks. Henry Anderson's approval is a linchpin for Chris's future as CEO. Confessing to Alissa could be like detonating a grenade in a glasshouse—fragile relationships would shatter irreparably. I've known Alissa for a mere week; she might have enchanted me, but she hasn't yet earned my trust.

In the suffocating silence, my mind runs in dizzying circles. I consider calling my mom, but what would I say? And Nicole, currently my best friend, would be equally clueless on how to help me untangle this royal mess I have gotten myself into.

A tired sigh escapes my lips as I sink into the plush pillows, my thoughts an indecipherable maelstrom. And as if pulling a protective cloak around me, sleep eventually envelops my worried mind, offering no resolutions but a brief respite from reality.

∞∞∞

Morning light filters through the curtains as Chris and I head to the stables. The Anderson family, decked in riding attire, has already assembled, their conversations filling the air with a mixture of tension and anticipation. Horses are saddled, and everyone is keen on the planned trail ride leading to a hillside picnic.

I greet them, maintaining a veneer of normality, but inside I'm a tempest. Alissa's gaze catches mine, an inscrutable look that sends shivers down my spine. Today, we ride together, but where we're all going—where I'm going—is a path shrouded in fog, the destination uncertain and fraught with hazards.

The horses neigh, impatient to be off. And for a moment, I envy them. They run because that's what they're born to do, uncomplicated by convoluted human games and secrets.

"You know, I was pretty much born in a saddle," Chris begins, trying not to sound too much like he's bragging. "I think I rode before I walked."

Alissa chuckles, "Wow, it's a miracle you can even stand upright now. Because from what I recall, I've outridden you more times than not."

Chris raises an eyebrow. "You challenging me, sis?"

"Sure am, cowboy. How 'bout a little race?"

Alissa gives me this look. "And let's make it more fun. Winner gets Sophia as their riding partner today. You know, since she can't really ride herself."

Chris turns to me, then back to his sister. "This family has already made us sleep in different beds, and now you want us to ride on different horses? I am beginning to think people around here are jealous of our love."

"Oh, please!" Alissa responds, "Sophia and I are becoming BFFs, and I have been taking better care of her on this ranch than you ever could!"

"Can't argue with that," I mutter under my breath, intrigued by Alissa's unpredictable antics.

Henry chimes in, clearly amused, "Alright, let's get this rodeo going! Whoever reaches that tree first is the undisputed champion. No recounts or appeals! It's not a democracy!"

Susie sighs like we're the ads she's forced to sit through before her favorite music video. Mary, the ever-concerned mom, speaks up, "Children, remember to be careful. Don't go too fast."

Henry glares at her. "For God's sake, Mary, do you always have to suck the life out of every room you enter?"

I watch Mary's face drop, a sudden cloud shadowing her beautiful features.

The tension snaps, and they're off! Hooves pound against the ground, dust billows, and I'm there, standing like a spectator at a Roman Colosseum. The horses are neck-and-neck, but just at the last stretch, Alissa pulls ahead, winning by no more than a horse's length. My heart is racing, but for entirely different reasons.

Alissa trots back triumphantly, looking like she should be on the cover of "Horsewoman Monthly" or something. She dismounts, a burst of flair in her every move. "I hope you're ready for this, Sophia. I promise to take you on the ride of your life," she says, her words dripping with double entendre.

I feel my face get so red you'd think I'd been slapped. Alissa helps me onto the horse, and the moment she takes the reins behind me, her arms are casually but deliberately wrapped around my waist.

The trail unwinds ahead of us, a serpentine path cutting through the heart of the Texas landscape. We're surrounded by a collage of green and brown, the wind playing with the trees like a symphony of whispers. With Alissa's arms wrapped securely around me, I feel a strange blend of peace and exhilaration—kinda like how you feel after that first sip of a really strong cocktail.

"So, about last night," Alissa begins, her voice low and tinged with mischief. Her chest is pressed against my back, and I can smell her luxurious perfume—expensive, yet earthy, just like her. "Have you decided you're ready to play fair?"

I chuckle. "I've been playing fair this whole time, haven't I? You're the one changing the rules."

"Changing rules can be fun, especially when the stakes are high." She adjusts her grip on the reins and her hands subtly tighten around my waist.

She continues, "You know, I couldn't help but notice

all your recent late-night viewing choices have something in common: the 'sister-in-law' trope. That's pretty...specific. Trying to hint at something?"

Caught off guard, I stammer a bit. "Umm, no, I'm just into taboo stuff, okay? Nothing to read into there."

Alissa leans in closer, her lips almost brushing my ear. "How taboo would it be if you just admit you're more into me than my brother, who's just a guy you know? Imagine the scandal, the intrigue."

My breath catches in my throat. "That would be really taboo. But unfortunately, that's not happening. I'm not into you."

Alissa places her hand on my thigh, her touch electric yet casual, and says, "We'll see how long you can keep fulfilling your fantasies through the screen."

The unspoken tension hangs thick between us, as tangible as the Southern humidity. I suddenly realize that being lost in the wilderness wouldn't be so bad, as long as I'm lost with her. But I also know, no matter how much I might fantasize, there are lines that can't be crossed.

The trail leads us through a sun-dappled forest, the light filtering through the leaves creating a natural kaleidoscope. We follow the Anderson family, our horse leisurely bringing up the rear.

"So, do you ride often in New York?" Alissa's voice, smooth as honey, buzzes in my ear.

"Yeah, the F train during rush hour, mostly," I quip. "Horses are a bit scarce between Manhattan skyscrapers."

She chuckles, her breath warm against my neck. "One doesn't just ride horses, you know?"

"I don't do any sort of riding."

"So you are a bottom?"

I almost fall off the horse, barely surviving being trampled to death — my nightmare come alive.

"It seems like you know more about being gay than the person you think is gay. Are you hiding secrets of your own, Ms. Anderson?"

Alissa laughs, and the sound makes me wanna ride things…and by things I mean her.

"Of course I am hiding secrets, Princess of Persia. What kind of a boring ass woman would I be if I had no secrets at all?"

"You would be Susie Anderson," I laugh, and she joins in my laughter.

I could get used to this—her laughter, the warmth of her body, the rhythmic movement of the horse. But just as I'm settling into the atmosphere, I see Henry leading the group toward a clearing. The family begins to dismount, laughing and chatting as they prepare for a mini-picnic.

Alissa seizes the moment. "You up for a little detour?"

"Do we get to dodge familial awkwardness?" I grin, already knowing her answer.

"Even better. I promise it's a view that'll knock the city skyline out of your head."

She guides the horse smoothly off the beaten path, making our way through a grove of trees with low-hanging branches, their leaves brushing against us like nature's flirtatious little nudges. After a few minutes, we arrive at what can only be described as a scene from a postcard—lush meadows under a sky painted with hues of gold and crimson, framed by the gentle hills.

Alissa helps me off the horse, and we tether them to a nearby tree. "Welcome to my secret escape," she whispers, looking into my eyes.

"It's no Central Park, but it'll do," I tease as she helps me off the horse. In the process, I almost topple over, my city slicker inexperience shining through.

"Whoa there, city girl! This isn't a New York subway. Hold your horses—literally!"

I burst out laughing as I find my footing. "Well, in the subway, no one's this handsy, so it's easier to balance."

We sit down on the grass, and the horse takes it as a cue to start grazing lazily. My eyes can't help but travel over Alissa, who looks every bit the part of a posh British equestrian—tight, white riding trousers molding her legs and a fitted shirt that does wonders for her figure.

"You know," I start, "you look like you could be on the cover of 'British Equestrian Weekly' or something. This is way better than the 'don't-mess-with-me' vibe you had last night."

She leans back on her palms, looking amused. "Well, I can play many roles. Last night, the serious demeanor was... necessary."

"Are we good, though?" I ask cautiously. "Last night was kinda intense."

Her eyes meet mine. "We never went bad, Sophia. But trust takes time." As if on cue, she pulls out a bottle of Château Margaux 2010 and two crystal wine glasses from her saddlebag.

"Since Anderson women don't drink with the men," she pours the wine, filling both glasses generously, "how about we show up a little buzzed and give 'em something to really talk about?"

I laugh, taking a sip of the luxurious wine. "Why not? A little alcohol never killed anyone—unless you're talking about my karaoke skills, in which case, it's murder on the ears."

"Karaoke, you say?" Alissa's eyes light up. "Please tell me you've got a go-to song."

"Um, does singing 'Bohemian Rhapsody' in the shower count?"

"It counts, but only if you hit those high notes," she says, eyes twinkling.

"And how about you?" I turn the question around.

"Whitney Houston's 'I Will Always Love You,' of course. But enough about karaoke divas, what about real-life divas?" Her eyes hold a mischievous gleam. "When did you realize you were into women?"

"Hmm," I ponder for a moment. "Have you ever watched 'V for Vendetta'?"

"Of course, Natalie Portman's a queen!"

"Right? That scene where she's like this beautiful, vulnerable, yet strong goddess? I was 15, and boom, it hit me. I was absolutely, irrevocably, bi."

Alissa looks thoroughly impressed. "Solid choice. So, spill the tea, who's better in bed? Men or women?"

"We're BFFs now, right? You have to promise this doesn't go beyond this magical forest of confessions."

She laughs, "Cross my heart, hope to—well, let's not get dramatic."

Slowly, as if drawn by an invisible thread, Alissa shifts closer to me. I notice how her body moves, the deliberate way her eyes meet mine. The tipsy haze makes her seem even more alluring, her scent intoxicating, wrapping me like a luxurious cloak I never want to take off.

"So?" she prompts.

I catch my breath. "Honestly? It depends on the person, but

the best sex I've ever had was definitely with a woman."

"Do tell," she says, her voice dropping an octave, her thigh now touching mine.

The aroma of the earthy grass below us mixes with the scent of the wine, the soft nickering of the horses in the distance adding a serenade to the tranquil atmosphere. I take a moment to absorb Alissa's essence, so strong and free. She seems eager to continue the conversation.

I think back to Kaylee, and then let it out: "Well, my ex, Kaylee, she was—oh god, she was stunning. She looked a bit like Alison Brie."

"Nice taste," Alissa teases.

"We once got stuck in a hotel elevator, and we had full-blown sex right on the floor. The risk of getting caught, the cramped space...it was exhilarating."

Alissa is visibly excited, her eyes dancing in the dim light. "Even scissoring?"

I nod, blushing more fiercely this time, "Yeah, even that."

"In a cramped elevator? That's gymnastic!"

"That was the thrill of it," I say, meeting her eyes.

Alissa chuckles, her eyes narrowing. "You, Sophia, are full of surprises."

"What about you?" I shift the focus, my curiosity piqued. "You've been so mysterious about your love life."

She hesitates for a moment. "Well, you see, it's more of a 'lust' life than a 'love' life. I've never really been in love."

"So, spill the details about this 'lust life' of yours," I prompt, "Ever been with a woman?"

Her eyes meet mine, curious, yet deliberate. She shuffles even closer, so close that I can feel the heat emanating from her body. Our thighs are almost touching; the tension between us is electric. In the background, the horse grazes, blissfully unaware of the human drama unfolding beside him.

"In college, in Britain, I had this friend, Sarah," she starts, her voice soft, almost whispering. "We got really close, one thing led to another, and we... experimented."

Her face moves closer to mine with every word, our lips just a breath away from each other.

"It was incredible," she continues, her voice even softer now, "Being with a woman was so different, so raw, so intimate. And ever since then, I've been craving that closeness, the scent of a woman, the touch of her skin, the taste of her lips."

The wine, the words, her proximity—they all swirl in my head, making me dizzy. My heart is thumping wildly in my chest, each beat screaming for the kiss that seems both imminent and impossible. The air between us is thick with desire, every second stretching out into an eternity as our faces inch closer.

"One evening, it was just the two of us left in the auditorium. We were rehearsing a particularly intense scene for a Shakespearean play, about lust, trust and denial... and something shifted. The lines between acting and reality blurred. It was...a magnetic pull, really. Neither of us could resist."

The way she articulates, deliberately drawing out words like 'magnetic' and 'resist' is intoxicating. Each syllable feels like a whisper against my skin.

"What happened then?" I ask, my voice almost trembling.

Alissa's eyes lock onto mine, piercing through me. "We kissed, and it was like we'd ignited something. The emotion was palpable. We became a tangled mess of moans...sighs...and screams. I clung onto her, and she clung onto me, and we kissed, and kissed, until our jaws hurt, and our clothes were ripped from our bodies. We didn't make love, Sophia. We fucked. And since then, I have been chasing that feeling, of being fucked by a gorgeous woman."

As she recounts her story, I find her hand gently resting on my thigh, her touch like a flicker of fire against my skin. My whole body is aching for that touch to escalate, for her to close the already nonexistent distance between us.

"So, Sophia," she whispers, her breath tickling my neck, "isn't life too short to keep fulfilling our fantasies only in our heads or, in your case, in porn?"

I'm so entranced by her words and so intoxicated by the wine that all I can do is let out a shaky breath. My mouth is dry, but my mind is vivid with imagination. I'm in sensory overload. It's as if the whole world has narrowed to this single, electrifying point between us. Every part of me is screaming to close that last millimeter of space, to taste the wine on her lips and feel the reality of Alissa.

"But what about trust?" I manage to whisper, clinging to the last thread of my self-control.

"Trust," she murmurs, "is often earned in the most intimate moments, don't you think?"

"Please don't do what I think you're about to." My voice comes out as a shaky, trembling mess.

"Why? I know you want it."

"Chris…"

"You don't love him."

"I do."

"Then push me away," Alissa says, and suddenly, I'm being pushed onto the grass. Alissa straddles me.

I watch her mount me, like she mounts those majestic horses, her eyes burning with the fires of passion and lust. Her cheeks are flushed, and her golden hair frames her as if she's some majestic Valkyrie.

I'm trapped, both under her body and under the weight of her aura.

She leans over me, and all I can do is watch as she places her lips on mine.

She lets out a soft sigh and starts kissing my lower lip. She wants access. She wants to break in.

And then, all of a sudden, I let her.

My mouth opens, and I let out a deep, dense, and daring moan of pleasure. Like an arrow from a bow, her tongue penetrates my mouth and starts exploring it like an adventurer.

My mind becomes a cocktail of lust and longing, and I can't control, can't stop my hand from caressing her back.

Fuck, she tastes like heaven.

My pussy throbs, screaming for delicious contact with her skin, but my shorts and her trousers separate us from the deepest pleasure, from crossing boundaries.

But isn't the boundary already crossed? Shit!

I push Alissa off me and scramble away from her.

"No! No! This is not who I am!" I mutter, more to myself than to Alissa.

Alissa, now sitting on her knees, is as calm as a lake.

"Stop fighting, Sophia. Trust me."

"Trust what? I can't cheat on my boyfriend with his sister. That's outrageous!"

"It's outrageous that you're still keeping up this charade. Chris is gay, I know."

"No, he isn't."

"Oh, for fuck's sake, Sophia. I'm also gay. Somehow, God played a very twisted, dark, and I have to admit, hilarious joke on the Anderson family. Henry Anderson, the guy who believes being gay is a disease, is blessed with not one, but two gay kids. I love that for him!"

"How do you know that Chris is gay?"

"I can put two and two together, honey."

"He and I had sex last night, after our little conversation in the cigar room."

"Bullshit!" Alissa snaps.

"He fucked me, Alissa. Hard. And I enjoyed his dick. I'm bi, not exclusively a lesbian, and Chris might be bi, I don't know. But he loves me, and I love him. Yeah, you're hot, and yeah, I would've loved to hook up with you if I wasn't happily committed to your brother. I can show you the used condom. It's still in the wastebasket in his room!"

Alissa glares at me, as if she's fighting the urge to tackle me to the ground once again. "You're lying," she whispers.

"I'm not. And don't try to force yourself on me ever again."

I stand up and look at the horse.

"I'll walk," I exclaim, and start walking back to the Andersons, tears filling my eyes.

Chapter Four

(Alissa)

The tension in the house is thicker than the Texas summer heat, and let me tell you, it's a scorcher out there. I'm used to being the life of the party, the firecracker, the girl everyone wants but can't have. To be denied by Sophia? That's a bruise on my ego I didn't see coming.

Work and horses—that's my medicine for the moment. Daylight finds me either in the stables with Whiskey, my prized stallion, or clacking away on my laptop in my Dallas office. The stable smells of fresh hay and horse, and my office smells of ambition. One soothes my soul; the other fuels my aspirations. CEO isn't just a title; it's the throne I've been eyeing for years.

Nights are the trickiest. I pull out the mattress and lay it on the floor, as far from Sophia as possible. She tries to make small talk— about the weather, the horses, the damn chipped paint on the barn door. Each attempt hangs in the air like an unanswered question, a story without an ending. I ignore her. It's as if she's not even there.

I flirt with the idea of exposing Chris. Wouldn't it be poetic justice? But then, I catch a glimpse of myself in the mirror. No, I'm not that petty. My eyes are set on bigger goals. Chris and his tangled love life can stay out of my thoughts. He's not my battle to fight. I owe it to myself to rise above it all.

Publicly, I'm cordial, flashing my practiced smiles at Sophia and Chris, laughing at the right moments, a master at keeping up appearances. But privately, I've erected walls thicker than the Great Wall of China between Sophia and me.

Days slither by like this, each more monotonous than the last. But somewhere between the heaps of paperwork and late-night rides, I find my thoughts drifting towards Sophia. When she calls out to me as I head to my car, or when she awkwardly steps into the kitchen as I'm brewing my morning coffee, there's this pull, this magnetism I can't seem to shake off.

Sophia tries to catch my eye, and for a second, a fraction of a heartbeat, I want to break. I want to turn around and share a simple, meaningless conversation to laugh like we used to, to exchange those silly, inside jokes that once meant nothing and yet everything. But the moment stretches and snaps, like a fragile thread tested too far. My eyes move away, focusing on anything but her.

Oh god, this is ridiculous.

I'm acting like a teenager with an insatiable crush. But this is different; it feels way more intense. That kiss in the meadow was like something out of a movie. The kind of moment you look back on and realize was a pivotal point in your life. It was passion personified, and dammit, why can't I stop reliving it?

At work, my mind drifts while in meetings—suddenly, the meadow appears, and I can practically feel Sophia beneath me, her hand finding its way to my hip. Even riding my horse, a normally liberating experience, is tainted. It's like I've swapped one saddle for another, except this one's a mental merry-go-round, and I can't seem to get off.

The shower offers no respite. The water trickles down my body, but all I can think of is how Sophia tasted, how she felt, how she matched my intensity until she—didn't. Why did she stop? What would've happened if she hadn't pulled away?

I imagine such a scenario, where we never stopped, where we stripped each other of every piece of clothing on our bodies, where we ended up tangled in a heap of limbs, and I can't stop my hands from sliding down my torso and ending up between my legs.

No one has ever made me question my self-control like she has. And honestly, it's driving me mad. I've never wanted to share my bed with someone this badly. It's both exhilarating and exhausting.

And then there's the songs. Bloody songs on the radio that suddenly have new meaning. Love songs, breakup songs—they all seem like they were written just to mess with me. Each lyric, each chord strums on my heartstrings, each one a haunting reminder of what could have been.

It's almost like Sophia's got this invisible tether wrapped around me, yanking me back whenever I try to get some distance. And the worst part? I don't entirely want to cut it.

So I dig. I dig deep into Sophia's past like some private investigator. What I find is fascinating, a narrative rich with complexity and drama. Her mother Ava, a Nobel Prize-winning astrophysicist, and her partner, Bella Foster, decades younger than Ava, Sophia's former roommate, a pop music sensation—both powerful women in their own right. I admire Sophia for her ability to handle such dynamics, especially her emotional maturity regarding her mother and Bella's relationship, and giving them her blessing to be together.

But what bugs me is Chris. Why isn't he part of this narrative? I can't find a single piece of credible information that links him to Sophia, apart from their well-scripted public appearances. It's like he's a ghost, an actor playing a role in Sophia's life. I know Sophia said they were intimate, but something doesn't add up.

And then there are those late nights. When the world is

quiet, and it's just her and me, separated by nothing but a few meters and a mattress. I see her in her sleep—peaceful, beautiful, so damn irresistible. And the walls I've built, they start to shake, to crumble, inch by inch, night by night.

What the hell am I going to do?

∞∞∞

The Andersons were headed off to Dallas for a night, some charity gala where Dad wanted the entire family to show a united front. I, however, declined, much to Dad's irritation. Others, the ones without balls as big as mine, succumbed to Dad's terror, including Sophia.

The day was supposed to be my own personal sanctuary —a day off from the world, from family drama, and yes, from Sophia's magnetic pull. I'd planned everything to a T. A luxurious, sinfully heavy breakfast: scrambled eggs topped with chives and a sprinkle of goat cheese, a tower of fluffy pancakes drowned in maple syrup, and freshly squeezed orange juice. All set against the backdrop of the morning sun spilling into the rustic kitchen.

Then, a long, soul-cleansing ride across the ranch, just me and my favorite horse, Whiskey. We'd ride through the trails and pastures until the city skyline became a distant blur. A shower would follow, but not before preparing a hearty Italian lunch. Handmade fettuccine alfredo sprinkled with a decadent amount of parmesan, a side of garlic bread, and maybe even a glass of white wine. I'd savor each bite while streaming something shamefully indulgent on Netflix. A classic rom-com or some new age trash TV, something I'd never admit to watching but secretly loved.

The evening would unfold in quiet productivity—emails, maybe drafting a few proposals. As the night drew near, I'd shift my focus to Bumble. I was officially on the prowl, ready for some no-strings-attached fun. A hot girl, a few flirtatious texts, and maybe even a naughty late-night chat. A little self-love and then, I'd wrap up the day in the most poetic way possible—in the library, hopefully with the rolling percussion of thunder as my background score, a gripping novel in hand, and a comfy armchair to curl into.

But as fate would have it, Sophia fell sick. Of all the damn days, she picks today to run a fever.

Chris, ever the concerned boyfriend, decided it was best for her to stay back. And who does he ask to play nursemaid? Me. Of course. Because Sophia and I are "besties," according to the world's worst-kept secret. I wanted to say no. But some masochistic part of me—the part that melts every time Sophia so much as breathes—wanted to say yes.

So, I did, albeit with a hesitant tone that screamed, "I'm not thrilled about this."

Sophia, never one to be sidelined, insisted she was well enough to travel. That's when I finally broke my silence. I looked her straight in the eyes, "Don't worry, I won't kill you if you stay here with me."

And just like that, her resistance melted away. She agreed, and as our eyes met, I felt a pang of something—longing, regret, excitement? I couldn't tell.

Finally, the Anderson convoy rolled out of the driveway, leaving behind a cloud of dust and two women locked in an emotional Mexican standoff.

∞∞∞

Sophia's eyes shift from her laptop screen to meet mine. "Look, I don't want things to get awkward today, so I'll stay out of your way."

I arch an eyebrow, a touch of sarcasm seeping into my voice. "Your loving boyfriend tasked me with taking care of you, which means I'll have to keep an eye on you."

Sophia shrugs. "I can take care of myself. It's just a fever."

"Guest rules," I counter, cutting off any room for argument. "As long as you're in my ranch, I'm responsible for you. Now, do you want some breakfast? I'm about to cook."

Sophia's eyes lighten up a fraction. "Only if it's not too much trouble."

"It's never too much trouble to eat," I quip, heading to the kitchen. I can feel Sophia's eyes on me, watching as I gracefully move around, pulling ingredients from cabinets and the fridge.

After a while, the kitchen is filled with the heavenly aroma of scrambled eggs and freshly flipped pancakes. I plate everything beautifully, just like in those fancy food blogs—scrambled eggs topped with chives and a sprinkle of goat cheese, a tower of fluffy pancakes drowned in maple syrup, and a glass of freshly squeezed orange juice.

I carry the breakfast tray into the living room where Sophia has made herself comfy on the couch. She looks up, clearly surprised. "I didn't know you could cook."

I set the tray down on the coffee table and settle into an armchair opposite her. "Well, I don't put all my talents on display. Some are reserved for special days or special fevers," I reply, the jibe smooth and subtle.

Sophia smiles, almost involuntarily, and we both dig into our breakfast, an air of awkward silence settling over us. It's Sophia who breaks it. "Should we watch something?"

I nod, pressing a button on the remote. The large flat-screen TV comes to life, filling the room with colors and sound. Unfortunately, the channel it lands on is airing a movie that couldn't be more awkward for the situation—a sultry, forbidden love affair between a man and his brother's wife.

Each scene feels like a gut punch, the tension in the room building with every frame. I catch Sophia sneaking glances at me, her cheeks flushed. This feels less like a movie and more like a mirror held up to our own convoluted emotions. Finally, I can't take it anymore.

"Alright, I'm heading to the stables. You should get some sleep," I announce, standing up abruptly, the movie still playing its awkward symphony in the background.

Sophia looks at me, her eyes filled with a mix of relief and disappointment. "Yeah, sleep sounds good."

I nod, my heart pounding, my thoughts a mess. I need the fresh air, the open fields, the smell of hay and horse—anything to escape the ever-growing complexity that is Sophia.

∞∞∞

I push open the creaky stable doors, the wood grumbling like it's got a case of the Mondays. The smell hits me instantly —hay, leather, and pure, unadulterated horse. God, I love that scent. It's like home, but the kind of home where no one's judging you for who you kiss or don't kiss.

I grab Sable's bridle off the hook. As my fingers run along the leather, I can't help but think of how Sophia would've reacted to all of this. "Look here, city girl, this is a bridle. It's not a purse, but it's damn important."

I approach Sable, who offers me a soft neigh. I guess horses can sense human bullshit because Sable's eyes almost seem to say, "You okay, boss?" I fit the bridle over her head, making sure it's not too tight. She's a good girl, deserves the best. Just like Sophia would have, if she were here. The idea of Sophia reaching up to touch Sable's snout dances in my mind, and for a moment, I almost smile.

Moving onto the saddle, I lift it over Sable's back and start tightening the straps. I picture Sophia watching me, her big eyes following my every move. "Keep your back straight when you lift," I'd warn her. "Unless you want to turn into Quasimodo by 30."

Finally, it's time to mount. Foot in the stirrup, I swing myself up onto the saddle. Damn, it feels lonely without Sophia's imagined arms around my waist, holding on for dear life, and maybe, just maybe, holding onto something more.

I give Sable the cue, and we're off. First a walk, then a canter, and then we're flying. The wind whooshes past me, almost like it's trying to carry away my clusterfuck of feelings. What would Sophia do right now? Would she be screaming in excitement or holding onto me tighter, scared and thrilled all at once?

I pull Sable back into a trot and then a walk, letting her know she's done good. We head back to the stable, and I start the unglamorous work of removing the saddle and bridle. I fill up a bucket with water and offer Sable some hay, which she devours like it's gourmet shit.

"Good girl," I whisper, giving Sable a pat. And then, leaning back against the stable wall, I let it all sink in. I'm alone, standing here covered in dirt and horse sweat. Sophia's not here. Those laughs, those stolen glances, that electric charge in the air—it's all in my head. For now, at least, these moments are mine alone. And it sucks more than I'm willing to admit.

Jesus H. Christ, as if today needed more drama. The sky darkens like it's got a mood disorder, and I can see the storm clouds rolling in fast. The thunder grumbles in the distance, a bass note of nature's playlist.

"Shit," I mutter. Horses get spooked easily in thunderstorms, their hearts racing faster than a teenager's in a haunted house. Last thing we need is a horse panicking and hurting itself, or God forbid, getting tangled in a fence.

I sprint outside, the rain already splattering down like it's in a damn rush. Sable's safe, but there are still two more horses out in the pasture. I whistle loud enough to wake the dead, hoping to get their attention.

And then it happens. Thunder cracks, sounding like the sky's splitting in half. One of the horses, Jasper, bolts like he's seen a ghost. His eyes are wide, the whites showing in stark contrast to his dark fur. Damn it. I make a grab for his halter, but he rears up. His hoof comes down fast, connecting with my leg. Pain shoots through me, and I feel the warm ooze of blood seeping into my jeans.

"Easy, Jasper, easy," I hiss through clenched teeth, forcing myself to stay calm. I reach out, my hand shaking, and manage to grab his halter. After a minute or so that feels like a lifetime, he finally calms down. I lead him and the other horse, Bella, back to the stable. Inside, I take a moment to catch my breath, my leg pounding in time with my heartbeat.

I swear, my leg feels like it's been used for target practice. But I can't deal with that right now. Jasper's still jittery, his flanks quivering like a leaf in the wind. I walk him slowly around the stable, talking to him in low, soothing tones.

"Easy, boy. I know, the sky's throwing a damn tantrum. But you're safe here, okay?"

Jasper's ears flick toward me, and he snorts softly, his eyes not quite as wild as before. Finally, I feel him relax, his body going from tense to merely cautious. With a sigh of relief, I lead him back to his stall and secure him safely. Bella follows suit, noticeably calmer.

"I'll be back to check on you two," I promise, brushing a hand over Jasper's mane. I give them some hay and fresh water, forcing myself to stay upright despite the lightheadedness that's starting to kick in.

Grabbing a towel, I wrap it tightly around my shin to stem the bleeding. Good thing the shin is the strongest bone in the body, or else I would have a broken leg. It's a makeshift tourniquet, but it'll have to do. As I limp out of the stable, the rain continues its torrential downpour, the sky lit up by veins of lightning. Mother Nature is clearly pissed about something. Join the club.

When I step back into the house, each step is a throb of agony. I'm doing my damnedest not to show it, but damn, it hurts. As I close the door behind me, I look up to find Sophia in the living room, her eyes glued to the storm outside. But she turns, and her eyes widen when she sees me.

"Alissa, what happened? You're limping... and are your trousers soaked in blood?"

"It's nothing," I say, gritting my teeth.

"Don't give me that 'nothing' crap," she snaps, suddenly all fire and fury. "Sit down. Now."

Her tone leaves no room for argument. And despite my instinct to push her away, I find myself captivated by the concern in her eyes, a concern that's mirrored by the violent flashes of lightning outside. I sit down, rolling up my jeans to reveal the hastily wrapped towel, now more red than white.

"Jesus, Alissa," Sophia gasps, "You need to get this cleaned and bandaged, like, yesterday."

"I told you, it's fine. I'll manage."

Sophia's eyes meet mine, and I see something there I haven't seen before—fear. But also determination. She's not backing down. Not this time.

"Where's your first-aid kit?"

"In the bathroom cabinet," I reply, my voice softer now.

She hurries away and is back within seconds, first-aid kit in hand. I watch as she kneels in front of me, her hands trembling just slightly as she removes the towel and begins cleaning the wound. Each touch sends a current through me, electrifying and tender, raw yet soothing. It's a paradox, much like the woman in front of me. And as she dresses the wound with care, I realize that I'm not just feeling the sting of antiseptic. I'm feeling something far more dangerous, far more intoxicating.

"Is this going to scar?" she asks, breaking the silence.

I look down at my leg, then back up at her. "Scars remind us that our past is real. But so is the present moment."

Sophia looks up, and our eyes lock, just as thunder rumbles and the storm outside reaches a fevered pitch. It's as if the universe itself is telling us something.

"So I guess that's a yes?" Sophia asks with a smile.

"Yes," I reply.

As Sophia ties off the last bit of the bandage, her fingers lingering on my skin just a moment longer than necessary, I finally break the silence. "Jasper got spooked by the thunder, kicked me when I tried to calm him down."

Her hands pause, and she looks up at me, clearly concerned. "That could've been so much worse, Alissa."

"Yeah, well, it wasn't, thanks to you." I try to lighten the mood, but the grimace of pain probably ruins the effect.

"How's the pain? Bad?" she asks, not fooled for a second.

"Just a little," I lie. My leg is screaming like a banshee in a heavy metal band, but I'll be damned if I let her see that.

Sophia narrows her eyes, clearly not buying it, and fishes a painkiller out of the first-aid kit. "Take this."

I consider arguing, but one look at her determined face

IN A WORLD OF OUR OWN

and I cave. Swallowing the pill, I lie back on the couch at her insistence.

"Do you want me to call a doctor?" Sophia asks, her voice tinged with worry.

"I'm fine," I snap, more harshly than I intend to.

She chuckles. "You're just like my mother—never wanting anyone to take care of her."

"And you're the same," I shoot back.

"I guess we're both a pair of stubborn fools, then," Sophia says, the corners of her mouth lifting.

"I was supposed to take care of you, not the other way around."

"Guess now we'll just have to take care of each other," she quips. But as soon as the words leave her mouth, the atmosphere changes, thickens, heavy with unsaid things.

Just then, thunder crashes again, the sound reverberating through the walls of the ranch. The place takes on an eerie vibe, like we're in some kind of haunted house movie.

"The ranch during a thunderstorm kinda feels scary. Ever had a close encounter of the third kind with a ghost?" I ask, partially to distract myself from the growing tension.

Sophia's eyes widen. "Once. It was in an old bed and breakfast my family stayed in when I was a kid. Doors would randomly creak open and shut, and I swear I heard footsteps in the hallway when no one was there. Creeped the hell out of me."

I shiver a little, not entirely from the cold. "I had something like that too. I was alone at the ranch, and I kept hearing the sound of hooves around midnight, but when I checked, all the horses were in the stables. To this day, I have no idea what it was."

"This ranch?" Sophia asks, her voice shaky and unstable.

"Yeah, but don't worry. I was a kid and I probably had too much to drink that night."

"As a kid?" Sophia laughs.

"Yeah, milkshakes were my alcohol, baby. I used to get high off of that shit."

Just as I finish my sentence, another roll of thunder shakes the house. Sophia jumps a little. "Mind if I join you on the couch?"

"Be my guest," I say, shifting over to make room.

Sophia settles down next to me, and for a moment, it's like the storm outside is in here with us—full of electricity, charged with tension. Then, out of nowhere, I burst into laughter.

Sophia looks at me like I've lost my mind. "What's so funny?"

"Look at us," I say, wiping away a tear of mirth. "We've spent days avoiding each other like the plague, and here we are—two wounded souls huddled on a couch during a thunderstorm. It's ridiculous."

Sophia starts to laugh too, and the sound of it mixes with the howl of the wind and the rumble of thunder. But none of that matters because, for the first time in days, the storm inside me feels a little bit quieter.

Sophia's fingers interlock with mine, as if the simple touch could bridge the gap that had grown between us. "How've you been? I mean, during these past few days when we weren't talking."

"Keeping busy, mostly," I say, a little too quickly. "Work, horses... you know, the usual."

"And?"

I hesitate, then let out a sigh. "Okay, fine. I was also...

stalking you online a bit."

Her eyebrows shoot up, a mix of surprise and curiosity painting her face. "Really? What did you find?"

"Your life's an open book," I reply. "Your mom and her girlfriend are quite the power couple, and you're... well, you're famous too."

"I was famous. Now I'm yesterday's news," Sophia retorts, but there's a bitterness to her words that tells me it's a sore subject.

"I beg to differ," I say softly. "Fame might be fickle, but the impact you leave isn't."

Sophia falls silent, digesting that. I press on. "Your mom and Bella, huh? How'd you handle your best friend ending up with your mom? That's like a plot twist right out of a soap opera."

"At first, it was surreal. Felt like I was stuck in an episode of a reality show I never signed up for," Sophia says. "But then... I don't know. I saw how happy Bella made my mom, and something in me just gave way. It's been years now, and they're still madly in love."

"But it's shifted your mom's focus. You don't like that, do you?"

Sophia takes a deep breath, clearly wrestling with something. "It's not that simple. Mom's always with Bella now—touring, going to concerts. Her own career, her own life, it's all taken a backseat. And yeah, maybe so have I."

"Ever talked to her about it?"

"I'm bad with confrontation, Alissa," Sophia admits. "Plus, I don't want to be that whiny, needy daughter. I feel like if my own life were fulfilling enough, I wouldn't be so hung up on this."

"Oh, come on. It's okay to want attention, especially from

someone as important as your mom," I say, giving her hand a reassuring squeeze. "And as for the fulfilling life part—sometimes the very thing you think is holding you back is what you need to confront to move forward."

Sophia locks eyes with me, like she's trying to read the fine print in my soul. "So what do you think I need to confront?"

I pause, choosing my words carefully. "I think you need to stop letting the world dictate your worth. Society's version of 'successful' isn't a one-size-fits-all, you know?"

She raises an eyebrow. "So you're telling me to lower my ambitions?"

"No," I clarify, "I'm telling you to find a balance. Ambition is great, but so is taking time to appreciate what you already have. So tell me, what's your ultimate goal right now, at this very moment?"

"To be happy," she murmurs, just as a bolt of lightning fractures the sky, illuminating her face.

"And what do you think will make you truly happy?" I prod.

"I can't answer that," she says softly.

"Why?"

"Because it'll change the dynamics between us. Again."

I can't help but frown. "We've already had our friendship-altering moment. How many curveballs are left in this game?"

"We've only scratched the surface, Alissa. Trust me."

"So, you're saying there's more to our story?" I ask, inching closer to her. Every rational part of me screams to keep my distance; one more rejection and I'm basically signing myself up for emotional bankruptcy.

But then Sophia leans in too, breaking every invisible boundary. Her eyes flicker to my lips, and she moistens her own.

"So much more," she whispers, her voice tinged with a promise that sets my heart racing.

I can feel the electricity between us; it's like the storm outside has seeped into the room, filling the air with tension. My heart is pounding in my chest, each beat screaming for her to close the distance between us.

"I really want to kiss you right now," Sophia whispers, her eyes locked onto my lips.

"Are you sure you want to?" My voice is barely a murmur, but laced with anticipation.

Sophia's gaze flicks up to meet mine, her eyes darkening. "I've never been surer of anything. It's as if every nerve ending in my body is drawn to you, and they won't rest until I've tasted you, felt you, known you in the only way that will quench this fucking relentless thirst."

My heart skips a beat. "What about your brother?"

Sophia sighs, her breath warm against my face. "I don't want to care about anything or anyone else right now. I want you, Alissa."

With that, she closes the gap, her lips finally meeting mine. It's like a dam has burst, unleashing a torrent of suppressed emotions and desires. Her lips are soft, yet insistent, as if she's making up for lost time. Her hands cup my face, drawing me closer, and I can't help but yield to the pressure, giving as good as I get.

I kiss her back passionately, my hands sliding into her hair, pulling her closer. The kiss grows in intensity, consuming us. My whole body is aflame, each touch and caress stoking the fire within. For a moment, the storm outside, the ranch, the world, they all fade away. It's just us, wrapped in our own tempest of feelings and wants.

Sophia's tongue slides against mine, and it's like adding fuel to a fire. It's hot and fierce, a delicious clash of wills, each of us vying for control, neither willing to back down. And yet, it's the kind of struggle that neither of us wants to end.

Sophia's hands leave my face and move to my shoulders, gently pushing me until my back hits the soft cushions of the couch. Even as I lie down, she's careful of my injured leg, placing it delicately on the coffee table. But then her eyes meet mine, and it's like she's been unleashed.

Her lips find my neck, and my entire body trembles. It's as if she can't get enough, as she moves her lips all over my neck, kissing, nipping, and then soothing the spots with her tongue. She knows exactly where to press, where to linger. Each flick of her tongue sends electric jolts straight down to my core. My hands clutch at her back, pulling her closer.

My neck has always been a sensitive spot, but Sophia's actions ignite something that's off the charts. Her mouth moves greedily, her breathing heavy and laced with desire, as she paints a trail of fire down my neck and collarbone. It's wild, frenzied, almost as if she's making up for all the lost time, for all the unspoken words and untaken actions between us.

My fingers dig into her waist as my back arches slightly, pressing myself further into her touch, granting her better access. "Sophia," I gasp, my voice tinged with a plea, almost begging her not to stop, to keep this intoxicating sensation going.

I feel her smile against my skin, a predatory satisfaction that makes my pulse quicken. And then she bites down gently, just below my ear, eliciting a moan that I can't keep in.

Sophia's voice drops to a sultry whisper, her breath hot against my skin. "You have no idea how sexy you look, all wet and drenched like this." Her eyes meet mine briefly, and there's a burning hunger in them that sends shivers down my spine.

With that, her lips start a descent down my chest, leaving a

IN A WORLD OF OUR OWN

trail of fire on my skin. My shirt is soaked through from the rain, sticking to me like a second skin, and Sophia's mouth finds my cleavage easily. The fabric is so wet that I can feel her lips as if there's nothing there at all.

But then she starts licking the front of my shirt, right where my nipples press tightly against the soaked fabric. I gasp, feeling myself tense with a desire so intense it's almost unbearable. It's as if she's trying to draw the very soul out of me through the wet material. Her mouth seals over one, her lips plump and warm, and sucks hard. The dual sensation of the wet fabric and her saliva is sensory overload, pushing me dangerously close to the edge of reason.

Her other hand reaches up to squeeze my other breast through the fabric, wetting it with her own saliva as she sucks on the first. My back arches off the couch involuntarily, pushing myself deeper into her mouth and hand. Every rational thought has fled my mind, leaving only this wild, intense need that Sophia is stirring within me.

For a split second, I consider flipping the tables, throwing her onto the carpeted floor and taking control. The thought is exhilarating, electrifying.

I grab Sophia by the back of her head, pulling her lips back to mine with a hunger that borders on primal. Our mouths clash, teeth and tongues fighting for dominance. I slide my hand inside her skirt, my fingers digging into the soft skin of her hips, eliciting a soft moan from her.

The tension is electric as we pant and whisper dirty things into each other's ears. "You have no idea how long I've fantasized about this," I growl, my fingernails running over the curve of her ass. The sensations are intoxicating, overwhelming, pulling us both deeper into this swirling vortex of lust and emotion.

Just then, my phone chimes on the table beside us. An incoming text from Chris, my brother, flashes across the screen, asking how Sophia is and thanking me for being a good sister and taking care of his girlfriend. The irony of it stabs me like a cold blade, arresting the fire that was consuming us.

Sophia's eyes meet mine, her gaze searching. The room hangs in a palpable tension, both of us suddenly painfully aware of the complicated web we're entangled in.

I pull back, looking her in the eye. "Sophia, are you and my brother really together?"

She hesitates, then finally speaks. "Sort of. I plan to break things off once we get back. I've been helping him for his father to give him the company. I'm not in love with him anymore, but I want to help him get what he wants."

Her words hang heavy in the air between us. The intimacy of the moment we just shared still lingers, but now it's tainted by the complications of reality. The urgency that had filled the room dissipates, replaced by a myriad of conflicting emotions.

Sophia and I sit on the edge of the couch, our hands still entwined. Her touch is warm, a striking contrast to the chill I feel running down my spine. "We should stop this," I whisper, "until you've talked to Chris."

Sophia looks at me with those piercing eyes, full of an emotion I can't quite place. "I agree. This isn't fair to any of us, especially Chris."

"And especially not to us," I add. My voice almost cracks as I say it, but I manage to hold it steady. I look at our intertwined hands, our fingers perfectly fitting like puzzle pieces. It's hard to believe that something that feels so right could be so complicated.

We sit there, the heaviness of our shared silence filling the room. Finally, I muster the courage to ask, "So, why do you want to break up with Chris? If you don't mind me asking."

Sophia takes a deep breath. "Chris is an incredible guy. He's ambitious, smart, and has a kindness that's really rare. But over time, I've realized that I don't feel the same thrill, the same excitement I used to feel. I can't keep stringing him along. He deserves better."

The sincerity in her voice is unmistakable, but it doesn't soothe the nagging question in my mind. I look at the massive bookshelf across the room, its spines filled with histories and romances, tales of choices and their outcomes. "Is it because of me? Please be honest. The last thing I want is to be the reason for my brother's unhappiness."

Sophia shakes her head fervently. "No, it has nothing to do with you, Alissa. My feelings for Chris had started to change long before I met you."

I sigh, relieved. Then a playful idea pops into my head. "So, you're helping Chris become the CEO, huh? The same position that I've been eyeing. What's the game plan here, Soph? You can be the kingmaker!"

She laughs, a sound that makes my heart flutter in spite of everything. "Well, I guess we've got ourselves a real 'Game of Thrones' situation here. I am very clear in my head, Alissa. I won't betray Chris. I'll be the girlfriend he wants me to be, until Henry decides who he wants as the next CEO."

"I'm not as power-hungry as Cersei, but I've got the cunning of Tyrion," I quip. "But don't worry, I want to play the game fair and square. I won't cheat against my brother. You know, I make a far better sister to Chris than he's ever been a brother to me. He didn't even let me ride his dirt bike when we were kids!"

Sophia leans against the back of the couch, crossing her arms. "I think you and Chris need to sort things out between yourselves."

I chuckle dryly, "And what's the point of that? In a few days, we'll be back at square one when he finds out I'm dating his ex." The words slip out, and I suddenly feel their weight in the room.

Raising an eyebrow, Sophia inches closer to me, her voice tinged with playful seduction. "Already laying out the roadmap for our future, are we? Ever heard of consent, Anderson?"

I shoot her a teasing look, the electricity between us almost palpable. "Ah, the irony. You're one to talk, Miller. You practically pounced on me just minutes ago!"

Sophia grins, eyes flicking to mine. "You were simply irresistible."

I smirk, folding my arms across my chest. "Irresistible? What was so damn irresistible about me?"

Sophia leans towards me, her gaze tracing over me like calligraphy on parchment. "Your wet hair, sticking to your face. Your shirt, hugging you in all the right places. And even your injured leg."

I chuckle incredulously, "My injured leg? Really?"

She leans in, her voice dropping an octave. "Absolutely. There's something incredibly sexy about how you got hurt trying to save those horses of yours. If it were me, I'd have hightailed it back to the ranch."

Feeling emboldened, I close the gap between us, my fingers lightly grazing the curve of her neck before tangling in her hair. "And what if I told you to hightail it straight back to me after all this family drama blows over?"

Sophia leans into my touch, her eyes hooded but intense. "You do realize all this touching is playing with fire, right?"

I smirk, letting the electricity between us spark. "So, should I continue sleeping on the mattress then?"

Her voice thick with desire, she says, "Not a chance. I want you right beside me, every night."

"And what about clothes?" I ask, my eyes twinkling with mischief. "Should they be invited to this slumber party?"

"Absolutely not," Sophia purrs, and I realize I am in for a few tantalizing nights in the near future.

∞∞∞

Sophia and I clean out the fridge, eating yesterday's scrambled eggs and bacon like we're at some five-star brunch. It's like a little slice of normalcy, but the way we lock eyes over bites of toast makes it clear: normal is long gone.

We head up to my room, collapsing on the bed together. The emotional toll of the last few days catches up, and we're out like a light. I never thought falling asleep next to someone could feel like such an adventure, but here we are.

Sophia's phone buzzes us awake. It's a call from Chris. Sophia talks, but her voice lowers when she mentions my leg injury. My mom overhears and panics, asking to speak with me. "Mom, chill. I'm fine. I didn't wrestle a bear."

"We're driving back tonight," she insists. I roll my eyes but agree. Moms will be moms.

As I end the call, I can see Sophia is puzzled. "Mom's got a Ph.D. in worrying," I explain.

"You know, your mom's sweet, but your dad?" Sophia trails off.

"Yeah, he can be a real piece of work. Mom's always tiptoeing around him, the perennial Southern belle. I've tried to tell him to be nicer, but you know old men—they're as stubborn as their outdated views."

We decide to ring up the staff, ending their day off a bit early. "We've got about an hour of privacy left," Sophia teases, a sly grin on her face.

I arch an eyebrow, "Is that an invitation or a challenge?"

"Could be both," she laughs.

I shake my head. "You do remember the boundaries we set, right? Besides, we are roomies. It's not like we're starved for alone time."

Sophia bursts into giggles. "I get to be the intimidating one now, huh?"

I saunter over to her and lock eyes. "Good luck with that, Miller. Intimidation is my middle name."

Chapter Five

(Sophia)

I lied to Alissa again. Well, it's more like I shaded the truth. I wanted to be as forthright as I could, but some things just aren't mine to disclose.

Chris's sexuality? That's his story to tell. I've got no business spilling those beans, even if my feelings for Alissa are getting complicated—intense, irrevocable, and somewhat overwhelming.

Alissa herself has turned into this irresistible force, a maelstrom of allure aimed directly at me, tempting me to cross a line.

What line, though? That's the question. Because, technically, I'm not with Chris. So, it's not like getting involved with Alissa equates to betrayal. But she's in the dark about all this.

Until Henry Anderson makes up his mind about who's steering the Anderson Corp ship, my hands are metaphorically tied. They're definitely not exploring the tempting territory of Alissa's curves. Oh, the struggle is real.

So here we are—Alissa and me—in a game of cat and mouse, with a ranch as our playground and lines we've promised not to cross. The funny thing about lines? They blur when you get too close, and boy, have we been testing those limits.

Instance one, the stables. With horses prepped for a group ride, I find myself alone, hands brushing over the mane of the gelding I'll be riding. It still feels weird to be touching the things that once were the main characters in my nightmares. Then, in walks Alissa, filling the barn with her earthy perfume—something like cedar and wildflowers. She finds me and pins me to a wall of hay bales. "Last chance to be my riding partner," she whispers, hot breath on my neck.

Just as my willpower starts crumbling like a cookie in milk, in walks Chris, as clueless as ever. "Hey, you two, ready to hit the trail?" he calls, blissfully ignorant of the electricity between us. Alissa steps back like she's been burned, and I adjust my hair and composure.

"Ready as we'll ever be," I answer, throwing Alissa a look that says, "We're not done here."

Instance two, a midnight raid on the kitchen. I'm alone, gobbling up the leftover apple pie like it holds the answers to my life. Alissa strides in, quiet as a cat, and leans against the counter. "Can't sleep?" she asks, a loaded question if there ever was one.

Our eyes lock as I take another forkful of pie, savoring it slowly to torture us both. The air gets so thick you could cut it with a knife. Suddenly, the sound of footsteps. Alissa and I both freeze like we've been caught stealing. It's just Susie, coming for a glass of water, but in that moment, we're guilty as sin. "Evening, ladies," she mumbles, bleary-eyed, as she leaves. Alissa and I break into guilty laughter as I set the fork down, leaving us both starving in more ways than one.

Third instance, the lake. We're there under the guise of fishing, but it's the two of us who are the real catch. Alissa stands close—too close—helping me with my casting technique, her body against mine as she takes my hands in hers. "Feel the tension but control it," she breathes into my ear, and it's all I can do not to turn around and kiss her senseless.

Just as I'm about to give in to this magnetic force between us, a sharp 'Ahem' interrupts us. It's Jared, Chris' friend, carrying a tackle box like he's ready to bait us into a confession. "Mind if I join you?" he asks, but he's already settling down before we can reply. Alissa and I look at each other, our secret safe but the tension undiminished.

"Lines, Sophia. Remember, we drew lines," Alissa whispers, her voice betraying her impatience and desire.

"Yeah," I say, feeling my voice tremble, "but lines can be crossed, erased, or redrawn, can't they?"

She gazes at me, her eyes aflame with the same turbulent emotions coursing through my veins. "It's not a matter of if, Sophia, but when."

And there we leave it, our vows to keep our hands to ourselves hanging by the thinnest thread, as fragile and taut as a spider's web after a storm. But one thing's for sure—sooner or later, the storm will break, and I'm not sure either of us will be ready for the deluge that follows.

Two weeks pass from the day I stepped into the world of the Andersons, and finally, I start feeling more at home than ever before. From nervous glances to stolen touches, I've found myself oddly attached to the rough yet vibrant pulse of this Texas ranch. Riding horses isn't a nightmare anymore; it's something I do. Alissa has been a good teacher, her eyes twinkling with mischief and pride each time I finally grasp something new.

Days at the ranch are a sweaty blend of horses, mud, outdoor picnics, walks by the lake, ogling at Alissa, cuddling with her while she sleeps and basketball games. Chris and his friend Mark have something of a bromance, always at the court, getting their game on. The chemistry between them intrigues me—there's more than just ball passes and three-pointers happening there. Mental note: I need to ask Chris what's up.

As the days pile on, it's not just horse manure and hay that add weight. My career back in New York, or the lack of it, casts a shadow. Yet, what gnaws at me is the radio silence from Ava, my mother. No calls, no texts, nothing. Three weeks of silence and my anxiety is ready to build its own ranch.

"Alissa," I finally blurt out as we're winding down for the night, the soft glow of her bedside lamp casting intimate shadows. "I haven't heard from my mother in almost three weeks."

Alissa turns on her side, her head propped up by pillows, and looks at me with concern in her ocean-blue eyes. "Did you try to call her?"

"No. I call her most of the time. Shouldn't she... I don't know, remember from time to time that she has a full-blown, human daughter existing, surviving somewhere in the world?"

"Maybe she's caught up with something?"

"Yeah, Bella Foster, the blonde bombshell who's ensnared my mom in her jaws."

"Sophia, you need to talk with your mother. This misunderstanding will keep gnawing at you until one day it becomes too severe to clear, maybe damaging your relationship with your mother beyond repair. Give your mom a call right now. I'll leave the room so you can talk to her in peace."

"You're not going anywhere. You're the spinach to my Popeye."

"The hay to your horse?"

I smile. "I wonder how much more cringe we can make this."

"The dildo to your pussy?" Alissa laughs, and I roll my eyes. "I wish."

"Call your mom, Soph. C'mon."

After a little internal deliberation, I decide to be vulnerable one last time.

My heart beats in my ears as I find mom's phone number, and tap the call button. Finally, my mother's voice comes through on the speaker phone. "Sophia?"

"Hi, Mom. How are you? Where are you?" The words come out, tinged with a mix of hope and apprehension.

"I'm back in New York. Just came back from a press tour for Bella's new cosmetic line," she responds, a flatness in her tone.

"New York? Mom, we planned to catch up once you were back. What happened?" My voice trembles, a cocktail of disappointment and anger building.

"We were tired, Sophia. Bella and I just wanted some time to ourselves," she states.

Time to themselves? My fist clenches involuntarily. Alissa, sensing my rising tension, places a comforting hand on my shoulder. "How's Bella doing, then?" I manage to ask, tightening my grip on the phone.

"She's... coping. I wonder how she handles so much stress on her own," Mom answers, a note of admiration in her voice.

I can't hold it in any longer. "On her own? Mom, Bella has teams and assistants, loads of money, and most importantly, you. She's not doing it on her own. I've been fighting by myself."

A heavy silence fills the line. "Sophia, it's not like—"

"Do you even remember you have a daughter? I've been alone, struggling to salvage my career, navigating a painful breakup. Bella used to call herself my soul sister. Where is she now? Where are you?"

Silence. The void fills with unspoken words and unsaid confessions. Finally, she asks, "Where are you, Sophia?"

"I'm in Texas, at the Andersons' ranch with Chris. I've wanted to share this experience with you, with Bella, with anyone who'd care to listen, but no one's been there. Nicole and Emma are off doing their thing in LA. I've had no one."

The phone line is quiet. "Sophia, listen, we do care about you. Things have been complicated here as well."

My chest tightens. "Complicated for who? For you or for me? I think we've been living in different realities, Mom."

"I love you, Sophia. Bella does, too. We've just been…busy."

"Busy is a luxury I can't afford," I snap. "Take care of your life, Mom. I'll handle mine," and I end the call, my eyes meeting Alissa's.

Her eyes hold a universe of comfort and understanding, and it's when I lock onto those celestial orbs that I feel the dam break. Tears stream down my face as my sobbing becomes uncontrolled, a reflection of unmet expectations and disappointment that I can't contain any longer.

Alissa's arms circle me, her whispered words of strength filling my ears, intermingled with the soothing scent of her perfume. But nothing seems capable of quelling this anguish.

I surrender to the comforting cradle of her body. As her fingers softly stroke my hair, I nuzzle against her chest, indifferent to the dampness my tears leave on her skin.

"Hey, Soph, it's okay to let it out," Alissa murmurs as she gently strokes my back. "You know, most people look at me and think I have it all—wealth, looks, a loving family. But that's far from reality."

I sniffle, intrigued despite my misery. "What do you mean?"

"My dad? Barely acknowledges me unless it has something to do with the business. My mom? She's amazing but she has a soft corner for Chris. Friends? Well, let's just say, when your life is this public, it's hard to know who's genuine."

Alissa's voice is a tender caress, and I find myself listening intently. "Sometimes we need isolation to realize that maybe, just maybe, we don't need a lot of people around us to feel complete or to achieve greatness. Take the example of J.K Rowling," Alissa whispers, her lips gently grazing my ears, as her words continue to soothe me,

"She was a struggling single mother, going through a divorce and living off welfare. Almost everyone in her life had abandoned her. Even after she finished writing Harry Potter, a story that came to her when she was at her lowest, twelve publishers rejected it."

"Twelve rejections, huh?" I manage to murmur through my lingering pain.

"Exactly. But she persevered, fought her way through depression, poverty, and the odds stacked against her. She's now one of the most successful authors on the planet, a literal billionaire. And she did it mostly on her own," Alissa concludes, her eyes meeting mine as if urging me to find a fragment of myself in Rowling's story.

I'm still reeling from my own emotional whirlpool, but I can't help but feel a spark of warmth, knowing how much Alissa is trying to lift me up. "That's cool and all, and it means a lot that you're sharing this with me, Alissa. But you know how fresh wounds are. They still sting."

Alissa nods, her eyes filled with a complex blend of understanding and compassion. "I know one inspirational story won't mend everything that's been broken, Sophia. But sometimes, hearing about someone else's journey can offer a glimmer of light in our darkest tunnels."

As she holds me, my soul still writhes with the fresh agony of maternal abandonment, but her arms feel like a sanctuary in a world that's showing its colder corners to me. "Thank you, Alissa," I say softly. The words are simple, but they carry the weight of genuine gratitude, admiration, and a tinge of unexpected warmth amidst a sorrow that's far from vanishing.

My heart skips a beat as Alissa murmurs into my ear, her voice a sultry blend of emotion and intent, "Can I cross that boundary tonight, Sophia? Just this once?"

"Why?" I find myself half-joking despite the whirlwind of emotions inside me, "You know I don't need pity sex, right?"

Alissa's eyes meet mine, illuminated by a raw, incandescent fire. "There's nothing pitious about you, Sophia. You're pure, innocent, and so goddamn raw that it makes me want to worship you. I want to show you how much I admire you, in every conceivable way."

Before I can even process her words, Alissa climbs on top of me, her body a warm promise against mine. She stretches an arm to the bedside control panel and presses a button. The room fills with the soulful melody of Taylor Swift's "Lover."

I hug her tightly as the music plays, my voice tinged with vulnerability. "What if this leads to more heartbreak for me?"

She silences me with a soft, lingering kiss. "Let's not think about the 'what ifs' for now. Let's just be in this moment. I want to taste every inch of you. I want to touch your soul, Sophia. Forget about the world, our families, our ambitions, and our insecurities. Let's just drown ourselves in each other, if only for tonight."

Her words hit me like a bolt of lightning, melting the last of my reserves. For the first time in what feels like an eternity, I feel wanted, seen—loved, in a way that's raw and unfiltered. And for that, I'm willing to risk the heartbreak that might come later.

I pull her down into a kiss, sealing a pact that's been silently forming between us. For tonight, the rest of the world can wait. Tonight, we drown in each other, no holds barred.

Alissa's eyes meet mine, their blues deeper than any ocean, as the last strum of Taylor Swift's "Lover" fades into silence. Her fingers lightly trace the outline of my jaw, sending shivers down my spine. In a move that's as natural as it is electric, our lips meet—first gently, then with increasing urgency.

Her hand travels down my neck, barely grazing the skin, yet leaving a trail of fire. She hovers over the buttons of my blouse, her eyes seeking permission. I nod, my heartbeat racing so fast it's all I can hear.

As she unbuttons my blouse, her eyes never leave mine. My blouse falls open, and her fingers softly graze the lace of my bra, as if she's memorizing the very texture of me.

My breath catches as she moves to kiss the curve of my neck, her lips gentle but insistent. The sensation is electrifying, each touch amplified by the weight of what's about to happen between us. Her hands find my waist, pulling me closer until our bodies are flush against each other.

Her lips move downward, exploring the valley between my collarbones. The warmth of her mouth leaves a tingling sensation, like the afterglow of a beautiful sunset. Her hands move to the small of my back, pressing me into her as if she could absorb me into her very being. I can feel her heartbeat, strong and steady, and it fills me with a sense of belonging I hadn't realized I'd been missing.

Breaking away for a moment, she looks into my eyes, and in them, I see a reflection of my own vulnerability and desire. She whispers softly, "Are you sure?"

In answer, my hands find the hem of her shirt, lifting it to reveal the expanse of her smooth skin. My fingers tremble, not from fear but from the sheer depth of my emotions. For once, my mind is silent—no fears, no what-ifs—filled only by the sound of our breaths, mingled in the air between us.

"Beyond sure," I whisper back, sealing our pact with another kiss.

Alissa smiles, the curve of her lips the most beautiful thing I've ever seen. Her hands return to my waist, and I feel her fingers slip beneath the fabric, tugging it free with a newfound confidence.

Her fingers dance over my stomach, tracing invisible patterns as if she's writing a secret message known only to us. She glides her fingers to my thighs, sending shivers that make their way up my spine, electrifying my every nerve. I find her waist and draw her toward me, my fingertips digging into her skin just enough to elicit a gasp. It's a sound that's part surprise, part exhilaration, and it pushes me further.

Our eyes lock again, and I can see my own lust mirrored in her gaze.

She lowers her lips to mine, and our kiss is hungry, urgent. It's as if we're trying to consume the passion, the pent-up emotions we've been carrying.

Her hand reaches my face, her thumb caressing my lower lip. I take the opportunity to kiss her thumb, tasting the saltiness of her skin. Her fingers then slide to my neck, her grip firm but gentle, as if she holds my very essence in her hands. I feel the pressure, a sweet ache that's paradoxically soothing.

"Do you trust me?" she asks, her voice heavy with an emotion that I can't quite name but understand all too well.

"With every fiber of my being," I breathe out, amazed at how true the words feel.

She smiles, the last barrier between us crumbling away, leaving nothing but pure, unfiltered connection. "Then let go, Sophia. Let go and let me take you to heights you've never imagined."

As she says those words, I feel a release, as if chains I didn't know were holding me back suddenly break.

I clasp my arms around her, pull her to me, onto me so that I can have her closer. Her lips are frantic, wild and wet on mine, her body as light as a feather as she rolls half on top of me. She's shaking, panting for air as I hold her with all of strength, trying to imprint her skin onto mine. Her fingers slide up along my ribs to my breasts, and her kisses are delicious and insistent. My need is almost unbearable but we need to slow down and take it slow. "Slow down, slow... slower," I beg, when I can. "Slow down. Slow down, you're..."

I trail off as she moans, "No. Fuck no!" Her voice is filled with longing and desperation.

"I've waited so long for you. I thought I would never have you and then, just when I was about to give up hope, you came back to me. I'm not going slow. I want to go crazy, I want you... I need you. I crave you."

I sit upright and shift. The fabric of her nightie brushes my skin as she pulls it up and off her. She slumps forward again, and this time I feel the warmth of her breasts against mine. A deep groan escapes me as I pull her closer, legs quivering and trembling as she squeezes my aching nipples. "Show me how to make love to you," she whispers desperately. "Show me how to be what you want...I want to be what you want..."

"You are. Oh god, just touch me. Kiss me," I beg her, and she responds by shuddering out an echo into my neck. I feel her fumbling at me and cry out a relieved yes as she manages to slip her hand inside my leggings.

My nails dig into her back as she finds me. She cries out in pleasure and shifts off of me so that she can lie beside me, gently teasing my swollen lips open with hers. I'm soaked, and she gives a breathy moan of desire as she finds my entrance. "Alissa, Alissa, please," I plead, moving desperately against her. "Put your fingers in me... like this..." Fumbling down, I take her hand and guide it into me with a cry of pleasure as my body tightens around her. My other hand moves to my clit and I start to frantically stroke myself as she pushes her fingers deeper inside me. She pants into my neck, biting down on my ear, grinding her belly against my hip as she takes me.

Her fingers penetrate me, my soul, my being, and I thrust my hips to meet her fingers. I have never wanted anyone so deep inside me.

We lock eyes. She growls and takes one my nipples in her eager mouth.

"Yes, Oh my god…yes!" Her tongue swirling around my nipples, her clawed fingers destroying my vagina…it's all too much.

She bites, nips and pulls on my nipples.

I grab her hair, and stuff her mouth full of my tit. Her fingers reach places in me I didn't know existed.

And then I wail—a howl that would have reached the stables outside.

"Fuck yes babyyyyy…my babyyyy!"

I writhe on the bed, on her hand, like a tortured soul, extracting every last bit of friction from her fingers, until I am cumming all over them. I press my forehead against Alissa's and look into her eyes as I cum for her…for the hottest blonde to walk the earth.

My back goes rigid, quivering like mad as Alissa's fingers find just the right spot. I can't even form words; I'm lost in this electrifying feeling that rocks me to my core. Alissa keeps me steady, her fingers still inside me, letting me come back to Earth on my own time.

She snuggles against me, laying her head on my shoulder. We're both catching our breath, and I'm still struggling to get my words back. When she finally pulls her hand away, my thighs clench around it like they don't want to let go. A kiss on my neck sends another shiver through me.

She's all softness when she says, "I've been dreaming of this, of making you totally mine."

Summoning some strength, I wrap an arm around her and pull her closer. She lies half on me, her hand, still damp, resting between my boobs. I catch a whiff of us mingled together, and it's intoxicating, making me twitch again.

"Sophia?" She's whispering, like even she's afraid to break the spell.

"I'm...wow. Give me a sec," is all I manage.

A laugh bubbles up from her. "So, a good time, huh?"

"Hell yeah," I say, finally finding my voice. "It was exactly what I needed."

As we lay there, hearts still pounding, I can't help but soak in the moment. Alissa's fingers lazily trace circles on my collarbone, and our eyes meet. There's this smoky intensity in her gaze, and I'm suddenly very aware that the night is far from over.

"Are you trying to hypnotize me with those eyes, Alissa?" I tease, catching my breath.

She grins, her eyes still locked onto mine. "If I had that power, do you know the naughty things I'd have you do?"

I chuckle. "Do I even want to know?"

"You'll find out," she says, her voice dropping to a sultrier tone. "But for now, how about we give your body a different kind of attention?"

Before I can ask what she means, she starts showering me with light kisses, beginning at my collarbone and traveling downward. Each kiss is like a spark, reigniting the fire that I thought had temporarily cooled.

"Turn over," she whispers, pausing her descent. "Lie on your belly for me."

I comply, flipping over and resting my face on a pillow. I feel the mattress shift as Alissa positions herself, straddling my thighs. Her hands find my back, lightly grazing my skin before settling into a more rhythmic motion. She starts massaging my tense muscles, her fingers expertly kneading away any residual stress.

"You're all knotted up here," she murmurs, pressing her thumbs into a particularly tight spot near my shoulder blades. "Does it hurt?"

"In the best way," I manage to groan. "Keep going."

She leans in close, her lips brushing against the nape of my neck, sending shivers down my spine. "Don't worry, I intend to cover every inch of you."

Her hands move lower, tracing the contours of my back before slipping down to my thighs. Her fingers squeeze gently, then more firmly, as if she's claiming each piece of me as her own. Her touch is electrifying, igniting a different kind of heat that courses through me.

"How are you so good at this?" I gasp, surprised at the sensation she's evoking.

"I aim to please," she says. "Besides, I've wanted to touch you like this for so long, I've practically choreographed it in my mind."

I laugh at her candidness, but my laughter catches in my throat as her fingers edge perilously close to more intimate areas. I feel her lean in closer, her breath hot against my ear.

"Are you ready for round two?" she whispers, her voice tinged with anticipation.

My heart pounds in response, my body already yearning for

her touch, eager for whatever she has choreographed next. "I've never been more ready for anything in my life."

∞∞∞

I pace around, alone in Alissa's room, looking at the crumpled sheets on the bed where Alissa rocked my world last night. The morning sun looms over the horizon, but the beauty of the Texan sunrise is lost on me.

I am an emotional mess.

From my mom's utter lack of care regarding my existence, to Alissa and her body, her face and her heart slowly pulling me into the quicksand of emotions…and probably love.

Yup. I am thinking of the L word, because I know what it feels to be in love, and this is eerily similar.

Alissa had to leave before sunrise—work emergency or something, but she had left a little note by the side of the bed, 'have to leave urgently, but I'll be back soon. You are always on my mind. Miss you.'

Now, that sounds like love-talk to me. Or relationship talk at the minimum.

Am I already in a damn relationship with my pretend boyfriend's sister who wants to take over the company he wants?

Yes, last night was incredible. It was more than incredible. It was the best sex I've had in years, and yes, I am completely head over heels for an American born, British educated cowgirl, but what about Chris?

I need to tell him the truth. I can't keep lying to both Chris and Alissa and risk losing them both!

I mull over my thoughts, when suddenly, I realize I need advice.

I sit on the edge of the bed, phone pressed to my ear, nervously twirling a strand of my hair.

"Nicole? It's me," I say, as Nicole screams over the phone.

"Oh my god, I was about to call you! How are you, girl?" Nicole's voice seems chirpy. At least *someone* is happy to talk to me.

"I am good. I know you are in LA, and you must be knee-deep with the opening of your studio, but I really needed to talk to someone. Do you have a min?"

"Of course, baby. What's up?"

So, you remember Chris, the guy who revived my career three years ago and became my best friend?"

"Uh…yeah the guy who owns Anderson Stores, right?"

"Exactly him. He asked me to pretend to be his girlfriend to impress his conservative family. He is gay, and the whole charade is supposed to help him secure the CEO position in his family's corporation."

"And you agreed to this because?"

"Because it's Chris. We've been through a lot, and if a pretend relationship can help him, why not?"

Nicole pauses, absorbing the complexity of the situation. "Alright, so you were sure you could handle being the conservative, pretend girlfriend of a gay guy, while hiding your own sexuality?"

I chuckle. "Initially, yes. But then I met his sister, Alissa. She's also vying for the CEO position. And she's… into women."

"You're kidding. Don't tell me you two—"

"Yes, we did. And it wasn't just a fling. Being with her feels like… finding a missing piece of myself, you know? But now I'm lying to her, to Chris, and maybe even to myself."

"Wait, hold on, does Alissa know about the whole pretend relationship setup?"

"No, she doesn't. Now it feels like I've dug myself into a hole so deep, I can't climb out."

Nicole pauses, offering a nugget of wisdom. "Relationships, especially new and passionate ones, have to be built on trust. Honesty isn't just a good policy; it's the only policy. Have you considered coming clean to both of them?"

"I've thought about it, but I'm terrified of the fallout. What if coming clean ruins everything for everyone? Chris's future, my relationship with Alissa—everything."

"But how would it ruin Chris's future?"

"He clearly doesn't trust his sister with his sexuality secret, so I want to respect his decision and not spill the beans. Plus, he's been adamant about me not doing anything that could jeopardize his chances of becoming the CEO. And I'm pretty sure me sleeping with his only competition isn't 'best-friend behavior.'"

"Who's in charge of deciding the next CEO?" Nicole asks.

"Henry Anderson. He's the head honcho of the Anderson clan, a man's man—homophobic and terrifying. Imagine my mom, but bearded, rugged, straight as an arrow, and Texan."

"Ew, not a pretty image. So Henry Anderson can't know his son is gay. He wants his son married, or at least in a stable relationship, before handing him the company. Meanwhile, Alissa knows her brother is dating a cheating whore?"

"Nicole! Shut up! She doesn't think of me like that!"

Nicole laughs. "Alright, so Alissa could theoretically tell her father everything and become the CEO, right?"

"She could, but she won't. She's an angel, Nicole, except in bed. There she's really the devil," I say, my cheeks turning red.

"Okay, assuming she does spill the beans, what's the worst that can happen? You tell Henry that she's gay too, and then what? He decides which gay child gets the company?"

"He'd probably rather die."

"I don't see the problem, Soph. Tell Chris the truth, tell Alissa the truth, explore whatever this is with Alissa, and stay neutral in the CEO competition."

"Chris won't appreciate my neutrality. I know that."

Nicole sighs. "What's the real deal with Alissa? Is she just a freak in bed, or is there more?"

"There's so much more, Nicole. I think I'm falling in love," I admit, finally saying the words that have haunted me since last night.

Nicole's voice softens. "Sophia, you're at a crossroads, and neither path is easy. But delaying the truth will only make things worse. If what you have with Alissa is as powerful as you say, and if Chris is a good friend, they both deserve the truth. And you deserve to speak it."

"I know. But it's so complicated."

We both fall silent, and I look out the window at the colorful sky.

"So, how's Emma? And when is the studio launch?"

"Emma's good. Keeps asking about you. The launch is this weekend. I was about to call and invite you, but I guess you won't make it, huh?"

"It's tough," I admit. "But let's catch up as soon as we're all back in New York, okay?"

"Absolutely. I have to go; Susie's down with a fever and Emma's not home."

"Take care of your Susie. The Susie here is nothing like

yours. Nice catching up, babe. And all the best for the dance studio. Keep teaching girls to pole dance; that's what the world needs right now—sexy women on poles. Bye."

∞∞∞

I sit next to Chris on the sundeck, my heart pounding like a drum solo in a rock concert. I am mustering courage to tell him the truth. The situation seems perfect for it. "Chris," I start, but falter. "Um, don't you just love these sunsets? They're really something."

Chris turns his gaze toward me, squinting as though he's trying to decrypt a complex equation visible only on my face. "You okay, Sophia? You seem a bit...off. Anything on your mind?" His voice is drenched in gentle concern, yet still holding that note of boyish curiosity.

He rises from his chair, an old leather thing that's seen better days, and comes to sit beside me. As he takes my hand, I feel his warmth radiate through the calloused texture of his skin —those hands that have worked the ranch but also held me in moments of need.

"I know it's been hard for you, Soph, and I want to thank you. Thank you, Sophia," he starts, his voice a caressing whisper tinged with an unspoken heaviness. "For everything, really. You've stepped out of your comfort zone, handled my insane family drama, put your own career on pause. Hell, you even pull off the cowboy boots like a natural now."

I chuckle softly, touched by his words, but the tension still lingers. "Well, maybe I like the drama. Keeps life interesting."

He grins, but then his smile fades a bit. "I talked to my dad today."

I feel a swirl of emotions rise within me—like a twister

made of both joy and sorrow. My lips curl into a smile, but it's mixed with a certain discomfort. "Oh? And?"

"It sounds promising, Sophia. I think I might actually become the new CEO. Our little charade is working wonders."

I hug him tightly then, my chest constricting, almost suffocated by the blend of emotions. "You've worked so hard for this, Chris. It's well-deserved."

Pulling back from the hug, he searches my eyes. "I can't help but feel a little bad for Alissa, though. She's dreamed of this ever since we were in college. But I want her involved, equally involved. CEO might be my title, but she'll be just as vital. I plan for us to work together."

He grows more introspective, sharing more of his personal history with Alissa. "She was my protector, you know? When kids at school would call me a 'bookworm' or 'teacher's pet,' she'd step up and tell them to back off, like a fierce little lioness."

As he speaks, I find myself getting lost in his recollections, a visceral empathy growing within me.

"She's been so welcoming to you, Sophia. Even though she knows you could be the 'deal-breaker' for her, she's never let that stand in the way. I want to celebrate both of you when all this is over—two incredibly strong women that mean the world to me."

His words slam into me, sending waves of guilt surging through my veins. The realization hits hard: I might be the reason Alissa loses her lifelong dream. "Why not tell her the truth, Chris? That you're gay? She's not like the rest of your family."

Chris deliberates, his eyes clouding with a momentary uncertainty. "I will, Sophia, but not until I officially have the job. Can't risk the boat capsizing when we're this close to shore."

I feel a slight change in the atmosphere as Chris steers the conversation toward more personal matters. "How are things with your mom and Bella?" he asks, his eyes a pool of genuine concern.

I sigh. "Complicated. We had a fight and aren't really on speaking terms."

Chris gently places his hand over mine, as if trying to pass some of his strength into me. "Once we're back in New York, I'll host an intervention or something. You two need to sort things out."

I chuckle, trying to dispel the tension. "God, is that your solution to everything? You sound like every self-help book I've ever read."

He laughs back. "Maybe I should add 'life coach' to my resume then."

Changing the subject, I tell him about my upcoming collab with 'Jewel,' the upscale hotel chain. "I've got this poolside shoot tomorrow. It's a big deal for my brand. I'll need to step out of the ranch."

"Don't worry about it," Chris reassures me, "I'll just tell Dad you have to go shopping or something. You and Alissa can make a girls' day out of it."

I can't help but tease him. "Aren't you the brave one, leaving me alone with your irresistibly hot sister?"

Chris snorts, obviously amused. "Trust me, the only things Alissa is interested in are rows and columns on an Excel sheet. She's practically a robot."

As he says this, a flood of memories engulfs my mind.

Me, on all fours, holding onto the headboard of the bed as Alissa plunged her fingers deep into me, the creaking of the bed as she humped my thighs until they were slick with her juices... the grunts coming from her as she attacked my pussy with her mouth.

I can't help but smile slyly, thinking, Yeah, she's a robot alright, but in ways you could never imagine, Chris.

Chapter Six

(Alissa)

"How long is this shoot?" Susie asks me, nonchalantly.

"As long as it takes for you to braid your hair," I say, looking over my shoulder at Susie, and the intricate web of braids covering her scalp. She has somehow persuaded her mom to allow her to accompany her to this girls day out.

I glance at Sophia, her eyes determinedly on the road, hands gripping the wheel like she's holding onto her sanity.

"How much are you getting paid for this?" Susie asks, her voice bordering on sleepy, her eyes practically glued to the window. "Not much, I bet!"

Sophia rolls her eyes but can't hide a small smile. "Enough to buy plenty of Vogue magazines, Susie." I wink at my younger cousin, who goes red in her cheeks.

"Susie, have you ever thought how you'd look in a bikini?" Sophia asks, joining in on the fun.

"No. Bikinis tempt the minds of men."

"Not just men, baby," I say and offer Sophia a sly smile.

"What do you mean?"

"Bikinis on a good body, like the one Sophia has, are hot enough to make women think naughty thoughts as well. Have you ever had naughty thoughts about women?" I can't help myself, I am having too much fun.

Susie makes a face as if she has seen human poo.

"Both of you need Jesus," she blurts out.

"And you need to get laid. You are 22. At your age, the only time I called out for God was when I was in bed with another human being," I say, making myself comfy on the passenger seat.

"What does that even mean?" Susie prods.

"It means your cousin would only pray with someone else. She never likes praying alone," Sophia adds, controlling her laughter, but barely.

"I would like to sit alone in silence please," Susie says, making another poo face.

"Sure, darling. As you say," I nod at Susie and turn up the volume as Nicki Minaj's Anaconda blasts through the car speakers.

Finally, we pull up at the Hotel Jewel, its grandeur unmistakable even from the parking lot. Sophia steps out, stretching her legs before reaching back into the car to grab her tote. And then we're off, making our way to the poolside, where a team of photographers and makeup artists await her.

The moment Sophia steps in front of the camera, she transforms. I've always known she was gorgeous, but this is something else. She's magnetic, ethereal. She's wearing this one-piece black swimsuit that's cut so high on the hips it should be illegal. And the way she moves in front of the camera is like pure poetry—every twist, every turn executed with a grace I didn't even know was possible.

Beside me, Susie watches, her eyes wide and mouth slightly agape. She's in awe, and honestly, so am I.

"I didn't know someone could be so... stunning," Susie finally manages to say, her voice tinged with disbelief.

I smirk. "You don't know the half of it."

The tension is unbearable, the air charged with a kind of electricity that can't be ignored. My body feels like it's on fire, my skin prickling with anticipation, arousal, a mix of emotions I can't even begin to untangle.

The first pose is Sophia lying on her side, the pool behind her, and her eyes making love to the camera. The camera starts clicking away, and Sophia points, eyes squinted, and legs draped over one another.

Those legs will be the reason I check into a mental asylum.

Pose two is even worse, or better, depends on who you ask. My vagina would say worse, because it sends it into a little throbbing bout. It is Sophia, standing in waist high water, and slowly, seductively, pulling herself out of the pool, while looking back over her shoulder at the camera. But the highlight is her bum, glistening with drops of water, clinging to her backside, those little lucky bastards.

I lick my lips, imagining licking them off her booty.

By the time Sophia hits the third pose, I am breathless, and have decided to stop looking in Sophia's direction. I try making small talk with Susie, but somehow, and unbelievably so, Sophia has managed to stun and mesmerize Susie as well.

"Susie, so do you like your virgin mojito?" I try to talk to Susie, who, wait for it, shushes me!

Keeps a finger on her lips, does not even look at me, and keeps staring at Sophia like she is an angel descended from heaven.

I am left with no choice but to ogle my ...girlfriend? No. My brother's girlfriend?

That's even worse.

Enough. I can't take it anymore. As Sophia wraps up her shoot and starts heading towards her suite, I follow. I pause at the door, glancing at the makeup artists and assistants who have been busily touching up her look. With a nod, I signal for them to leave. The urgency in my eyes is unmistakable, and they quickly exit, closing the door behind them.

"Sophia," I begin, my voice laden with intent.

She turns around, her eyes locking onto mine, and in that moment, I know she feels it too. I close the distance between us, my lips meeting hers in a hungry kiss. It's as if we've been holding back a flood, and now the dam has broken, unleashing a torrent of pent-up emotion, desire, need. She responds fiercely, her hands clawing at my back as she pulls me closer.

"I am sorry, but I…can't…I just can't…when you are looking this…fucking…sexy!" I say through kisses, and Sophia chuckles.

"I can't as well. Chris will understand…aaah, easy there, lady!" Sophia's request falls on deaf ears as I yank her one-piece swimsuit off her body, like a sex depraved convict living in prison would, and give myself only a few seconds to admire Sophia and the luxurious curves of her Persian body.

"Do a spin for me," I say, my voice husky with anticipation and burning desire.

Sophia complies and does a wonderfully seductive twirl, hands on hips and all, and winks at me, almost challenging my desire to show her what it can do.

My desire responds, grabbing Sophia by her waist, turning her around, hair flying everywhere, and pinning her against the glass window overlooking the city of Dallas.

"Alissa…you can't keep pampering me like this, baby. I feel selfish."

"Then stop tormenting with these…" I say, getting on my knees, and kneading Sophia's ass with both my hands, my eyes droopy with lust as I eye her gorgeous behind.

I take one last look at the tall supermodel, looking over her shoulder at what I was planning to do to her, and then with a little spank on her bum, I dig in.

∞∞∞

We saunter back to the poolside, both of us a touch disheveled but otherwise looking like we've just sashayed out of a fashion spread. That's when we hear it—giggles intertwined with strained conversation.

Rounding the corner, we spot Susie engrossed in what can only be described as the most cringe-worthy flirtation I've ever witnessed. She's chatting with one of the cameramen, and it's obvious she's clueless about the art of seduction.

"So, you, like, take pictures and stuff? That's so cool," Susie ventures, twirling a strand of her hair.

"Uh, yeah, it's my job," the cameraman responds, visibly bemused.

"Do you do this often?" Susie plows on, seemingly oblivious to the awkwardness she's generating.

"Um… yes, it's my job, so I do this quite a lot," Steve, the cameraman, answers, clearly entertained by her awkward advances. "Would you mind telling me more about it? Perhaps if I give you my number?" Steve cuts to the chase.

"I… actually don't remember it. I don't give it out often."

"Got your phone on you?"

"Yeah," Susie mutters, still engrossed in her hair-twirling

routine.

"Then give me a call. My number is…"

Unable to contain ourselves, Sophia and I exchange glances before bursting into giggles.

"What do you think set that off?" I ask Sophia as we abandon Susie to her newly-awakened hormones.

"Freedom from the Church of the Andersons, perhaps? Plus, Susie is kinda pretty, you know."

"Whoa, you can't go seducing the whole Anderson clan!" I jest, leading us toward the poolside bar.

"I've only seduced one. What are you talking about?"

"Chris?"

Sophia hesitates for a beat before saying, "Oh yeah, him too."

"Is the sex that forgettable?" I inquire, my curiosity piqued.

"Let's just say he's never dropped to his knees, held my waist, and lavished as much love on my backside as you did a few minutes ago."

"Okay, okay, let's not venture into TMI territory," I caution, as I order us a couple of Piña Coladas.

After the hysterical display at the pool, we decide to shift gears and venture out for a shopping spree. Since we're already in Dallas, Sophia suggests a detour to one of the Anderson stores. You'd think I'd get tired of my own family's retail empire, but nope, I get a kick out of the royal treatment every time.

We wander through the upscale boutique, pulling Susie along who's reluctant but curious. She eyes the trendy outfits skeptically, but Sophia and I are on a mission.

"How about this?" Sophia holds up a figure-hugging, little black dress. "You'll look killer in it, and who knows, might even attract a date."

I wink at Sophia, and she grins back. "Exactly. You never know when you'll bump into Mr. Right—or Mr. Right Now," I add, handing Susie another outfit.

After we've selected an armful of date-worthy clothes for Susie, Sophia and I find ourselves in adjacent fitting rooms. She's trying on a sultry red dress that hugs her curves like a second skin, and the sight of her sends a jolt of electricity through me. Our eyes meet, and without a word, we lean into a deep, passionate kiss. Our hands start to roam, and things are just about to go from hot to volcanic when...

"Um, guys? Could you help me with the zipper?" Susie's voice punctures our little love bubble, pulling us back into the role of responsible guardians, or at least semi-responsible in my case.

Laughing off our thwarted escapade, we help Susie fit into her new body-con dress. She looks stunning, a modern woman ready for modern love.

The drive back to the ranch is quiet. Susie, worn out from the day's adventures, is dozing in the backseat. Sophia takes advantage of the solitude and slides her hand onto my thigh. The sensation is electrifying, sending tingles up my spine.

She leans closer, her breath warm against my ear. "You looked so sexy today," she whispers, her hand inching higher, causing my breath to catch.

My eyes dart to the rearview mirror, confirming that Susie's still deep in slumber. Sophia's fingers dance across my body, tracing circles around my waist before venturing to cup my breasts. I stifle a moan as she gives them a firm yet gentle squeeze. It's like we're two teenagers again, stealing touches and trading giggles. It's electrifying, tantalizing, and utterly addictive.

"Are we really doing this?" I ask, grinning like a Cheshire cat.

"You've hogged too much of my body for too long. It's my turn now, cowgirl," Sophia replies, sealing her words with a quick but intense kiss.

For the rest of the drive, I multitask between driving the car and screaming out in pleasure, as Sophia and her fingers, eager and hidden inside my leggings, keep driving me to the edge and back.

Finally, with the ranch just ten minutes away, I beg Sophia for release, and she thrusts two fingers in, while pinching my nipples, and makes me cum like a leaky faucet.

I mouth the words 'Fuck', 'oh my god', and 'Sophia' several times, as the car slows down to a crawl, but my heartbeat goes crazy.

And then once we are back at the ranch, Sophia greets Chris with a hug, but with her eyes locked onto me, she licks the two fingers that were inside me a few minutes ago, almost making me faint.

As I am recovering from the visual treat, Chris pulls me aside almost immediately. "Alissa, can we talk? Maybe take a walk?"

I shoot a quick look back at Sophia, who mouths "Go" to me.

"Sure, what's up?" I ask as we step away from the arriving throng. But in the back of my mind, my thoughts are still lingering on the way Sophia sucked my juices clean off her fingers.

I shudder with pleasure and follow Chris towards the old oak tree.

Chris and I find ourselves in a secluded part of the sprawling ranch, walking side by side but not touching. A stream is quietly burbling nearby, probably whispering secrets like the two of us are about to.

"Look, Alissa," Chris starts, his gaze trained ahead, "I wanted to thank you. You've been an unexpected surprise these past few weeks. With Sophia, and well, with me too. I was half-expecting you to be icy, especially toward her."

I can't help but chuckle at that. "You were expecting Elsa from 'Frozen', and you got, what? Belle from 'Beauty and the Beast'?"

"Something like that." He smiles. "Remember when we were kids, and we used to play superheroes? I'd be Batman, and you'd always insist on being Wonder Woman because you didn't want to be a sidekick."

I laugh at the memory, my eyes getting misty. "Hell, yes. Batman and Wonder Woman were equals. And I made sure you acknowledged that, remember? We had to shake on it."

Chris laughs. "I remember. I want us to be like that again. Equals, sharing secrets, fighting imaginary villains together."

"In my heart, you're still that big brother who acted like a little one. You taught me how to fight, but you also cried when you watched 'The Lion King.'"

He chuckles, visibly pleased. "Well, Mufasa's death was traumatic."

"Yeah, for a seven-year-old. You were fourteen!"

"Let's not get bogged down by the details," he jokes, and we both laugh. Then, his expression turns serious again. "Should we address the elephant in the room?"

For a split second, my mind wanders to Sophia. "Sophia is not as fat as an elephant," I blurt out before catching myself.

159

Chris laughs uproariously. "Not her, you goof. I meant the CEO position. The competition between us."

I nod, realizing the gravity of what he's about to say.

"Look, whatever happens, I won't harbor any ill will against you. And if I do get the position, it'll only be on paper. You'll still have hands-on involvement in everything. We're a team, Alissa. Always have been, always will be."

I let Chris's words sink in. I'm touched, of course, but it irks me how confident he is that he'll be the CEO.

"And I'll make sure to do the same, you know, if Dad chooses me," I reply.

Chris looks like he's about to argue, but then he smiles. I'm surprised by his maturity. "I hope you do."

We walk in silence for a few meters before he abruptly asks about my love life. "Got a boyfriend?"

"Me? No! You know me. I'm too busy trying to prove that women are as good as men, and in the process, I forget that men exist."

Chris smiles. "You'd make a great girlfriend, you know?"

"Really?" I chuckle. "This is coming from a guy who once claimed I was a cyborg without emotions that Dad found in a dumpster and adopted?"

"Yeah, you did display scary levels of emotional disconnect, but now that I can read between the lines, I know you have a beating heart in there somewhere—just like mine."

"You're such a softy." I playfully punch him in the arm.

"So, when do you think Dad will, you know, announce who his favorite child is and plunge us into more trauma?"

"I don't think he'll give the CEO position based on who his favorite child is. If that were the case, I'd definitely lose," I reply.

"Why do you think he's stepping down in the first place?" I ask.

"I think it's Mom. They've been having issues lately," he reveals.

"Mom?" My eyes go wide. "No way, she's his shadow."

"Yeah, and she's tired of being one. She's started to push back," Chris confesses.

"Wow. I didn't see that coming, especially since Mom never shares anything with me," I say.

"That's because you don't try with her," Chris argues, slightly irritating me.

"Yeah, because she tells Dad everything!" I counter.

"Alissa, things are changing. She's pushing him to retire to spend more time with her and the family. She's not happy, and you should talk to her about it," he advises.

"Yeah, I'll try," I agree.

We continue walking under a blanket of stars, a soft breeze making the leaves rustle.

"How are you and Sophia? Everything fine in paradise?" The guilt and emotional turmoil of being with my brother's girlfriend make me ask the question.

"Things are great. She's perfect, you know? Being with her is like being wrapped in a warm hug. Her presence alone calms you down," he says.

I know.

"That's nice," I whisper into the night. "You really love her, don't you?"

"Yup. She's the one, Alissa."

His words are like sharp shards of glass, tearing through

the veil of denial I've wrapped around myself. "She's the one I'll marry," he says, and my stomach drops as if it's in free fall. He's talking about Sophia, my Sophia, in a way that sends ripples of guilt crashing over me. A storm of doubt starts to gather in my mind, dark clouds blotting out the clarity I thought I had.

Until now, I'd rationalized my feelings for Sophia. Told myself her relationship was temporary with Chris, a mess bound to untangle itself. But what if I'm the one sabotaging this tapestry, snipping at the threads that keep Chris's life woven tightly together?

He keeps talking about Sophia, recounting their intimate moments like they're lines from a love poem. But his words now clang like loud cymbals in my ears. My brother, blissfully unaware, is laying his heart bare, while here I am, a thief in the night, stealing the very love that fills it.

Is Sophia lying to me? She whispered in the darkness that things with Chris weren't the same. She'd said she'd be ending it after the vacation. Had those late-night confessions been a smokescreen? Could she be a pawn in some elaborate game to ruin my chances at the CEO position? No, that doesn't make sense. Chris is many things, but a schemer he is not.

I cast a side glance at him. His face is glowing in the soft light of the moon, eyes full of dreams I fear I'm about to shatter. A voice in my head screams, what are you doing, Alissa? What have you done?

I make an excuse to Chris about a sudden stomachache and make a beeline towards the house. I am almost running, as the realization of what I might have done keeps stabbing me, each stab causing more pain than the last.

The word 'homewrecker' echoes in my head. I feel like a monster.

I stumble into my room and find Sophia perched in front of the vanity mirror, brushing her hair.

"We need to stop, Sophia," I breathe out, panting like I have been running a marathon.

Sophia looks up, her eyes catching mine in the mirror. "Stop? Stop what?"

"Us," I choke out, my voice laced with a desperation I can't hide. "This thing between us, it needs to end. Now."

She turns, her eyes widening, a mix of confusion and hurt swirling in them. "Why, Alissa? I thought we were... I thought this was real."

"It is real, Sophia. Too real," I confess, pacing around the room as my thoughts spin out of control. "But have you listened to Chris? He's talking about marriage, about a lifetime with you. And what am I doing? Sneaking around behind my brother's back like some sort of... of traitor!"

Sophia stands up, approaching me cautiously, as if I'm a wounded animal ready to bolt. "Alissa, you're overthinking this."

"Am I?" My voice rises, almost hysterical. "Am I really? Because the way I see it, I'm the villain in this story, Sophia. I've let my desires, my feelings, cloud what should be crystal clear. Chris loves you, and what am I doing? I'm jeopardizing his happiness, our family's unity, for what? A fling?"

Sophia tries to interject, but I can't stop, the dam of my emotions has burst, and years of self-discipline and control go spiraling down the drain.

"I've been fighting my whole life to prove myself, to be someone who my father, my family, can be proud of. To be worthy of the Anderson name. And here I am, risking it all because I can't control my feelings? What does that make me, Sophia?"

She hesitates, her eyes filling with tears. "It makes you human, Alissa. We're all human. We make mistakes, we fall in love, often with the wrong people. That's life."

"But at what cost?" My voice is almost a whisper, a shaky exhale of defeat. "I really like you, Sophia, God help me, I do. But I also love my brother, and I can't... I won't be the one to break his heart."

Sophia steps closer, her hand reaching up to touch my face, but I pull away.

"I need space," I murmur, backing away. "Space to think, to weigh the enormity of what we've done and decide what comes next."

"I can tell you exactly what comes next," Sophia says in a soft voice, an expressionless face staring at me.

"What?"

"Chris and I will break up, he will go on to become the CEO, and you and I will be free to…"

"But I don't believe you! Chris wasn't talking like someone whose relationship is on the rocks!"

"That's because he doesn't know!"

"That's even worse, Sophia! You've been stringing him along! At least start dropping hints, fight a little, I don't know, throw tantrums or something. You can't crush the man like this."

"I am not crushing anyone." Sophia's voice is stern, and I can't believe how little emotion she is showing for someone who is going to break the heart of someone she used to love once, and who loves her still.

"Wow, do you have any empathy at all?" I walk over to where Sophia is standing and look her straight into her eyes. "Just because I slept with you doesn't mean I will go to any lengths to hurt my brother. You need to come clean to him, or to me. What the hell do you want, Sophia?"

"I want you."

"Then, tell Chris, before he keeps dreaming of making you his wife, for god's sake!"

"He isn't dreaming of any such thing. He is only dreaming of that CEO position." Sophia's voice is still calm, and it's throwing me off.

"He just told me…"

"He is lying. He is acting. It is all a set-up, Alissa."

"But he told me that…"

"Alissa…he is gay."

I stop mid-sentence and just stare at Sophia for a while. "The rumors are true. The gods *have* played a great joke on Henry Anderson—both his children are gay. I am just his friend from New York, a very good friend, but we've never dated. He is like a brother to me, who I had to kiss on the lips, and it was as weird for me as it would have been for you."

My mind is a whirlwind, struggling to process everything Sophia's just revealed. "So, you and Chris… you're both… acting? Is that it?"

"Yes," she admits, her voice barely above a whisper. "It's a façade, for the company, for the shareholders, and for your father. Chris was never comfortable coming out to your dad, fearing it would affect his chances of taking over Anderson Corp."

"And you agreed to this?" I'm incredulous.

"We're best friends. He needed me, and I wanted to help him. Plus, it gave me an opportunity to get to know you." Her voice softens as she says this, her eyes filled with a strange mix of sincerity and caution.

My thoughts spiral further into chaos. "So all those plans he shared about marrying you were… a lie?"

"A convenient story," she says.

Sophia reaches out and takes my hand, her fingers gently intertwining with mine. "Alissa, listen. You've done nothing wrong, and neither have I. Chris is my best friend, and I care about him. He'll be happy as long as he gets the position of CEO."

I pull my hand away slowly, my eyes meeting hers. "I want to be CEO, too, Sophia. What then?"

For a moment, Sophia's face is a tableau of conflicting emotions, before it settles into a somber mask. "I know, and that's what makes all of this so complicated. I feel stuck between the two of you."

"So, what does that mean for us?" My voice cracks, the words heavy with the gravity of our entangled lives, our entangled ambitions.

She takes a deep breath before speaking. "It means we have difficult choices to make, not just about our careers but about us. How real is this, Alissa? How serious are we?"

"Are you asking me or are you asking yourself?" I counter, staring intently into her eyes.

"I'm asking us, both of us," she responds, meeting my gaze without flinching. "Because if this is something real, something serious, then we both need to decide how far we're willing to go for it."

I pause, weighing her words. This is uncharted territory for me.

"Sophia, listen," I begin, my words heavy with a vulnerability I rarely show. "You've only been here for a short period, but you've already become so important to me. The first night you stayed at the ranch, I went to your room. Not to offer you a cup of sugar or some neighborly advice. I went there hoping you'd be scared or uncomfortable and might want to share a room with me, because I was really, really attracted to you."

I take a deep breath, feeling the weight of my confession, then continue, "But then I got to know you, Sophia. I got to know your humor, your heart, your dreams, your fears—your entire beautiful, complex self. And what I found resonates deeply with me. Your struggles echo my own. Your ambition mirrors the fire that's always been in me but was never acknowledged."

I close the gap between us, taking her hands in mine. "I see myself in you. I see the same need to prove ourselves, the same complicated family issues, the same hesitancy to give love a chance. Hell, I see two people waking up each day unsure of what they really want from life but still giving it their best shot."

I pause, my eyes searching hers for some sign that she feels the same. "These days at the ranch, they've been the highlight of my year. No, not just the year—the past few years. I don't know what the future holds, Sophia, but I do know that I don't want to lose you. That's all I know."

For a moment, the room is silent, filled only with the loud pounding of my heart and the hopeful look in Sophia's eyes.

"Say something." I search Sophia's face, and she stands still in front of me, a manuscript I can't read.

Sophia doesn't say anything, but lunges at me, wrapping me in her arms and pulling me into a hug I would go on to remember for the rest of my life.

All of the times that we've made love, pale in comparison to that one hug. The urgency of it, the clawing at each other's back, the need to be consumed by each other, fuels us, drives us, to not want to let go. Ever.

The candles around the room go out, as a gust of wind sweeps into the room. The pages of a book I had been reading flutter, and the curtains frolic.

But we stay still, locked in embrace.

The clouds roar, the rain starts lashing the ranch mercilessly, but I hold Sophia close to me, she holds me, like I am hers.

Have I become hers?

Every fiber in my body seems to think so, My heart, beating, pounding against the walls of my chest, seems to think so.

I close my eyes and breathe in the scent of her hair, and if you believe Phoebe from Friends, that's a definite sign you're in love.

"Alissa," Sophia finally speaks, her eyes brimming with a complex mix of emotions. "I want you. And what terrifies me is that I've never wanted anyone as much as I want you right now."

"Then have me. I'm yours."

Without another word, Sophia surges forward, her lips finding mine as if guided by some magnetic pull. The force of our collision sends us tumbling back onto the bed.

"I've been waiting for my turn to worship this body," Sophia murmurs, her fingers deftly working at the hem of my crop top.

With a quick assist from me, the fabric is lifted over my head. But even during those fleeting seconds of disrobing, Sophia can't resist planting kisses up and down my arms, each touch like a brand.

My fingers find their way to her mouth, and I watch, entranced, as she delicately kisses their length before taking them into her inviting lips.

"Can I make you mine tonight, baby?" She poses the question as her hands deftly unbutton my baggy jeans, pinning one of my arms behind me.

"Yes," I manage to gasp out. "Take me. All of me. Imprint yourself on me, baby."

My jeans are swiftly dispatched, sent flying through the air to land unceremoniously on the floor. I watch as Sophia, too, sheds the layers of her clothing, each piece falling away until she stands before me—naked, raw, divine.

She climbs over me, locking eyes as she whispers, "Open your mouth for me, babe."

I comply, sticking out my tongue, and she leans in to envelop it with her own, softly sucking on the tip. Her dark eyes, framed by kohl, seem to smolder with a fire that mirrors my own burning desire.

Our initial gentleness gives way to a frenzied passion, Sophia's hands mapping out every inch of my body. Each place she touches feels like it's been kissed by molten wax, searing and electric.

We're all tongues and teeth and fingernails. It's a glorious, primal battle for supremacy, a battle I have no desire to win. I want her to dominate me, to own me. I need her to take my body and make it her own, to use it to sate her every whim and fantasy. To leave her mark on it.

On me. I'm hers, and hers alone.

As if sensing my need, Sophia's fingers slip down my belly to the waistband of my panties. They brush gently against the sensitive skin of my abdomen, teasing me, taunting me. I feel myself tense in anticipation. Then, her fingers hook into the waistband, and she begins to tug them down. My heart flutters in my chest. I'm so nervous, but so eager. My entire body is on fire, my mind swimming with thoughts and emotions.

Sophia's fingers brush over my pubic mound, her nails lightly scraping the sensitive skin. I shiver in response, goosebumps breaking out across my skin. I can feel the heat of her fingers as they draw closer to my aching center, the tension mounting.

She pauses for a moment, her fingertips just barely grazing the surface of my clit. It's as if time itself has stopped, the universe holding its breath as Sophia hovers on the precipice of making her first move. In that moment, I am hers. Heart, body, and soul. Whatever happens next, I will submit to her.

"Sophia," I murmur.

"Yes, babe?"

"Take me. Use me. I'm yours."

"Are you sure?"

"I've never been more sure of anything in my life."

"Let me take care of you," she says, her voice husky with desire.

"Yes," I whisper.

She moves down my body, her hands caressing every inch of me. Her lips find my nipples, her tongue teasing them into hard peaks.

"Oh, God," I moan.

She continues her exploration, her hands and lips moving lower. She kisses a path down my stomach, her tongue tracing circles around my navel. My hips buck involuntarily as she nears my aching center, my body craving her touch.

"Sophia, please..." I beg.

"I've got you, baby," she murmurs, her fingers dancing over my folds.

She spreads my legs apart, her mouth descending on my clit. I cry out as she sucks and licks me, bringing me closer and closer to the edge.

Her tongue slips out from between her lips and glides up my slick folds.

"Oh, God, yes," I moan, my fingers tangling in her hair.

I pull her closer, my hips grinding against her face as she feasts on me. I can feel my body tensing, my thighs quivering. I am close, and I can't wait to go over the edge.

"Don't stop," I pant, my hips bucking against her face.

"I won't," she murmurs, her tongue delving deeper into my hot center.

She slides two fingers inside me, curling them to hit that spot that makes me scream her name. I cry out, my back arching as my orgasm crashes over me.

My screams echo off the walls, and my body writhes beneath me as I ride out the waves of pleasure.

"Holy shit," I gasp, my chest heaving.

"Are you okay?" she asks, pressing a soft kiss to my inner thigh.

"Never better," I say, my lips curling into a grin.

She crawls up my body, my lips meeting hers in a passionate kiss.

"I thought the British were all about manners," Sophia husks into my ear, "and the Texans were all about hospitality, and here, you claim to be both, but don't care that I am still waiting for my…"

I kiss Sophia hard and stop her mid sentence. "What do you want, love?" I ask, stroking her hair.

She bites her lip, her eyes flicking down.

"Tell me," I murmur, tilting her chin up so our eyes meet.

"I want to grind my pussy on your thigh," she whispers, her cheeks flushing even darker. "I want to ride you like you ride your horses."

Sophia's boldness makes me laugh. "Anything for you, city

girl," I say, pulling her close.

She settles her legs on either side of mine, her heat resting against my thigh. She lets out a soft moan as she starts to grind, her clit brushing against my skin.

I lean back, watching her as she slowly grinds her pussy on my thigh. Her eyes are closed, her face relaxed, and her breasts bouncing with each movement.

Never in my life had I previously been exposed to something more beautiful. A literal goddess is perched on thigh, as if it was her throne, and extracting pleasure for herself by using me as she wished.

And I was here for it.

My eyes linger over her breasts, two mounds of flesh that have become my obsession.

I can't resist cupping them in my hands, my fingers lightly brushing over her nipples.

"You're the life...that was missing from my life," I murmur, and her eyes flutter open, her gaze meeting mine.

"So are you," she says, leaning down to kiss me.

Her lips are soft and warm, her tongue sliding into my mouth. I moan into her mouth, my hands tightening on her breasts.

She gasps, her movements becoming more erratic as she grinds her clit harder against my thigh. I feel her arousal leaking out, coating my skin.

"You're getting my leg all wet," I whisper against her lips, and she lets out a groan, her hips bucking against me.

"God, that's so hot," she moans, her fingers digging into my shoulders.

"Do you like the way you're grinding your pussy on me, love?" I murmur, trailing kisses down her jaw.

"Yes," she breathes, her eyes closing as she arches her back.

"Do you want to cum all over my thigh?" I ask, gently biting her earlobe.

"Fuck, yes," she gasps, her movements becoming almost frantic.

I can tell she's close, so I lean in and whisper, "Cum for me, Sophia."

Her eyes squeeze shut, and she throws her head back, a loud moan escaping her lips.

She grinds her clit harder against me, her hips bucking wildly.

"That's it, love," I murmur, holding her close.

"Come for me."

"Alissa," she cries out, her whole body trembling as her orgasm hits her.

"Alissa."

"I've got you, love," I whisper, kissing her softly.

"I've got you."

She collapses against me, her breathing heavy.

"Are you okay?" I ask, stroking her hair.

"Better than okay," she murmurs, a soft smile spreading across her face.

"What do you think of how you made a mess on my thigh?" I joke.

She looks up, her cheeks flushing slightly.

"Can I clean it up for you?" she asks, her voice low.

"You want to taste yourself on my skin?"

"Yes."

God, she is driving me crazy.

She crawls down my body, her lips finding my skin. She licks and kisses her way down my stomach, before settling on my thigh where she had been grinding herself like a maniac a few seconds ago.

I watch as Sophia, the woman who was a stranger to me three weeks ago, starts gently lapping up her own juices off my legs, giving me a visual that would sear itself on the walls of my brain.

∞ ∞ ∞

In the afterglow, we find ourselves entangled in a mess of limbs and bedsheets, our bodies still humming from the intensity of our connection. I'm laying on my back, Sophia nestled in the crook of my arm, her head resting on my shoulder. One of her legs is thrown over mine, and her arm drapes across my waist, as if claiming me for her own. It feels possessive yet tender, and I wouldn't have it any other way.

The large windows of the room are slightly ajar, and the wind—carrying with it the fresh scent of rain—gently billows the curtains. The aroma mixes with the residual warmth and intimacy hanging in the air, creating an atmosphere that feels almost sacred.

Sophia draws circles on my abdomen with her fingers, her touch light but infinitely comforting.

Sophia traces her finger along my collarbone before meeting my eyes, a slightly mischievous glint shining through. "So, when was the last time you had it that good?"

"Wow, confident much?" I chuckle. "But if we're getting down to it...hmm, can't really recall a time that's up there with this. I guess you've set a new benchmark, Miss Sophia."

Sophia grins widely. "Well, you're not so bad yourself. You're full of surprises."

I raise an eyebrow, a playful smirk on my lips. "I had no idea you were such a wild card, Sophia. You're really something else in bed."

Sophia laughs, the sound light and carefree. "That's where us city girls shine, darling. We bring a touch of kink to the table."

"You certainly do," I nod appreciatively. "And I am all in for discovering more of your city girl tricks."

Sophia grows silent for a moment, her playful demeanor shifting. She looks at me, her eyes searching, slightly anxious. "Can I ask you something?"

"Shoot," I say, sensing the change in mood.

She takes a deep breath. "If you don't get the CEO position, will you hold it against me? Will you think that maybe, somewhere along the line, I could've done something to swing it in your favor?"

I look deep into Sophia's eyes, understanding the weight of the question. "Listen, you made a promise to my brother. And the fact that you're doing the right thing, even when it's hard, even when you could easily be swayed by our newfound... ahem, physical chemistry? That's what I love about you, Sophia. You're a woman of your word, and that means more to me than any title or position."

Sophia lets out a breath, visibly relieved. "I can't tell you how much that means to me, Alissa."

"Good, because that's how it's gonna be. No doubts, no what-ifs." I pull her closer to me, locking my eyes onto hers. "We're in this, all the way, no matter where our careers take us."

She smiles, her face glowing with genuine happiness. "I couldn't have asked for anything more."

***

Our dates have that forbidden allure—dark bars, dim lighting, and this time, a dance pole in the corner. As soon as I see it, I lean toward Sophia, sharing my secret fondness for pole dancing. Her eyes go wide, and she nearly spits out her margarita.

"You do what now?"

"You heard me. Pole dancing. A girl's got to have her hobbies," I retort, full of sass. Sophia grins ear to ear.

"Funny you mention that. I've got a friend—Nicole. You know, the star from Bella's video?" Sophia leans in, lowering her voice. "Nicole used to be a stripper, met this single-mom schoolteacher named Emma, and boom! Their love story's straight out of a romance novel. Bella played a hand in helping their love story flourish, and since then, they've been our tight-knit friends."

I'm spellbound. "Oh God, I've got such a crush on Nicole. Can I, you know, maybe get a private lap dance?"

Sophia's eyes narrow playfully. "Sure, if I'm in the room. And only then." I burst into laughter. "You really are a kinkster, aren't you?"

"But you, why haven't you tried it, given that Nicole, the pole goddess herself, is your bestie?"

Sophia laughs. "Tempting, but some things are better admired than attempted."

"Maybe you can attempt this for me?" I cock my eyebrow.

"Decide who you want the lap dance from, woman!"

"Can't I have both?" I risk my hand.

"Oh, getting a little too brave, aren't we? Let's see. You play nice with me, and who knows, you might get a special performance from me and Nicole, although it will be weird performing with her. She is like my sister."

"I don't care. I am already envisioning it, and I need it, baby."

"As I said, we'll see," Sophia says, winking at me as she takes a sip of her margarita.

Our steamy romance isn't just confined to obscure bars; we're leaving our love marks all over the ranch, including some dangerous spots. We coin it "Ranch Roulette" after a near miss in the hayloft. Another night, Chris walks into our room just when Sophia's under the sheets and, well, between my legs. I've never seen myself scramble that fast to pretend we're having a 'deep conversation.'

Amidst this heady rush of new love, I see Susie sneaking around, phone in hand, giggling away. She's been chatting with Steve, the cameraman, and even plans a date. Hilariously, she once pocket-dials Sophia, trying to snap a sultry selfie, unaware she's live on video. The uproarious chain of awkward angles and confused expressions that follow is the comic relief Sophia and I didn't know we needed.

Chris and I have also been getting closer, acting on our promise of strengthening our bond. I use this opportunity to get him to spill his secret. He's close to Mark, his childhood friend, so close that they practically finish each other's sentences. I poke at him, trying to get him to open up. "You guys are so adorable. So when's the wedding?"

Chris is clearly annoyed but slowly gets into the swing of the banter, but never gives away the secret to his sexuality. It's sealed up tighter inside him than Fort Knox. But I don't relent; that's not my style.

Slowly, Sophia's integrating into the family as well. Uncle Daniel is teaching her the charm of gardening, and it melts my heart to see them plant roses together. Mom too starts sharing kitchen secrets with Sophia, forcing me to join their kitchen operations, even though getting ginger paste on my fingers is the last thing I want.

I use these moments to try to get Mom to confide in me about Dad, but she's a sealed vault. Someday, that vault will have to open. But for now, the mysteries remain.

So here we are—Sophia and me—sneaking around, stealing moments, breaking a few rules, but never each other's hearts. It's messy, it's exhilarating, and it's a hell of a lot of fun. But most importantly, it's ours.

∞∞∞

I walk into Dad's study and the atmosphere hits me like a wall—a storm cloud of tension, ready to burst. The room is filled with heavy furniture and even heavier silence. Books and portraits that seem to carry generations of expectations surround me. I sit down, my boots sinking into the plush carpet. Dad's behind his desk, eyes locked onto mine.

"Sit down, Alissa," he says, his voice soft, almost tender. I know better. I comply, trying to appear as collected as he is.

"I understand there are delays with the New Orleans store," he starts, staring at me with a level of calm that has my stomach in knots. "Explain."

"We've got some issues, Dad. Design hiccups, permit delays, but we're sorting it out," I reply, my voice steady, hiding the frustration simmering beneath.

Dad sighs, and I can see the storm cloud darkening. "The New Orleans store is crucial, Alissa. I expected better."

"I've got it handled, Dad. It's just a small hiccup," I counter.

He leans back in his chair. "You and Chris are my bets for the future of this company, Alissa. Don't make it difficult for me to defend you."

Defend me? Is he serious? "Why bother defending me when it seems like you've already chosen Chris?"

His eyes narrow. "You're the head of the Southern Division. My daughter. An Anderson."

"An Anderson second to being your daughter, right?" I shoot back.

He clenches his jaw. "I've given you every chance to prove you're both."

I almost blurt out the truth about Chris and Sophia, but stop myself. "I've proven it, time and again. The question is, do you see it?"

He looks at me, eyes probing. "So you think Chris is too soft to lead?"

"He has qualities the world needs more of," I reply, vaguely.

"And what about you? Did you dig into Sophia's background like I asked?"

Alissa felt a knot tighten in her stomach but remained quiet.

"Exactly," Henry sneered. "You can't play dirty either. You both have hearts. Unfortunately, the world is more forgiving of a soft man than it is of a soft woman."

"And that's my fault?" Alissa almost spat out the words.

Dad leans forward, a calculated glint in his eye. "We're about to acquire a small retail chain, run by women. It's going to be a brutal takeover. Do you have the stomach for it?"

I feel sick. Crushing someone else's dreams for business? Is that what being an Anderson means?

"Do you want this project, or should I hand it to Chris?" he asks.

I take a deep breath, squaring my shoulders as I ask, "What are the details of this takeover?"

Dad opens a drawer and slides a file across the desk toward me. "It's a small chain—Mae & Lyn's. Two women started it a decade ago. They've managed to carve out a unique space, a focus on sustainable, locally sourced products. Quite impressive, actually. But they're struggling. Market pressures, competition—you know the drill."

"And we're swooping in like vultures?" I can't hide the disdain in my voice.

He leans back, a slight smile on his lips. "Business is business, Alissa. We're offering them a buyout. They get a nice sum; we get to expand our footprint. Win-win."

I thumb through the file. The numbers catch my eye, and I feel a pang of guilt. We're lowballing them. Offering just enough to be tempting, but far below what the business is worth, far below what they've invested in dreams, sweat, and years.

"So, do you want it?" Dad's voice pulls me back to the room.

"I'll give it a read," I say, taking the file and standing up. My heart's pounding in my chest, but I try to keep my composure.

Before I leave the room, I pause at the door, my hand on the knob. "You know, Dad, the world is changing. Ethical business isn't just a trend; it's the future. And maybe, just maybe, being ruthless isn't the only way to show strength."

He raises an eyebrow, unspoken questions filling the space between us.

"But then again, what can I expect? If you've been too blind to see the changes in your own house, it's a bit much to expect you to notice when the world changes," I add, my voice steady but edged.

I don't wait for his reply. I pull the door open and step out, file in hand, a heavy weight settling in my gut. I've made my point, but at what cost? And now I have to decide: will I be the kind of Anderson that Dad wants, or the kind of Anderson that I can live with being?

∞∞∞

I'm staring at the blue light of my laptop screen, my thoughts circling like vultures around a kill. The words, the numbers—they're all blurring together. I'm so engrossed in the moral dilemma unfolding in my mind that I hardly notice Sophia snuggled beside me. She tries to grab my attention, running her fingers gently down my arm.

"Hey, what's eating you? You've been lost in that screen for a while now," she murmurs, her voice tinged with concern.

I look up, locking eyes with her. For a moment, I'm tempted to shut the lid and lose myself in the comfort that only she provides. But the weight of today sits heavy on my soul.

"I had a talk with Dad today," I start, forcing the words out, "about the business, a takeover we're planning."

She props herself up on her elbow, clearly sensing the gravity in my tone. "Go on."

"We're taking over a small retail chain, Mae & Lyn's. It's run by these two women who've built it from scratch. And we're offering them an amount that's... It's unfair, Sophia. We're squeezing them when they're vulnerable, and I hate it."

Sophia's eyes meet mine, full of understanding and yet questioning. "So, what are you going to do about it?"

"That's just it. I don't know. This is how the Andersons do business. It's how we've always done it. I'm supposed to lead this negotiation. And if I don't, Chris will."

Sophia lets out a long sigh. "You're between a rock and a hard place, aren't you?"

"I've been bending my morals for years, Sophia. For the company, for Dad. I play by his rules because they're the only rules I've ever known. And each time I do, I feel a piece of me erode away. Now I'm wondering how much is left."

Sophia reaches out, cupping my face, forcing me to look at her. "I see plenty left, Alissa. More than you think. You're strong, you're kind, and you're burdened by this because you're good. But being good also means knowing when to say enough."

"I wish it were that easy, Soph. Saying 'enough' might mean giving up on the idea that I could be the one to change how the Andersons do business. To make it better, ethical even."

Sophia smiles at me, and I feel my heart give a slight flutter, despite the heaviness of our conversation. "Well, you can't change a dynasty overnight. And you definitely can't do it alone. But maybe, just maybe, you start with one ethical decision. One step to show that an Anderson can be both powerful and good. How about you talk to Chris? Maybe he's fed up with being unethical as well?"

"I doubt it. He's mostly been on board with Dad's age-old business practices. But he's been surprising me lately. Maybe he's changed. I don't know, Soph. It's all very complicated." I close the lid of the laptop and snuggle next to Sophia, my head on her shoulder. "Can I be honest with you?"

"Yeah."

"I don't like the life I'm living," I say, the words finally coming out of my mouth after hiding inside me for years. "I don't like getting up each morning, feeling the pressure of proving myself, having to do things that go against my morals, all just to impress an old man who's way out of touch with reality."

Sophia shifts to look at me, her eyes searching for something within me that I know I've lost. "What kind of life do you actually want to live?"

"A life of raising horses, riding them, grooming them. A slow life, you know, away from everything."

"And do you think you will find your freedom and fulfillment in that life?"

I lick my lips and close my eyes for a few seconds.

I imagine the wind on my face and a dipping sun on the horizon. A horse beneath me, talking with the breeze. I feel arms around my waist, and I look over my shoulder and see a face as beautiful as the sunset in front of me.

A face I have come to love.

I see Sophia.

I open my eyes and find Sophia looking at me intently. "What did you see?"

"Freedom," I reply.

Chapter Seven

(Sophia)

I sit there, taking in the laughter and chatter under the Anderson's mighty oak tree. The sun is shining, the air filled with the scent of fresh flowers and the elaborate breakfast spread in front of us. It's so...storybook perfect, or would have been if I wasn't forced out of bed at 7 freaking am.

"Hey, Soph, you haven't touched your French toast," Chris says, grinning at me. "Missing your health shakes?"

I chuckle. "Oh, you know me too well. But no, the food is delicious. I'm just not a morning person."

Meanwhile, Alissa is engrossed in a conversation with her cousin Susie. "I'm telling you, that lavender essential oil works wonders for stress relief," Susie insists.

Alissa raises an eyebrow. "Lavender, you say? I might just need a whole barrel of it these days."

I chuckle at her comment, but just then, my eyes catch something—or rather, someone—in the distance. Two figures walking along the trail that leads here. I squint, trying to get a better look. A sense of familiarity tingles at the back of my mind.

As they come closer, my heart climbs into my throat, nearly choking me.

At first, I think it is my early morning drowsiness that

is making me hallucinate, because surely, it can't be. But as I continue staring at the approaching figures, their silhouettes becoming more defined, I realize I am not hallucinating, but might just be watching my worst nightmare come to life.

Holy shit. It's my mother, Ava, and Bella—her partner and my former roommate—walking toward us as if they're here for a casual weekend visit.

My hand clenches around the fork, and I nearly spit out my mimosa. This is bad, very bad. They have the potential to blow up everything, ruin this picturesque moment, and unravel the tightly wound threads of my life here.

Everyone around the table seems to notice my sudden tension, but it's Alissa who catches my eye, her gaze sharpening as she tries to read my expression. I try to signal her discreetly. Her eyes narrow in confusion, then widen as she follows my line of sight.

"Tell me I am not looking at your mother, and her very hot, very gay girlfriend approaching us?" Chris asks, following my gaze.

My voice gets caught in my throat as Ava and Bella reach the edge of the clearing, their eyes locking onto mine.

This is a disaster waiting to happen.

I shoot up from my seat, nearly catapulting my mimosa into the next county. "Uh, looks like we have some unexpected brunch guests!" I squeal in a voice so high-pitched it probably sends dogs in a five-mile radius into a frenzy.

Everyone swivels their heads from me to where I'm pointing, like they're at a tennis match. The patriarch, Henry Anderson, looks as if he's trying to solve a quantum physics equation, but it's Mary Anderson who comes to the rescue.

"Ah, those must be the new renters from the ranch by the lake. Shaun must've brought them here for introductions," she chimes in.

Oh goodie, what alternate universe have I stumbled into? One where your most awkward family gatherings are broadcast live for entertainment?

As Shaun, the caretaker, leads my mom and Bella toward our lavish spread, I snap into crisis mode. I bolt toward them, nearly tripping over my own feet, leaving a bewildered pack of Andersons behind me. Someone yells my name, but I couldn't care less. I've got a bomb to defuse, and the clock's ticking.

As I reach them, I hiss through my teeth, "Hi! So great to see you! I'm Sophia, another guest here. And who might you fine folks be?"

My mom, ever the queen in her flowy summer dress, gives me a look that suggests she thinks I've had a recent lobotomy. Bella, on the other hand—dressed in shorts and a crop top that would have Mrs. Anderson clutching her pearls—cracks a grin.

"Play along, for the love of God," I whisper urgently.

Bella gets it; Mom, not so much. "What?" Mom squints, clearly confused.

"Babe, I think we've just stepped into the middle of a soap opera," Bella explains. I shudder at hearing her call my mom "babe."

"Okay, time-out. Here, 'babe' isn't a thing. You're both straight as rulers, got it? Bella, you're my long-lost friend, and Mom, you're her kickass manager."

"What?" Mom is still stuck on repeat, bless her.

Seizing the moment, I pull Bella into a hug. "Are they watching?" I whisper.

"Like a hawk eyeballing a field mouse," she confirms, "What are you up to, Soph?"

"You would know if you took a little interest in my life," I whisper, before pulling back from the hug.

My palms are sweaty as I lead Mom and Bella toward the breakfast table. Shaun, the caretaker, falls into step beside me. "Sophia, you want me to—"

"I've got it from here, Shaun. Thanks," I say, nodding at him. I appreciate his concern, but right now, the last thing I need is another variable in this already volatile equation.

I feel like I've just pulled the pin on a grenade as I approach the table. All eyes swivel toward us, forks hovering mid-air. The clatter of knives and forks has gone silent. Even the sizzling bacon on the stovetop seems to hold its breath.

"Morning, everyone!" I announce, trying my best to sound upbeat. "What a coincidence it is that my friend Bella—" I gesture toward her, "—has rented the ranch near the lake for a few weeks!"

Bella steps up like the pro she is, taking her cue effortlessly. "Yeah, it's an incredible place you've got here. Perfect for the music video we're planning to shoot."

Mom, picking up on the act, chimes in, "I'm Ava, Bella's manager. We wanted to scout the location, maybe even involve some local talents." Her eyes roam the room, finally landing on Henry, who hasn't taken his eyes off his breakfast plate.

Henry, either unfazed or uninterested, simply continues munching on his toast. Mary, the eternal sweetheart, stands up first and extends her hand toward Mom and Bella. "Well, you're certainly welcome here. I'm Mary Anderson. Please, join us."

The tension ebbs slightly, but not by much. I take my seat, and Bella and Mom sit next to me. Across the table, Chris is fidgeting with his knife, eyes wide as saucers. Alissa shoots me a look, a blend of confusion and what-the-hell-are-you-up-to.

"You're scouting for a music video, you say?" Henry finally speaks up, wiping his mouth with a napkin before casting a skeptical gaze at Bella and Mom.

"That's right," Bella answers, oozing confidence. "We heard Texas landscapes offer the perfect backdrop for country music videos."

"And you, young lady, are a music producer?" Henry inquires, eying Bella intently.

"Guilty as charged," Bella replies with a wink, clearly enjoying the role she's playing.

Oh boy, she just winked at Henry Anderson.

"Ooh, what genre of music do you produce?" Henry asks, eyeing Bella as she serves herself a plate of sausages and cheese.

"Mostly pop and EDM. Occasionally, I transform movie soundtracks into club bangers," Bella replies with a grin.

"Club what now?" Martha interjects, her eyes narrowing on Bella as if she's a puzzle to be solved.

"Club bangers—those are songs you'll typically hear in nightclubs," Alissa explains, suppressing a smirk.

"It's lovely to have you both here. We've recently renovated the ranch you're staying at. I trust you're finding it comfortable?" Daniel adds, breaking the awkward silence.

"Absolutely, it's wonderful," Mom—aka Ava—replies, locking eyes with me for a brief moment.

Silence returns before Henry, still munching on his bacon, poses another question. "So how did you come to know our Sophia?"

Bella exchanges a glance with me, and I see her pondering the same question that's clouding my mind: Since when did I become an Anderson?

"We were roommates in New York," I jump in. "Both of us trying to find our feet in the Big Apple."

"Roommates?" Martha's voice raises a pitch, and I realize she hasn't touched her food since Bella and Mom arrived.

"Exactly," Bella chimes in, squeezing my hand gently. For a fleeting moment, my irritation with her dissolves. "In fact, seeing Sophia work so tirelessly inspired me to step out of my comfort zone. That girl's a machine."

A warm smile takes over my face, but from my peripheral vision, I catch Alissa's frown.

"Have I seen you somewhere before?" Susie finally speaks up, turning to Bella. A lump forms in my throat.

Our cover is about to be blown.

"Perhaps at a club where I was DJing?" Bella suggests.

"My daughter does not go to clubs," Martha snipes.

"Or maybe you've seen one of my interviews on TV?" Bella tries again.

"She doesn't watch TV either," Martha continues, digging the hole deeper.

Alissa intervenes, "Susie is quite religious, you know."

"In that case, I've got nothing. I doubt you would have seen me at a church," Bella cracks, breaking into laughter. But the only Anderson to share her humor is Alissa.

This is turning out to be even more awkward than I'd anticipated.

"Bella, find an excuse to leave," I whisper to her urgently.

Henry then turns his attention back to Mom, pointing his fork at her. "So you're the manager?"

"Yes, I manage Bella's career," Mom confirms, momentarily gripping Bella's hand under the table.

Seriously, Mom, cool it.

Martha and Daniel both notice the entwined hands, but Henry seems indifferent. "Well, you should know, Sophia is set to become an Anderson soon," he announces.

Mom's hand jerks back as if stung, knocking over a jar of pickles in the process.

"Kelly, would you mind cleaning this up?" Mary directs one of the house staff with practiced ease.

"As I was saying, she will be marrying my son, Chris. So, Sophia's friends are our friends, and if you ever need anything during your stay, feel free to let us know."

"Oh my god, Soph! Why didn't you tell me? I am so happy for you, baby!" Bella pulls me in for a hug, and whispers in my ear, "I thought Chris liked dick and you liked pussy?"

"Long story," I whisper back, letting go of my former roommate, who still smells like Dior and money.

"It's been wonderful reconnecting, Soph, and meeting all of you, but I'm afraid we must dash. My team is arriving soon, and I've got to prep for their welcome," Bella says, rising gracefully from her seat. She gives Mom a gentle pat on the shoulder, signaling her to do the same.

"How about we arrange another meal together? Mr. Anderson, I'd be particularly keen on picking your brain about business management," Mom suggests, casting a charismatic glance at Henry Anderson.

Henry chuckles, a deep, hearty sound. "I manage billions of dollars, you manage a human being. Quite different domains, I would say."

Hold it together, Mom!

"With all due respect, Mr. Anderson, I manage something that generates art and touches lives. You manage... well, a corporate empire. So, you're absolutely right; they're not the same. Till next time," Mom replies, offering a congenial smile to the Anderson clan. Her eyes lock onto mine for a split second, conveying an unmistakable 'we need to talk' message before she exits the room, Bella trailing behind her.

"I actually enjoyed that," Alissa murmurs, leaning in to whisper in my ear.

"You're a bit of a sadist, aren't you, Ms. Anderson?" I retort softly, throwing Chris a reassuring smile as the color finally returns to his face.

"That's precisely why I enjoy choking you in bed," Alissa purrs, her hand surreptitiously venturing between my legs under the table.

∞∞∞

As I stroll up the winding road to the ranch Ava and Bella have rented, I can already tell that this place is different. It's perched atop a hill, offering panoramic views of the shimmering lake below. While it's not as sprawling as the Anderson estate, it possesses its own unique allure. The building, more a Tuscan villa than a Texan ranch, is adorned with warm, terracotta tiles and sun-kissed stucco walls. As I step out of the car, a sense of awe washes over me. This place is an absolute dream.

Taking a deep breath, I approach the front door and knock. It swings open, and there's Bella, looking radiant as ever. "Hi there, future Anderson!" she exclaims, pulling me into a warm hug.

She ushers me inside, and my gaze immediately sweeps through the inviting architecture. Wrought-iron details, geometric terracotta floor tiles, and rustic wooden beams add a dash of Italian flair to the Texan landscape. Archways replace doors, fostering an open, welcoming atmosphere. The vibe here is so different from the more traditional ranch I've been staying at. "Do you like it?" Bella asks, reading my expression.

"Like it? I think I am moving in," I reply, still taking in the aesthetic details.

Just then, another door bursts open, and out steps Nicole. Decked out in a sultry outfit that highlights her Kylie Jenner-esque features, she's a vision. "Nicole?" I exclaim.

Bella's eyes twinkle, and she says, "Nicole! I was wondering when you'd show up."

"Surprise," Nicole grins, "I thought you could use another friendly face."

I dash over and wrap Nicole in a hug, our laughter filling the room.

"So, you're joining the party too?" I ask Nicole, already knowing the answer.

"Wouldn't miss it for the world." Nicole beams.

"Why didn't you give Bella and Mom a heads-up about what I'm doing here? They almost blew my cover this morning," I say, sinking into the plush couch beside Nicole.

"Hey, I would've warned them if I'd known they were coming, babe," Nicole replies, flashing me a smile that's almost too dazzling to look at directly. "They wanted to surprise you, and I only got here after the whole breakfast drama. But don't worry, I've filled them in now."

"Where's Mom?" I ask, glancing around the cozy living room.

"In the shower. For the third time since this morning," Bella chuckles. "She can't stand how sweaty she gets here."

"I've actually gotten used to it," I admit.

"Well, you've had plenty of 'practice,' given all that bedroom cardio you've been doing with your lovely roommate," Bella quips, her eyes twinkling mischievously. I feel my cheeks heat up and shoot Nicole an accusing look.

"You told them?" I groan.

"Sorry, Soph, but that tea was just too hot not to spill," Nicole replies, still wearing that irresistible smile.

"So spill the tea about this Alissa Anderson," Bella leans in, eager to gossip. "The one who's made you break your 'no relationships for three years' rule."

"We're not officially together... yet," I clarify.

"Babe, you're not the friends-with-benefits type, and you know it," Bella retorts, effortlessly sweeping her platinum blonde hair into a loose bun.

She's just as stunning as I remember—those piercing blue eyes, that Livvy Dunne-esque face, her petite yet athletic frame. It's like time has frozen for her since our Brooklyn flat-sharing days.

Just as we're engrossed in our conversation, the sound of footsteps approaches, and my mom, Ava, appears in the doorway. Her hair is still damp from the shower, tendrils sticking to her face, and she's wearing a luxurious robe that perfectly suits her. We share a somewhat awkward hug, the air heavy with things unsaid, and then she gracefully takes a seat next to Bella.

The moment that follows feels like it's pulled straight from a telenovela. Mom leans over and kisses Bella softly on the lips. It's tender, genuine, but also sort of surreal to witness.

I can't help but feel a mix of awe and discomfort. There's this weird undercurrent, seeing my mom so romantically involved with Bella, who's decades younger. But then again, Mom could easily pass as my elder sister; she has that Negin Mirsalehi vibe—effortlessly chic, eternally youthful. They both look happy, genuinely so, and that should be what matters.

But still, the oddness of it hangs in the air, like a perfume whose scent you can't quite place.

I take a deep breath, feeling the weight of their collective gazes on me. "So, about Alissa and me…"

Mom leans forward, her wet hair still clinging to her shoulders. "Yes, what's really going on there, Soph? You seemed a little flustered at breakfast, and I can't blame you. That was… intense."

"I've been seeing her, more like a friends-with-benefits kind of thing. But I can't deny there's some kind of electricity between us. It might be getting serious. I'm still figuring it out," I admit.

Mom frowns slightly. "Sophia, it's good that you're finding some happiness, but this is moving fast. Especially with a family like the Andersons involved."

"I know, Mom. But, honestly, Alissa and I are both adults. We can make our own decisions."

Bella chimes in, her eyes narrowed. "Look, Soph, I'm all for you going for it. But remember, the Andersons are not the kind of people you can take lightly. You stroll in there, pretend to be Chris's girlfriend, then seduce their daughter? Henry is a pretty terrifying dude, you know."

"I get it, Bella. But there's something about Alissa. She's… different. I don't know how to explain it."

Nicole sits back, smirking. "Why do you need to explain it? If it feels good, go with it. Just keep things casual for now. Wait until Henry announces the next CEO. Then, think about getting serious."

"You make it sound like I'm part of some corporate strategy," I say, slightly irked by the transactional way she's framing it.

Mom puts her hand on mine. "Nicole has a point, darling. You may not like to think of it as a game, but you're stepping into a high-stakes world."

"I'm not naive, Mom. And this isn't some calculated plot. I have genuine feelings for her, messy as they are."

Bella grins. "Well, she must have some kind of feelings for you too, Soph, or she wouldn't be caught dead in this sort of romantic quagmire. Just remember, love doesn't exist in a vacuum. There are external factors, like an entire empire of a family, who will have a say in this, whether you like it or not."

"I just wish I knew what she was really thinking," I sigh, frustrated. "She can be so hard to read sometimes."

Mom leans closer. "That's the intrigue of love, isn't it? The mystery. But Soph, everyone has their own ways of expressing their emotions, and maybe, Alissa is more of a closed book than you are, if that was even possible. Especially in a family trained more for boardrooms than heart-to-heart conversations."

"Which is why you should be extra careful," Bella adds. "In their world, you're stepping onto a chessboard. And you better know how to play."

Nicole grins. "Or at least enjoy the game while you're at it. The future will be here soon enough, and there's no rush to decide it all today."

I take a deep breath, gathering my thoughts before I speak. "You know, it's not just the chemistry between Alissa and me. We're both going through similar struggles. She's not happy with her career, just like I'm not thrilled with mine. We both have complicated relationships with our parents, and let's not even get started on our non-existent love lives before we met each other."

Mom looks at me, her eyes analytical. "Sophia, I hear you. But you need to understand, Alissa is already a successful businesswoman. She has the backing of her family, their resources, their network. You're on your own, darling. You need to keep giving it your all."

I shake my head, my frustration bubbling over. "But what's the point, Mom? Should I continue running a rat race that I don't even enjoy? Just to prove a point?"

Mom leans in, her voice tinged with a scientist's rationality. "Work gives life meaning, Sophia. What will you do without work? Sit around and ponder the mysteries of the universe?"

I chuckle at her sarcasm but then grow serious. "Work might give life structure, but does it give it meaning? I've been questioning that a lot lately. And being with Alissa, feeling this... this incredible connection, it's made me realize that maybe there's more to life than just climbing the corporate ladder or achieving some arbitrary measure of success."

"So, you just plan to sit around and be in love?" Mom's voice takes on that condescending tone that I hated as a teenager, reminding me that she is a scientist and I am just a model... correction, a former model.

"No, I plan to take a break and re-evaluate my life. I have enough in savings, and I think I need to just... be with myself for a bit, maybe decide on what kind of life I want to live," I say, my eyes wandering to the lake that shimmers back at me, looking majestic. "Maybe I'll live on a ranch like this, raise horses, eat breakfast under a tree every day, away from the back-biting and the politics of the modeling world, the influencer world."

"And what does Alissa want from her life?" Bella asks, leaning forward and placing her little chin on her knuckles.

"She wants the same."

"To raise horses?" Mom asks, in disbelief.

"Yeah," I reply, trying to keep my cool.

"So, she is fine with going from the head of Sales and

Marketing of a billion-dollar company to an average ranch... woman?"

I scoff at Mom. "Not everyone defines life's success based on titles and numbers, Mom."

"I don't get it, Sophia," Mom sighs, leaning back into the couch. "You fought with me, left home to stay all by yourself in New York because you wanted to be a supermodel, and now you want to throw it all away?"

"Who I was when I was 15 was different from who I was at 21, which is different from who I am at 26. And maybe at 31, I'll decide to open a restaurant, become a scuba diver at 40, who the fuck knows? And why should I keep doing something that is not giving me any happiness?"

"All of this is happening because of that girl," Mom snaps, tearing her eyes away from me.

"Really? You want to blame an innocent girl for something your daughter thinks that you don't agree with? Are we really doing this again, Mom? I left your house all those years ago because you thought I was taking decisions under the influence of *your* girlfriend, and now you're again blaming someone else? Have I blamed Bella for how little time you've been spending with me? Did I ever blame Bella for sleeping with my mother? Have I?" I glare at Bella, who looks defeated.

"But you do think that I've stolen your mom or something, right?"

"Maybe, but I never voiced it out loud. I did my best not to fucking blame you for my insecurities. And now, you're going to sit here," my eyes find Mom again, "and lecture me about being influenced by the girl I am fucking? Mom, you really need to be more self-aware."

I stop screaming.

I feel tears pricking the sides of my eyes.

I am out of breath, and I am out of patience.

"I have been alone for a year now. Kaylee left me, and then I lost most of my modeling gigs, and during all this time, how many times have we met?" I direct the question to both Bella and Mom.

None of them answer.

"You have always been so guarded about your emotions..." Mom begins.

"Because I had to. It was instilled in me. I wanted to be like you, Mom, all strength and reserve and... 'I can handle everything on my own.' Look what it has turned me into."

"Sophia..." Bella finally speaks. Her voice is soft and laced with hurt. Her beautiful blue eyes are shimmering with tears. "It was because of me. I have become selfish..."

"No, don't do this, Bella. She needs to know the truth," Mom says, and Bella is about to argue when Mom shushes her.

"Bella has Broken Heart Syndrome, which is a kind of heart disease induced by stress. She has massive chest pains frequently due to her heart muscles becoming weak. But she keeps insisting on working, touring, and I can't let her tour alone, so... I was so occupied with making sure nothing happens to her that I sort of... put you at the back of my mind, mostly because you've always shown so much strength that I thought you'd take care of yourself. But I was wrong. I should have been more aware."

I listen to Mom but keep looking at Bella. A girl who was more like my sister a long time ago. A girl who had been with me through my lowest lows.

"Bella," I whisper, "I am so sorry. I had no idea. Why didn't you ever tell me, you idiot!"

"Because I already felt like a loser in front of your Mom. I didn't want you to think of me as weak. Plus, you had your own things to worry about."

"I see what's going on here," Nicole speaks, and all eyes turn to her. "Bella and Sophia are both, more or less, in the same boat. But the difference is, one has found a woman who has pushed her to question the real meaning of success and happiness, while the other is in a relationship with a woman who defines it for all her loved ones." Nicole eyes Mom, and I can't believe she just said that. But then, that's Nicole. She will always say the right thing, no matter how controversial.

"Ava," Nicole begins, "once upon a time, you saved me and my relationship, and I will always thank you for it. But I think it's time that you allow yourself to listen to someone else. Both Bella and Sophia need a break. This life is crushing them. Instead of touring with Bella, force her to stop touring, ask her to stop working all the time. And Sophia, you go and do you. Take a break, have mind-blowing sex with your Southern bombshell, and live life a little. And you two," she continues, "listen, this girl will never tell you a few things because it will be too awkward for her, but I will say them on her behalf. Tone down the PDA in front of her. Don't forget, she did a major thing when she gave her blessing to your relationship. Because trust me, it would have been hard for me to see my mother with my best friend. And now, the two of you need to reciprocate by being there for her. By checking up on her, because she might not show it, but she needs you guys too. She needs us." Nicole's eyes meet mine, and I feel like rushing over to her and giving her the tightest hug of all time.

Mom takes a deep breath, her eyes meeting mine with a newfound clarity. "Sophia, I've realized how difficult this must have been for you. I've been so wrapped up in my own world that I've neglected to see the struggles you've been facing. I'm sorry."

She then turns to Bella, her eyes softening. "And Bella, if you ever got the impression that taking a break would make me think you're weak, then please know that's not the case. I love you for who you are, not for what you can endure."

Bella smiles warmly, her eyes meeting Mom's. "You've been my biggest strength, and I would never blame you for anything. But I agree with Sophia; we all need to stop and re-evaluate our lives. Take a break."

"Well, except for Nicole," Bella adds, "who seems to be crushing it with her dance studio."

Nicole chuckles, flipping her hair back with a flair. "I was a former stripper; running a pole dancing studio is light work compared to 20-hour shifts dancing on sweaty old people."

We all burst into laughter, the tension in the room dissipating like morning fog under the sun.

"So," Mom says, turning back to me, "when can we meet this Alissa? And how else can we help you get the girl of your dreams?"

I pause, considering her words. "First, I need to decide if Alissa really is the girl of my dreams. And then, you guys can help me by just playing your roles for now, until Henry decides on the CEO. As for meeting Alissa, how about we all have dinner tonight? Chris and Henry are going away on a business trip, and I think Alissa is free. You guys can get to know each other."

Nicole grins. "Does Alissa know what she's getting into? Meeting the family is a big step, especially this family."

Bella chimes in, "Yeah, we're like the Avengers of emotional baggage."

Mom laughs. "Well, every superhero team needs a good origin story, right?"

"And a villain," Nicole adds. "Who's the villain in this story?"

"We all take turns," I say, smiling. "But for now, let's focus on assembling our team for dinner tonight."

Mom nods, her eyes meeting mine one more time. "Assembled we shall be."

And just like that, the room fills with a sense of unity, a newfound understanding among us. It's a slow burn, but it's a start, and sometimes, that's all you need.

∞∞∞

Before I even get to my own dress, I find Alissa standing in her lingerie, holding up the black jumpsuit she's picked for tonight. Her eyes meet mine, a playful glint in them.

"Need some help there?" I ask, walking over to her.

"Would you mind?" she says, handing me the jumpsuit.

I take it from her, my eyes briefly lingering on the delicate lace of her lingerie. "You know, you could just go like this. I'm sure my mom would find it very... avant-garde."

She laughs, stepping one leg and then the other into the jumpsuit. "As tempting as that sounds, I think I'll stick to the traditional 'clothed' approach for meeting the parents."

I help her pull the jumpsuit up, my hands grazing her sides as I do. The fabric slides over her curves, and I can't help but think how I'll be taking this off her body in just a few hours.

"Zip me up?" she asks, turning her back to me.

"With pleasure," I reply, pulling the zipper up slowly, and kissing the nape of her neck when I am done.

Once she's zipped up, she turns back to face me, her eyes meeting mine. "Your turn," she says, gesturing to the emerald-green wrap dress I've laid out on the bed.

And so, we switch places, and the ritual of getting ready

continues.

I'm standing in front of the full-length mirror, examining the emerald-green wrap dress that I've chosen for tonight. Alissa walks up behind me, her eyes meeting mine in the reflection.

"Can't we just go back to the part where we were just in lingerie?" she nuzzles the side of my neck, while tracing a finger down my abdomen.

"We'll be late. My mom is very particular about timing."

"And I am very particular about making her daughter orgasm."

"Really? I don't think she'd appreciate this little info."

Alissa giggles and runs the tip of her tongue down the side of my neck while gently cupping my breasts. "Guess I'll just have to make do with mentally fucking you all night."

"Yup, that will have to do for now, baby."

Alissa groans. "So, how are you feeling better after that emotional breakthrough with your mother?" she asks, reaching around me to help tie the sash of my dress into a neat bow.

I take a deep breath, still amazed at the emotional breakthrough that unfolded earlier. "It was... intense. Finally telling Mom that I need a break from this rat race of money and success was a relief. And Bella... I am just happy to know she's also decided to take a break before her heart condition gets serious."

Alissa's eyes soften. "It was a lot to take in, right?"

"Yeah," I agree, as she moves to stand beside me, picking up a tube of mascara from the vanity. "But it was good. We all needed it."

She leans in, carefully applying the mascara to my lashes. "And what about you? Are you really serious about taking a break? Living on a ranch?"

I look into her eyes, seeing the sincerity there. "I've never been more serious about anything."

She smiles, setting down the mascara and picking up a lipstick. "Can I join you on this little fantasy ranch of yours?"

"As I'm imagining living on *your* ranch, I guess the answer is yes," I say, grinning as she carefully applies a soft rose shade to my lips.

She caps the lipstick and sets it down, her eyes meeting mine in the mirror. "I'm nervous about meeting your mom, you know. She's a literal Nobel Prize winner."

I laugh. "You've met the freaking President of the USA."

"That was easy," she says, moving behind me to help zip up the back of her jumpsuit. "Meeting your girlfriend's mother? Now that's hard."

I stop what I'm doing, my hands still on the zipper. "This is the first time you've called me your girlfriend."

She laughs, her eyes twinkling. "Well, get used to it."

Unable to resist, I turn around and pull her into a kiss. It's soft, sweet, and filled with promise.

"Oh, by the way," she says as we break apart, "Susie might want to come with us."

I chuckle. "Don't worry. I told her Mom will be drinking and watching 'Sex and the City.' Susie must be in chains by now."

We both laugh, and I finally manage to zip her up. She turns around, and I'm smitten by how good she looks. The jumpsuit complements her figure perfectly, and her makeup is subtle but stunning.

"You look amazing," I whisper, my eyes meeting hers.

She smiles, her eyes filled with warmth. "So do you. But

more importantly, you look happy, and that's all I've ever wanted for you."

I feel my heart swell at her words. "And you, Alissa, are a big reason for that happiness."

She leans in, her lips meeting mine in a soft, lingering kiss. "Then let's go make some more happy memories, starting with tonight."

∞∞∞

We're all seated around the rustic wooden table at Mom and Bella's ranch house, the atmosphere warm and inviting. The table is set with an array of delicious dishes, and the wine is flowing freely. Alissa sits beside me, her hand occasionally brushing against mine under the table, sending little jolts of electricity through me.

"So, Alissa," Mom starts, "Sophia tells me you studied at both Oxford and Cambridge. That's quite impressive."

Alissa chuckles. "Yes, I did. It was an interesting experience, to say the least. Once, during a formal dinner at Oxford, I mistook a finger bowl for a soup bowl."

Bella bursts into laughter. "Oh, that's nothing. During one of my concerts in Britain, I tried to get the crowd going by shouting, 'Are you all right?' and everyone just politely responded, 'Yes, thank you.' Totally killed the vibe!"

We all laugh, the tension of the first meeting slowly dissipating.

Mom turns to me, a mischievous glint in her eye. "Speaking of setting vibes, Sophia here was so passionate about modeling as a kid that she used to strut down our hallway as if it were a runway. She even made her little cousin announce her, 'Ladies and gentlemen, presenting the fabulous Sophia, the greatest, most beautiful female on Earth, Solar System and the Universe!'"

I feel my cheeks flush but laugh along. "Well, someone had to appreciate my talents."

Alissa shoots a playful grin my way before swiveling her attention to Mom and Bella. "So, spill the tea. Was it a 'see-you-and-the-world-stops' kind of love, or more like a slow-burning candle?"

Mom chuckles, "Oh, it was a slow burn, alright. We first crossed paths at a party where Bella was the DJ. I had no idea she was Sophia's roommate at the time."

I roll my eyes dramatically. "So she claims."

Bella bursts into laughter. "Trust me, if I were acting, you'd know. Have you seen me play charades? I couldn't fake my way out of a paper bag!"

I chime in, "Yeah, Mom's only Oscar-worthy role is playing the stern matriarch. But deep down, she's a total softie." Our eyes meet, and for a moment, the room fades away. That old, comforting warmth floods through me, just like it used to.

Alissa, ever the inquisitive one, nudges the conversation along. "So, after Bella's set, what happened?"

Bella covers her blushing face with her hands but can't contain her excitement. "We hooked up! I saw her in the crowd, and I just had to dedicate a song to her. One of my Interstellar remixes, as fate would have it. And then, get this—I find out my club crush is an astrophysicist! Talk about stars aligning, and I mean that literally."

Mom takes over, "It was complicated, to say the least. The age gap, Bella being Sophia's friend, and roommate—there were a million reasons it shouldn't have worked. But love, as they say, finds a way."

Alissa dabs her mouth with a napkin, inadvertently

smearing her lipstick. "And Nicole, where's Emma tonight? Sophia's been raving about your love story. A high-school teacher and a former stripper? It's like you guys are characters in a romance novel!"

I lean over and help Alissa smooth out her lipstick, our eyes meeting for a brief, electric moment.

Nicole leans back, swirling her wine glass. "Ah, Emma. She was the quintessential prim and proper teacher, still nursing a broken heart. I was a stripper and a single mom, jaded from searching for love in a club teeming with the city's most unsavory characters. Then, one fateful night, Emma walks in for her sister's bachelorette party."

Alissa, her hand now entwined with mine, asks, "And she agreed to a lap dance? Just like that?"

I shoot her a look that says, 'Easy, cowgirl. We're in mixed company.'

Nicole grins, her eyes twinkling like stars. "Oh, you'd be surprised what a little peer pressure can do. So yes, I gave Emma the lap dance of her life. And let's just say, by the end of the night, she was utterly captivated. It was as if I had cast a spell on her, one she couldn't—and didn't want to—break."

Nicole takes a sip of her wine, her eyes meeting Alissa's. "Sometimes, love shows up in the places you least expect, wearing a disguise you never saw coming. And when it does, you don't question it; you just dance to the rhythm it sets for you."

"True," Alissa murmurs, her voice barely above a whisper. Then, as if pulled by an invisible force, her eyes meet mine.

In that fleeting moment, her gaze transforms into a poetic language all its own. It's as if her eyes are whispering to me, 'I am that unexpected love, the one you never saw coming, yet here I am, irrevocably changing your world.'

And in that instant, I realize—where indeed is the lie?

∞∞∞

So, the dinner? A total slam dunk, and let's just say Alissa is the MVP. She's got this social game down to a science—every word out of her mouth is like a perfectly aimed arrow, hitting the bullseye between 'classy' and 'cool as a cucumber.'

Big props to Mom, Bella, and Nicole for not turning dinner into an episode of "Who Wants to Interrogate My Girlfriend?" I shoot them a 'thank you for not being Sherlock Holmes' look later, and they get the memo.

Tonight's not about grilling Alissa like she's on the witness stand. Nah, it's her debutante ball, her chance to show off why she's the leading lady in my life's rom-com.

As for the 'are we or aren't we' debate about our relationship? That's a can of worms for another day, thank you very much.

As the dinner winds down, Alissa pulls me aside, tucking us into a cozy corner of the living room. "So, did I pass the Mom test? Or should I start studying astrophysics to impress Ava?"

I raise an eyebrow, playing it cool. "Astrophysics? Honey, you'd need a whole new galaxy to impress my mom. Her initial reaction was 'You can do better, Sophia.'"

Alissa's eyes widen for a split second before I burst into laughter. "I'm kidding! You were a hit, babe. Even Mom's impressed, and that's like getting a nod from the Nobel committee."

"Are you sure? Was she okay with all the astronomy puns I couldn't help myself from making?"

"Yeah, what was all that about?"

"I don't know. They just kept coming to me, and I didn't

even try to keep them in my mind. My brain works in weird ways sometimes."

"That's because it is half-British and half-Texan. If *that* isn't the definition of a weird brain, I don't know what is."

Later, Bella sweeps me away for a mini-tour of the house. "So, how are you holding up? Any lingering grudges?"

I look at her, my soul sister in every sense. "Grudges? Please, we're way past that. We're back to being Thelma and Louise, minus the cliff dive."

"Good, because I've missed my partner in crime," Bella says, her eyes softening. "You know, the one who'd stay up with me watching rom-coms and dissecting every line."

"And I've missed my go-to DJ for every emotional crisis," I reply. "We're back, Bella. Soul sisters for life."

"And listen, I promise to be in touch. In fact, I plan to bombard you with calls, texts, and all the emotional drama you can handle," Bella says as we step into the cozy library on the first floor.

"As long as you refrain from discussing your sex life with my mom, we're golden," I reply.

"Obviously. But I'm dying to hear all the juicy details about your escapades with that Anderson you've snagged. So, spill—how good is she?"

"In bed?" I ask as we approach the massive window overlooking the lake.

"No, on MS Excel. Duh," she retorts.

I can't help but smile, recalling Bella's signature sarcasm.

"She's the best I've ever had," I say, arching an eyebrow for emphasis.

"Even better than Kaylee?" Bella counters, raising her own

eyebrow.

"Kaylee was... malleable. She did whatever I asked her to, which was fun. But Alissa? She takes charge. Makes Nicole look like a vanilla cone."

"Oh, come on. You can't compare her to Nicole. That girl is a freak."

"Well, so is Alissa. And tonight, we might just let our freak flags fly." I wink at Bella, who gives me two thumbs up and a nod of approval and admiration.

Finally, it's time to say our goodbyes. Nicole's up first. "You two better visit soon. Don't let the Andersons chain you up. No offense, Alissa."

"None taken," Alissa replies, hugging Nicole goodbye. "And about that private lap dance—Sophia was joking. I didn't actually express a desire to get one from you."

"Really? Now that's disappointing. I thought you were a genuine fan," Nicole says.

"Don't listen to her. A few days ago, she made me stay up all night to watch all your live performances and practice sessions on your YouTube channel. Trust me, it got weird after a while," I interject as Alissa looks like she'd rather jump into the lake than continue this conversation.

"Alright, I am a fan, and I would really like that lap dance," Alissa finally admits.

"Then let's plan another dinner, and I'll be the dessert," Nicole says, her voice dripping with sultriness.

Next up are Mom and Bella. "You girls take care," Bella says, hugging us both. "And Sophia, I need the deets for the 'freak on,' okay?"

"Shut up, Bells," I reply, grinning from ear to ear.

Mom hugs me, then turns to Alissa. "It was lovely meeting

you, Alissa. We must do this again soon."

"Absolutely," Alissa agrees, her face lighting up.

As we're about to leave, Mom pulls me aside. "Sophia, I'm really happy for you. Alissa seems like a wonderful young woman."

I catch the subtle emphasis on 'wonderful,' and my heart does a little happy dance. Mom's approval is the cherry on top of an already perfect evening.

∞ ∞ ∞

We're walking back to the Anderson ranch, the night air thick with the scent of fresh grass and the intoxicating buzz of alcohol. Our hands find each other naturally, like magnets drawn together.

"How about a game?" Alissa suggests, her eyes twinkling with mischief.

"Do tell," I reply, intrigued.

"We walk in a straight line toward the lake, taking ten steps each time in turns. Whoever stumbles has to remove a piece of clothing. Let's see who's more dressed by the time we reach the water."

I chuckle, loving her audacity. "You're on."

Alissa goes first, taking ten careful steps. "Your turn, hotshot."

I step forward, feeling the grass beneath my feet. I make it, but just barely. "Looks like we're both still in the game."

Alissa takes her next turn, and this time, she stumbles. "Ah, damn it!"

"Looks like it's strip o'clock," I tease.

With a playful roll of her eyes, she removes her sandals and tosses them aside. "Your move."

I take my steps, but this time I stumble too. "Guess it's fair play," I say, removing my sandals as well.

We continue, the tension building with each step and each piece of discarded clothing. Alissa loses her jacket, and I lose my belt. By the time we're halfway to the lake, we're both down to our essentials, and the stakes have never felt higher—or more exciting.

"Okay, final stretch," Alissa says, taking her steps. She stumbles again, laughing as she removes her watch.

I follow suit, but my tipsy state betrays me, and I stumble as well. Off goes my watch as well. We're both standing there, half-dressed, half-exhilarated, and completely smitten.

"So, what's the tiebreaker?" Alissa asks, her voice tinged with anticipation.

I lean in, my lips inches from hers. "I think we both win," I whisper, and pull Alissa into my arms.

My mouth is hungry on her lips, and my fingers impatient on the clasps of her bra.

The cool wind flirts with our bodies as I rip Alissa's bra off her body.

"In the mood for skinny dipping, huh?" she whispers, breathless, watching me shed the last remaining layers of her clothing, as if I am attempting to break a world record.

"In the mood for fucking," I reply, through clenched teeth.

It is unbelievable how horny this woman makes me.

I slide Alissa's panties off her legs and give her thighs a few hungry licks before shedding my own undergarments.

Alissa licks her lips and pounces on me as we fall onto the

moss covered ground. My eyes briefly admire the moon and how bright and full it is tonight, before Alissa's entire body envelopes me, and she starts kissing me wildly.

We roll around on the grass, drunk with alcohol , lust and what now seems to be love as well.

I wrap my legs and arms around Alissa, and we moan into the night.

Soon, Alissa has her legs around my waist, and our centers are thrusting into each other while the lake shimmers a few meters away from us.

"Allis… Alissa… Alissaaa…"

"Yes, baby, look at me….yes, oh god I love your body so fucking much!"

We come together, under the twinkling stars, amidst the rustling of the leaves, illuminated by a full moon that casts its spotlight on two naked women, glistening with sweat, laying in each other's arms like lovers from a forgotten century.

Finally, we realize it's getting late and reluctantly start looking for our discarded pieces of clothing with the help of our phone's flashlight.

Once we've found everything, we help each other dress, taking little breaks in between to kiss, lick, or simply hug each other.

If this isn't the onset of love, I don't know what is!

Once we're fully dressed, we embrace one last time and kiss as if our lives depend on it, then let go.

"I want to take this moment, store it in a cute, rustic jar, and keep it tucked away," I say, touching my forehead to Alissa's.

"I want to tuck you away in a little corner of my heart."

"I think I love you, Alissa," I finally say the words.

The wind around us seems to suddenly drop and the leaves stop rustling as if the world is waiting with bated breath for what comes next.

I see Alissa take a deep breath.

Here it comes, Soph. Brace yourself.

But before she can say the words my ears have been desperate to hear, another voice pierces the stillness around us.

"What the fuck?"

Alissa and I turn around at the same time to see Chris standing a few feet away from us, his face illuminated by the moonlight, eyes burning with rage, nostrils flared, and chest heaving with fury.

The air is thick with tension, each of us locked in a standoff. Chris's eyes are ablaze, darting between Alissa and me.

"Chris, let me explain—" Alissa starts, but he cuts her off.

"Explain? You're out here, half-dressed, with Sophia, and you think you can explain this?"

I step in, feeling the weight of the moment. "Chris, it's not what it looks like. We—"

"Oh, it's exactly what it looks like," he snaps, his voice tinged with bitterness. "Sophia, couldn't you keep it in your pants for just a few days? You've put everything I've worked for at stake!"

I wince at his words, the sting of his accusation cutting deep. "Chris, I never intended for any of this to happen. But feelings aren't something we can control."

He turns his glare toward Alissa. "And you, is this how much you want to be CEO? You'd pretend to be gay just to jeopardize my chances?"

Alissa's eyes widen, her cheeks flushed. "Chris, you're

misunderstanding. This has nothing to do with the CEO position or any scheme. This is real."

Frustrated, Chris throws his hands in the air. "I don't even know what to believe anymore. Who should I believe? How long has this been happening?"

"We didn't orchestrate this, Chris. It just unfolded," Alissa replies, her voice tinged with a desperate sincerity.

"What unfolded? Explain," Chris demands.

"I fell for Alissa, Chris. I tried not to, believe me, but damn it, I think she's the one."

"The one who'll run to Dad and spill everything to usurp my chance at being CEO?" Chris retorts, his words like daggers.

"Chris, I have no intention of exposing you or playing dirty to become CEO. That's not who I am," Alissa insists.

"So you're saying you're *actually* gay?"

"Yes, Chris, I've always been gay. Just like you."

Chris looks as if he's been blindsided by a freight train.

"You told her?" He turns to me, his voice more tinged with hurt than anger. "You didn't even give me a chance, did you? You slept with her and then spilled all my secrets, trusting her blindly?

"It was MY fucking decision to make! You had no right—absolutely no right—to tell her something that could ruin me, especially to the one person who could use it against me!" Chris's voice roars, the veins in his neck pulsating with each syllable.

"I'm sorry," I murmur, my voice barely above a whisper. "I fucked up, but Chris, she's gay too. Why does it matter?"

"Because no one's whispering rumors about her," Chris retorts, pausing to catch his breath. "She didn't ask a friend to masquerade as her girlfriend to appease a conservative father.

There's no evidence against her. But me? I have you—a living, breathing piece of evidence. Once she spills the beans, Dad will dig deeper. And then, it's game over for me."

"That won't happen, Chris," Alissa interjects.

"Why? Because you've suddenly lost interest in being CEO?" Chris challenges.

I turn to Alissa, who takes a deep, steadying breath.

"Swear on our mother that you don't want the job, and I'll believe everything you're saying. Remove yourself from the running," Chris says, his eyes locked onto Alissa's.

"Alissa?" I prompt, my voice tinged with a sense of betrayal.

Alissa's eyes meet mine before shifting back to Chris. "I want the job, but I want to earn it fair and square. You keep your secret, maintain this façade with Sophia, and let's compete on even ground. We can pretend tonight never happened."

"But you told me you didn't want the job!" My voice cracks, the hurt evident as I look at Alissa.

"I was contemplating it, Sophia. I haven't made a final decision yet."

"Seemed like a done deal to me," I retort, my words laced with a bitterness I can't conceal.

Chris clenches his fists, his face a storm of conflicting emotions. "You know what? I can't even talk to either of you right now. I need space." Without another word, he storms off into the night.

I turn to Alissa, my eyes searching hers for some semblance of the truth. "Why couldn't you just tell Chris you didn't want the job? Why keep him—and me—in this agonizing limbo?"

"Because I don't know if I want it or not, Sophia!" Alissa exclaims, her voice tinged with frustration. "I'm allowed to be uncertain. I'm allowed to weigh my options."

"Options? Is that what I am to you? An option?" The hurt in my voice is palpable, even to me.

"No, Sophia, you're not just an option. But I can't just throw everything away on a whim. I have to think about this."

"Think about what? Us? The job? What is it that you're so confused about, Alissa?"

"Everything! I'm confused about everything, okay? This is all so new to me."

I take a deep breath, trying to calm the whirlwind of emotions inside me. "I thought I had finally figured out what I wanted in life, but you... you're still so unsure. Maybe you need to take some time to figure out what you really want."

Alissa looks at me, her eyes filled with a mixture of regret and understanding. "Maybe you're right."

"I need to be with Chris right now," I say, my voice softer. "I feel like I've betrayed him in some way, and I need to make it right. Plus, I suddenly feel suffocated, like I can't breathe."

Alissa nods, her eyes downcast. "Go. Be with Chris. And I'll... I'll take some time to figure things out."

I nod, feeling a strange mix of relief and sadness. "Let me know when you do."

With that, I turn and walk away, each step widening the emotional distance between Alissa and me, leaving us both to ponder what we truly want from life—and from each other.

As I walk away, my heels crunching on the gravel path, I can't help but glance back. Alissa stands there, a solitary figure bathed in the soft glow of the moonlight, her eyes meeting mine for a fleeting moment before I turn away. The weight of our unresolved feelings hangs heavy in the air, making me feel like a prisoner in a cell where the walls are closing in on me.

I find Chris sitting alone against the bark of the oak tree, his face buried in his hands. As I approach, he looks up, his face softer than it was a few moments ago.

"Hey," I say softly, taking a seat beside him.

"Hey," he replies, his voice barely above a whisper.

"We need to talk, Chris."

He sighs, looking away. "Do we? Because I just don't have the energy in me to face any more betrayals."

"I messed up," I admit, "I should've never shared your secret with Alissa. But I thought—"

"You thought what? That she'd be different? That she wouldn't use it against me?"

"I thought I could trust her. And I still think I can. She's as scared and confused as we are, Chris."

Chris shakes his head. "That's just it, Sophia. We can't afford to be scared and confused. Not when so much is at stake."

"I know," I say, my voice tinged with regret. "And that's why I'm here. To figure out how we can make this right."

Chris looks at me, his eyes searching mine. "And how do we do that?"

"I don't know," I admit. "But we can start by being honest with each other. No more secrets, Chris. If we're going to get through this, we need to trust each other completely. Can you trust an old friend?"

"I can try," says Chris, looking away into the distance where the massive Anderson mansion lies cloaked in the silvery garment of the moon.

"I really like your sister, Chris. I don't know how else to put it. Before you showed up, I had just confessed my feelings to her. I had told her I loved her."

Chris's eyes narrow, his jaw tightening. "And what did she

say?"

"That's just it," I say, my heart pounding in my chest. "Before she could reply, you showed up. I still don't know what she would have said."

Chris shakes his head, his eyes skeptical. "Sophia, do you really think Alissa is capable of loving someone? All her life, she's loved herself and her work more than anything else."

I look into his eyes, searching for understanding. "You're wrong about her, Chris. I've spent time with her. She's different from what you think."

Chris snorts, his eyes drifting to the Anderson mansion, its silhouette haunting in the moonlight. "And you think she's wrong about me too?"

"Yes," I say, my voice firm. "Both of you have misconceptions about each other."

Chris leans back, his eyes meeting mine again. "So what do you have in mind?"

I take a deep breath. "There's only one thing we can do right now. Pretend none of this happened. You and Alissa wait for Henry to make his decision. Whoever loses concedes gracefully. And the two of you need to have a conversation and start trusting each other."

Chris rubs his temples. "That sounds good on paper, Sophia. But can Alissa play fair?"

"She will," I say, my voice tinged with conviction. "You have my word."

Chris sighs, then looks at me, his eyes piercing. "What happens to you and Alissa if she becomes CEO? Because that would mean she can't date you publicly."

My heart sinks at his words. I feel a lump forming in my throat, and I swallow hard. "I guess Alissa has made the decision for both of us," I say, my voice barely above a whisper. "Maybe I read her wrong. Maybe my feelings were deeper than hers."

Chris leans back against the tree, his eyes searching mine. "How did you and Alissa even start this fling? When was all of this happening?"

I chuckle, brushing a stray lock of hair from my face. "While you were out shooting three-pointers and slam-dunking in your basketball games, Alissa and I were playing a different kind of game. One of emotions, not points on a scoreboard."

Chris laughs, his eyes twinkling. "Well, I hope you were at least scoring some emotional baskets."

We sit in silence for a while, the night air thick with unsaid words and lingering questions. Finally, Chris speaks.

"You know, Sophia, it hurts me to say this, but I probably know you better right now than I know my own sister. I've had more in-depth conversations with you than with Alissa, and that's why I'm a little doubtful of her intentions."

I look at him, touched by his vulnerability. "Chris, I get it. But I also know Alissa. She's not the person you think she is."

He sighs, his eyes meeting mine. "I trust your judgment, Sophia. If you think there's a future with Alissa, then you should go talk to her. Ask her straight out what she wants. And don't accept a vague answer. Because once she becomes CEO, there's no future for the two of you. Dad will make sure of it. I'm not saying this to make her drop out of the race; I'm saying this to save you another heartbreak. You've already gone through one a year ago with Kaylee."

I feel a warmth spread through me, grateful for his concern. "Thanks, Chris. That means a lot."

He leans in closer, his voice dropping to a whisper. "Sophia, Dad is planning a family meeting. He's going to ask both Alissa and me to tell him—and the family—why we're better suited to run the company."

My eyes widen, shocked by this revelation. "Really? Why?"

Chris shrugs. "He thinks it might help him make a decision. The meeting is day after tomorrow. He'll announce his decision that night."

"Do you think Alissa knows about this?"

Chris shakes his head. "Dad planned to tell her tonight."

I sit there, my mind racing. "A family meeting to decide who gets to be CEO? That's... intense."

Chris nods, his eyes clouded with uncertainty. "Yeah, it's a big deal. Dad's always been unconventional, but this takes it to a whole new level."

We both fall silent, contemplating the gravity of what's to come. Finally, Chris breaks the silence.

"You know, Sophia, the past month has changed both our lives in ways we couldn't have imagined. And who knows what the future holds? I might go back to New York as the CEO of Anders Corp, and you might go back with a girlfriend."

I look at him, my eyes meeting his. "Honestly, Chris, I don't want to think about girlfriends right now. I'm just relieved that you and Alissa know the truth. That I don't have to hide anything anymore."

Chris smiles, a soft, understanding smile that warms my heart. "So, what happens now? Do we go back to being pretend boyfriend and girlfriend?"

I pause, searching for the right words. "Yes, from tomorrow, I can go back to being your pretend girlfriend and..." I take a deep breath, my voice tinged with a sadness I can't hide, "just an acquaintance to Alissa."

Chris looks at me, his eyes filled with a mix of understanding and regret. "Sophia, whatever happens, know that you've got a friend in me. And if Alissa doesn't see how amazing you are, then she's the one missing out."

I smile, touched by his words. "Thanks, Chris. That means the world to me."

As we sit there under the moonlight, the looming family meeting casting its shadow over us, I can't help but think how much has changed and how much more could change in the days to come. But for now, in this moment, I find comfort in the friendship that has stood the test of time and trials.

Chapter Eight

(Alissa)

So Sophia's moved out of the big, fancy Anderson ranch to the smaller one her mom and friends are renting. Honestly? Good for me. I need the headspace and zero distractions to absolutely nail the presentation Dad's got planned for Chris and me. And why's he making us present to the whole family? No idea. Dad's a wildcard, always has been.

Sophia leaving didn't sit well with the Anderson clan, but Chris, bless him, finally grew a backbone. He's been going all out with this 'loving boyfriend' act lately, and for once, he put his foot down. About time, too. He needs that spine for the company, especially when I take over as CEO.

Yeah, you heard me. I'm that confident.

And now, I want that CEO title more than ever. I've got to show Sophia why I can't just drop everything for her. I can't just forget about a dream that's been my driving force for years.

For the past 24 hours, I've been a machine. Slide after slide, point after point, I've been crafting this presentation like it's my magnum opus. Coffee on my left, laptop in front of me, and a mountain of research papers to my right—I've got my war room set up. Sophia? She's been blocked out, tucked away in some corner of my mind. I can't afford distractions, not when the CEO position is almost within my grasp.

But that was last night. Tonight's a different story. It's the eve of the big presentation, and my nerves are frayed. I've rehearsed my speech a dozen times, tweaked the slides until my eyes hurt, and now, there's nothing left to do but wait. And it's in this waiting that I find myself missing Sophia. Terribly.

I miss the little things. The way she'd be next to me in bed, her face glowing from her nighttime skincare routine. The way she'd pull out her phone and start creating Instagram stories, narrating the highlights of her day to her followers. It was like living in a cozy, real-time rom-com.

Unable to resist, I find myself scrolling through Instagram and landing on Sophia's profile. My thumb hovers over her latest stories, and then I tap. There she is, laughing and playing charades with Ava, her mom, and her friends Bella and Nicole. They're all having a blast, and I was supposed to be there, right in the thick of it. But I'm not.

I watch as Sophia acts out a word, her face animated, her hands flying around as she tries to get her point across. Ava guesses it right, and they share a high-five, their faces lighting up with pure joy. And it hits me—this is what I'm missing out on. This is the life that's passing me by while I chase after titles and corner offices.

I put my phone down, my heart heavy. I've made my choices, set my priorities, and now, all that's left is to face the consequences. Tomorrow, I'll stand in front of my family and make the pitch of my life. But tonight, just for tonight, I allow myself to feel the weight of what I've given up.

∞∞∞

The living hall of the Anderson mansion has been transformed into what could easily pass for a corporate conference room. Plush chairs are neatly aligned, a projector is set up, and the grand chandelier overhead lends an air of gravitas to the setting. I walk in, my heels clicking against the marble floor, dressed in a pencil skirt and a tight blouse. My hair flows freely, framing my face like a cascading waterfall.

As I scan the room, my eyes land on every person present. There's Aunt Martha and Uncle Daniel, looking as smug as ever, and even their daughter Susie has shown up. My mom, Mary, is also there, her face grave. I know she disapproves of how Dad is turning Chris's and my sibling rivalry into a public spectacle.

Then my eyes meet Dad's—Henry Anderson in his finest suit, puffing on his most expensive cigar. His face is like that of a predator, his hair slicked back and oily, his full white beard giving him an air of patriarchal authority. And then I see them—the entire board of directors of Anderson Corp. A smile creeps onto my face. I love it when the stakes are high; I thrive under pressure.

But my smile fades as my eyes land on Chris and Sophia, sitting side by side, her hand in his. Even though I know their relationship is a charade, a pang of jealousy hits me. Sophia should be by my side, whispering words of encouragement into my ear, not sitting there holding my brother's hand.

Sophia looks up, and our eyes meet. She's more beautiful than ever, dressed in a long, flowing bohemian skirt and a black full-sleeve blouse. Her bohemian necklace and makeup accentuate her exotic beauty, and my heart aches with longing.

Shaking off the emotion, I clear my mind and walk up to the table, greeting everyone with a smile that hides the whirlwind of feelings inside me.

I reach the table, and Dad is the first to greet me. "Ah, there's my star player," he says, puffing out a cloud of cigar smoke.

"Only star player, Dad. Chris is still in the minor leagues," I quip, shooting a playful glance at my brother.

Chris rolls his eyes but grins. "Keep dreaming, sis. You might need it."

I turn to Sophia, our eyes meeting for a brief moment. "Sophia, you look stunning as always."

"Thank you, Alissa. So do you," she replies, her voice soft yet distant.

I nod to the board members, exchanging pleasantries and handshakes, before taking my seat. The setting is formal: a long, mahogany table surrounded by plush leather chairs. I sit next to my mother, her face still a mask of concern. Across from me is Chris, with Sophia by his side. At the head of the table, Dad sits like a king holding court, the board members flanking him on both sides.

A household staff member comes by, offering me a glass of lemonade. I take it, savoring the tart sweetness that momentarily distracts me from the tension in the room.

Clearing his throat, Dad stands up. "Ladies and gentlemen, family and esteemed board members, thank you for gathering here today. We're about to witness a presentation that will help decide the future of Anderson Corp. I believe that everyone, even family members who aren't directly involved in the business, should know the views of the next potential leaders of this company."

He pauses, a sly grin forming on his lips. "And don't worry, this won't be as boring as one of Martha's book club meetings."

A few chuckles fill the room, and Aunt Martha rolls her eyes but smiles nonetheless.

"So, without further ado," Dad continues, "I'd like to invite Chris to kick things off. Son, the floor is yours."

As Chris rises, I take a deep breath, steadying myself for what's to come. The game is on, and I'm more than ready to play.

Chris clears his throat and begins. "Ladies and gentlemen, Anderson Corp isn't just a chain of department stores; it's a legacy. A legacy that I've been a part of since I was old enough to understand the value of a dollar."

He smoothly transitions into his background, talking about his business degree, his hands-on experience in various Anderson stores, and his vision for the future. "Now, let's discuss what lies ahead," he says, pulling up a slide, "I propose we expand our online presence, introduce a line of eco-friendly products, and venture into international markets."

I can't help but smile as I jot down notes. Expanding online is good, but without a solid digital marketing strategy, it's a shot in the dark. Eco-friendly products are trendy but can be costly to produce and less profitable. And international markets? That's a logistical and financial minefield.

Chris starts to stumble over his words, his eyes meeting mine. I offer a smile that I know unsettles him. My fingers continue their dance on the keyboard, each click underscoring his hesitations.

A text notification pops up on my laptop. It's from Sophia. "Go easy on him," she writes.

I smirk and reply, "You should know by now, I don't like going easy."

"How would I know?" she texts back, with a smiley.

"Because you've screamed and begged for me to go easy on many occasions," I retort.

Our eyes lock, and Sophia's smile sends a shiver down my spine. She texts, "Pity you won't get to hear me scream ever again. I guess you've chosen CEO over my moans."

I pause, then type, "Who says I can't have both?"

As I hit send, my focus shifts back to Chris, who's wrapping

IN A WORLD OF OUR OWN

up. My mind is already formulating counterarguments, but part of me is also pondering Sophia's last message.

Chris finishes his presentation with a rehearsed flourish, looking somewhat relieved. "I'll now open the floor for questions," he announces.

Dad nods approvingly. "Alright, anyone have questions for Chris?"

My hand shoots up instantly, and Dad gives me a nod to proceed. "Chris, you mentioned expanding our online presence. Could you elaborate on the digital marketing strategy you have in mind to drive traffic and increase sales?"

Chris hesitates, clearly not expecting to be grilled so soon. "Well, we'll be investing in social media advertising and SEO—"

"But what's the ROI you're expecting on these investments?" I interrupt, my eyes flicking to Sophia for a moment, just to show her how effortlessly I can do this.

Chris stumbles over his words. "Um, we're still working on those figures—"

"Interesting," I say, cutting him off again. "And what about the eco-friendly product line? Have you considered the production costs and the impact on our profit margins?"

Chris's face reddens. "The eco-friendly line is more about brand image than immediate profits—"

"So, it's a long-term investment with no short-term gains? In a market that's already saturated with eco-friendly options?" I press, my eyes meeting Sophia's again, relishing the challenge I was born for.

"We want to stay competitive—"

"And the international markets?" I continue, relentless. "Have you considered the logistical challenges, the cultural differences, the financial risks?"

"That's something we'll navigate as we go along," Chris almost snaps.

"Navigate as we go along? That's not a strategy, Chris. That's wishful thinking," I retort, my voice tinged with a mix of triumph and regret.

By now, Chris is visibly furious, his voice elevated. Before things can escalate further, Dad intervenes. "Alright, Chris, I think that's enough. Please take your seat."

Chris storms back to his seat, shooting me a glare that could melt steel. Dad turns to me. "Alissa, you're up."

As I rise, my eyes meet Sophia's one last time. I can't read her expression, but it doesn't matter. Right now, I have a presentation to nail and a future to claim.

I walk to the front of the room, my heels clicking with each step, echoing the beat of my heart. I take a deep breath and look at the faces before me—my family, the board members, and Sophia. Especially Sophia.

"Ladies and gentlemen, esteemed board members, and beloved family," I begin, my voice steady and confident. "Anderson Corp is more than just a business; it's a legacy, a legacy that I intend to honor and elevate."

I launch into my presentation, laying out my plans with precision and flair. Unlike Chris, I have the numbers to back up my claims, the logistics worked out, and a strategy that's both innovative and practical.

As I speak, I can't help but glance at Sophia occasionally, each look a silent message. I was born for this, and she knows it. I wrap up, confident that I've made my case, and open the floor for questions, ready for whatever comes my way.

Dad stands up. "Any questions for Alissa?"

The room is silent for a moment, then a board member

raises a hand, and I prepare myself to answer, my eyes meeting Sophia's one last time. This is it—the moment of truth.

The board member clears his throat. "Alissa, your plans are ambitious and well-thought-out. But how do you propose to fund these initiatives without affecting our current operations?"

I smile, ready for this. "Great question. I propose a phased rollout, starting with our most profitable stores. The revenue generated from these will fund the subsequent phases. Additionally, I've identified potential partnerships that could offset initial costs."

Another hand goes up, this time it's Uncle Daniel. "Alissa, you mentioned partnerships. Can you give us an idea of who you're considering?"

"Of course," I reply, my eyes briefly meeting Sophia's. "I've been in talks with several sustainable product suppliers who are interested in exclusive deals with Anderson Corp. This not only aligns with our eco-friendly initiative but also gives us a unique selling point."

Troy, another board member, chimes in next. "You've laid out a comprehensive plan, but what's your strategy for employee retention? We've had a higher turnover rate lately."

"Employee satisfaction is a priority," I assert. "I plan to introduce performance incentives and growth opportunities within the company. Happy employees make for a successful business."

Finally, Chris asks, "Your plans are clearly geared towards the future, but what immediate changes can we expect to see in the next quarter?"

His voice is squeaky. He is clearly off his game. I see Sophia whisper something in his ear, and it makes my blood boil.

"Immediate changes would include a revamp of our online shopping platform to improve user experience," I answer, locking eyes with Sophia for a brief moment, "Our UI is clunky and outdated, and we lost more than 13% in sales because we are not able to retain customer attention on our website and app. The detailed analysis has been mailed to all of you, including future projections and estimates."

Dad stands up, effectively cutting off any further questions. "If there are no more questions, I think we've heard enough. Thank you, Alissa. You may take your seat."

I nod and make my way back to my seat, my heels clicking in a rhythm that matches the pounding of my heart.

Dad clears his throat, pulling my attention back to the room. "I'll be making my decision tomorrow night. I expect everyone to be present. This meeting is adjourned."

The room starts to empty, board members filing out with handshakes and murmured conversations. Chris avoids eye contact with me, still smarting from the Q&A session. But none of that matters now. What matters is the decision that will be made tomorrow and the unspoken words that hang heavy between Sophia and me.

As I pack up my laptop, Sophia approaches. "You were brilliant," she says softly.

"Thank you," I manage to say, but the words feel inadequate, almost hollow, as they leave my lips.

Sophia looks at me, her eyes brimming with a sadness so deep it's like staring into an abyss. "I guess this is it then," she murmurs.

"What do you mean?" My heart pounds, each beat echoing the urgency in my voice.

She sighs, her gaze unwavering. "Your presentation, Alissa. It was like you were announcing your decision to the world, to me. It felt like you were saying we were just a fling."

I step closer, the space between us charged with a tension

that's both electric and heartbreaking. "Don't say that, Sophia. You were never 'just a fling' to me."

"But not enough to be your love," she counters, her eyes searching mine for something—anything—that might contradict her words.

"You won't believe anything I say right now," I admit, the truth stinging as it passes my lips.

"You're right, I won't," she confirms, her voice tinged with a bitterness that cuts through me.

"But I have to say it anyway. I love you, Sophia."

She chuckles, but it's devoid of any real humor. "Bullshit."

"See? I knew you wouldn't believe me," I reply, my own voice tinged with regret and a longing that I can't fully express.

"Do you really want all of this?" Sophia's question hangs in the air, heavy and loaded. I open my mouth to say 'yes,' to affirm my ambitions and my plans. But the word gets caught, tangled in a web of emotions, leaving me staring into Sophia's deep, soulful eyes.

"This is all I've ever known," I finally manage to say, my voice softer than I'd like.

"That's not a good enough reason to continue doing something," she replies, her words tinged with a wisdom that makes my heart ache.

"What would you have me do, then?" I ask.

Sophia's eyes soften, the hurt that had been there replaced by a kind of empathy that feels even worse. "If you hadn't just lied to me about your feelings, I would have told you. Please, Alissa, don't ever tell someone you love them just because you feel you owe it to them. It does more harm than good."

Sophia's eyes meet mine, then drop to my lips, and back up again. For a moment, it feels like time is suspended, like we're the only two people in the universe. Then, she turns on her heel and walks away, back to where Chris is waiting for her. I'm left standing alone in a room that's a strange hybrid of a corporate conference hall and a rustic living space, the remnants of our family's legacy and my own ambitions.

I should be elated. My presentation was a triumph; I could feel it in my bones. The CEO position was practically mine.

So why did I feel so devastatingly alone? Why did it feel like I had lost something irreplaceable, even as I stood on the cusp of a monumental win?

My eyes drift to the last slide of my presentation, still projected on the screen. It reads, "Anderson Corp: Onwards and Upwards." The words, meant to be a rallying cry, now feel like an ironic commentary on my emotional state.

I look back at the empty hallway through which Sophia had exited, not just the mansion but perhaps my life as well. And in that moment, the weight of what I might have lost settles in, heavy and unyielding, making my triumph feel more like a defeat.

∞ ∞ ∞

The room's air feels thick, almost as if it's holding its breath along with me. My eyes stray to the duvet, crumpled and untouched since she left. It's as if Sophia's essence lingers there, a silent, invisible presence. I can almost feel the warmth of her body, the curve of her smile, the softness of her words. I sit on the edge of the bed, not daring to disturb the duvet, as if it's a sacred relic.

My laptop sits open in front of me, its screen glowing in the dim light. The report on Mae and Lyn's stares back at me, words and numbers that should mean something. My eyes catch on a particular section—Mae and Lyn, the founders, are married. To each other. They've been fighting the takeover, not just because of numbers but because of principles. My father's endorsement of an anti-LGBTQ presidential candidate is a deal-breaker for them.

I pause, my eyes frozen on the screen. The cursor blinks, as if urging me to react, to feel something. I think of Sophia, her activism, her fierce sense of justice. I imagine her reading this report, her eyes darkening, her lips parting in disbelief or perhaps disappointment.

I shut the laptop with a soft click, its sudden darkness mirroring the uncertainty clouding my mind. I've always prided myself on my ability to compartmentalize, to keep my personal and professional worlds separate. But now those worlds are colliding, crashing into each other with a force I can't ignore.

My gaze drifts back to the duvet, its folds and creases telling a story I'm not ready to read. It's as if Sophia's asking me, without words, whether this seat at the corporate table is worth the personal cost. Whether this version of success is worth losing a part of my soul, a part of us.

A soft knock interrupts my reverie. "Come in," I call out, my voice tinged with a weariness I can't quite shake off.

The door creaks open, and she steps in—dark eyes, youthful face, a hint of nervousness in her posture. She looks like Jenna Ortega, and I've always found her disarmingly cute. Her name escapes me, a casualty of my preoccupied mind, but her presence is a welcome distraction.

She carries a tray with a cup of coffee and a bowl of salad, her hands slightly trembling as she sets it down on the bedside table. "Is there anything else you'd like, ma'am?" she asks, her voice tinged with a mix of deference and curiosity.

As I look at her, a realization washes over me. The absence of a permanent attachment means a return to a life I once relished—nights of fleeting intimacy, mornings without strings. A life where the heart doesn't weigh as heavy as it does now.

A slow smile creeps onto my face, a stark contrast to the emotional turmoil I was swimming in moments ago. "Tell me about yourself," I say, gesturing for her to sit beside me on the bed.

She hesitates, then sits, her eyes wide and filled with a sort of awe that I find both flattering and slightly disconcerting. We engage in small talk, her words gradually losing their initial stiffness. Her name is Vivian, and she tells me about her day, her aspirations, the mundane details that make up her life. And as she talks, I find myself listening—not as the would-be CEO of Anderson Corp, but as Alissa, a woman at a crossroads, seeking connection in a world that feels increasingly disconnected.

"Do you like me, Vivian?" I ask her, cutting her autobiographical monologue short.

She smiles. The kinda smile that tells me I can have her if I wanted to.

"You are amazing, ma'am. So clever, so pretty."

"Is it okay if I ask you to kiss me?"

Vivian's eyes go wide, "I have always fantasized about kissing you, ma'am."

"Then, let's turn those fantasies into reality."

I pull the girl into my arms and attack her eager mouth. She opens wide, giving me her everything, serving her tongue on a platter for me.

Soon, I have her tits in my mouth, and she is grinding on top of me. Her tight body thrusts back and forth, outline of her abs visible under the soft glow of the night lamp.

Ah, yes. This is the life I deserve, I think as I chew on her erect nipples, grabbing her ass with the other hand, and using her as I will.

This is the life that waits for me. Power, girls, and respect. This is how I am supposed to feel, like a queen, conqueror, a badass boss bitch…with an empty, hollow heart, devoid of love.

The girl twists, grab's Sophia's duvet, and throws it on top of our naked bodies.

"No!" The word bursts from my lips, a guttural scream that shatters the moment.

The cup of coffee crashes to the floor, dark liquid splattering across the tiles. The salad bowl follows suit, its contents painting a chaotic mural on the wall.

My eyes snap open, the haze of the fantasy dissipating. Vivian stands there, fully clothed, her face a mask of shock and confusion.

Even in my daydreams, I can't escape the weight of my own conscience. That's a new low.

"Vivian, I'm so sorry," I stammer, my heart pounding. "I was lost in thought. Are you okay?"

"I'm fine, ma'am," she assures me, already bending to clean the mess. "Don't worry about it. I'll take care of this."

As I watch her sweep up the shards and wipe away the stains, a wave of self-reproach washes over me. What kind of person would I have been to exploit her vulnerability? And what kind of person will I become if I proceed with the takeover of Mae & Lyn's?

∞∞∞

My hand hovers over the doorknob, a cold piece of metal that feels like the gateway to my future—or perhaps my undoing. I take a deep breath to steady my racing heart and turn the handle, pushing the door open.

The study smells of aged leather and mahogany, a scent that's always been synonymous with my father's authority. He stands with his back to me, contemplating a large portrait that hangs above the fireplace. It's a family tableau, a lineage of Andersons frozen in time, including my grandfather in his military uniform, a relic from his days in Vietnam.

As the door creaks shut behind me, Dad turns, his eyes meeting mine. A smile stretches across his face, and he opens his arms in a silent invitation. Each step toward him feels like a journey across a minefield, my heart pounding in my chest as if it's trying to escape.

Finally, I'm enveloped in his embrace, the familiar scent of whiskey and cigar smoke clinging to his clothes. For a moment, I allow myself to be his little girl again, seeking refuge in the arms that once seemed capable of shielding me from the world's harsh realities.

Outside the window, the sun casts its golden glow over the ranch. Horses graze lazily in the fields, their tails swishing away flies. Among them is Buttercup, her coat shining in the sunlight. Sophia's favorite. The sight of her, so carefree and unburdened, twists something inside me, a painful reminder of the complexities I'm entangled in.

Dad clears his throat, breaking the silence that had settled between us. "You were exceptional at the presentation, Alissa. Always knew you'd outshine Chris."

His words should fill me with pride, but they settle in my stomach like stones. Outside, Buttercup prances around the field, her hooves barely touching the ground, as if she's floating on air. She's the epitome of freedom, a stark contrast to the walls closing in on me.

"I'll admit," Dad continues, "I had my reservations. Couldn't fathom how a woman could lead this company into the future. But you've changed my mind."

My eyes remain fixed on Buttercup. One of the new stable hands is attempting to tack her up, but she's having none of it. She rears, her front hooves slashing the air, refusing to be bridled. I can't help but smile at her defiance.

"Tonight, in front of the entire family, I'll announce you as the new CEO," Dad says, pulling me back into the room.

I hear him, but the words feel distant, like they're coming from another world. Outside, Buttercup finally shakes off the stable hand, bolting across the field in a burst of unrestrained joy, while the stable hand runs after her.

Dad follows my gaze. "Did you even hear what I said?"

I tear my eyes away from the window and look at him. "Yes, Dad. I heard you. Thank you. I can't wait to take on the responsibility."

He smiles, but then his expression turns serious. "It's a big job, Alissa. The spotlight will be on you, now more than ever."

Dad's words flow like a gentle stream, but each one lands like a stone in my gut. "You'll need to come clean about anything that could be a PR issue—any ex-boyfriends who might have dirt on you. And it's high time you start thinking about settling down. I've taken the liberty of lining up some suitable men for you to meet."

Suitable men. The phrase hangs in the air, heavy and suffocating. Outside, Buttercup bursts into view, her mane flowing in the wind. But it's not the stable hand who's managed to mount her; it's Sophia. She's dressed in loose-fitting clothes, her face almost bare. She's not creating content; she's simply living, her laughter echoing across the field as she whispers sweet nothings into Buttercup's ear.

"Chris will throw a tantrum, of course," Dad continues, oblivious to the scene unfolding outside. "But you need to be firm with him. You need to stop being soft, Alissa. That's one flaw you need to work on. And as for the Mae and Lyn merger, make that your first victory after becoming CEO, show the world you are your father's daughter."

Victory. The word tastes like ash in my mouth. Sophia looks so free, so unburdened, her joy radiating like the sun that's shining down on her. How can I think of victories when all I feel is defeat?

"And another thing," Dad adds, "Chris will have to break things off with Sophia. She's too rambunctious, too wild, not what the Andersons need—"

"Dad, I'm gay," I interrupt, the words tumbling out before I can stop them. "And I'm in love with Sophia."

For a moment, the room falls silent, the weight of my confession hanging in the air. Dad's eyes meet mine, and for the first time, I see a flicker of uncertainty there. Outside, Sophia pulls Buttercup to a stop and dismounts, her eyes meeting mine through the window.

"I'm gay, Dad," I say, shrugging my shoulders. "And Chris and Sophia are almost broken up already, so you don't have to worry about that. Give the job to Chris."

"What?" The impact of my words leaves Henry Anderson speechless, a rare occurrence.

"You are what?"

"Lesbian. Love women. Can't live without them, like horses. I like to ride both."

"What the hell are you talking about, you silly girl!" Ah, the lion finally roars. But he's got a lioness in front of him this time.

"Here's what I think you need to do. Listen up. First, you need to educate yourself on a lot of things: LGBTQ issues, women's struggles and rights, ethical business norms, and even a bit about racism. I have a few books lying around; I'll send them to you. Second, make Chris the CEO and give him all the power. He's intelligent, efficient, and most importantly, morally conscious. Spend some time with Mom, listen to her opinions, help her fulfill some of her dreams. And last but not least, let people live, Dad. Anderson this, Anderson that—who the hell cares what makes an Anderson? I don't. I know what makes a good human being, and you know what? I think I'll concentrate on being that first."

Henry Anderson stands like a boulder in front of me, expressionless and stoic.

"Do you know what this will mean for you?" he finally speaks.

"What?"

"If you act on your... ungodly thinking and desires, you'll be removed from the family. You'll no longer have any right to stay with us or be part of anything that we, the Andersons, whom you suddenly hate so much, do or say."

"Ah! That would be great! I never wanted to be associated with the Andersons in the first place."

"All of this for that girl?" Dad screams, his voice a tsunami wave in the stillness of the study.

"No, this is for me. For my mental health and peace. She just nudged me a little."

"Does Chris know his girlfriend..."

"Chris has an idea. But he's innocent in all of this. He just wants the job, Dad. Give it to him, and I hope he can survive this prison you call Anderson Corp."

"Get out of my fucking sight," Dad growls.

"Happily," I say, my eyes lingering on Sophia, who is stealing glances at me through the window.

∞∞∞

My first stop after storming out of Dad's study, is Chris' bedroom, where he is still sulking after being outshined by me.

I burst into his room and find him lying in bed, scrolling away on his phone.

"Get up, lazy ass. You have a company to run," I say, with a smile on my face.

I kick the door shut behind me, and Chris looks up, startled. "Alissa? What are you doing here?"

"Making a house call," I say, leaning against the doorframe. "You're the new CEO of Anderson Corp, so you might want to get out of bed."

Chris sits up, his eyes widening. "What? Are you serious? What happened?"

I walk over and sit on the edge of his bed. "Let's just say I had a very enlightening conversation with Dad."

Chris sets his phone aside, suddenly all ears. "Enlightening how?"

I take a deep breath, my eyes meeting his. "I told him I'm gay, Chris. And that I'm in love with Sophia."

His eyes go wide, then narrow, as if he's trying to read the sincerity in my gaze. "You did what?"

"Yeah, I did. And I told him to give you the CEO position."

Chris looks stunned, his mouth opening and closing like a fish out of water. "But why? You've worked so hard for this."

I shrug. "I realized that there's more to life than titles and boardrooms. And I don't want to be part of a company, or a family, that can't accept me for who I am."

"How did he take it?"

"What do you think? Threatened to kick me out of not just the company, but the family. I will be ostracized if I act on my 'ungodly thinking and desires'. Boy, how the hell did that homophobe birth two gay children? I love God and his sense of humor sometimes."

"I thought you were an atheist?" Chris says, throwing the covers off his body and sitting up straight.

"I am everything now, Chris. I can be whatever I want to be," I say, spreading my arms wide. "You should join me, Chris. Tell Dad you're gay too, and then he'll have no choice. He won't give the company to an outsider; I know it."

"So, he doesn't know about me and…"

"Nope, I just told him I'm gay and that Sophia and I are in love. I told him you had no idea. You're in the clear."

"But what about Sophia and my relationship?"

"He doesn't want Sophia as his daughter-in-law, bro! What made you think you'd parade a supermodel in front of him, and he'd be like, 'Great, we'll have that bikini-wearing, self-made, progressive, Persian-origin bombshell as our daughter-in-law!' I think he'll be glad the two of you are over. But heads up, he'll start finding a wife for you, so I don't know how you'll get out of that."

"Ah…there's a catch," Chris says, his voice dropping.

"What?" I eye him curiously.

"He can't find a wife for me because… I'm already married."

"Umm…excuse me? I thought I was going to be the one blowing people's minds today. Don't steal my thunder!"

Chris laughs, "Well, it happened last night, or early this

morning."

"Explain!" I snap at Chris.

"Well, after your presentation, I knew it was over for me. I had lost the position, and I was pretty bummed about it. Mark and I…have this thing going…"

"I knew it! I called it! I told Sophia there was something going on between the two of you, but…" I suddenly look at Chris with suspicion. "You married him over a 'thing'?"

"Well, it's more than a thing, and it's been going on since we were in school. We were high school sweethearts, then I became ambitious, told him we couldn't be together…yada yada yada… we stayed in touch, had this toxic thing going on, and then everything got rekindled once I came back to stay on the ranch. Over the past month, I realized it's him. I sabotaged my own presentation subconsciously, I guess, because I didn't want to lose him."

"Chris, you're blowing my mind every second here. So, hold on, you and I were living the exact same love story, at the same time? Both fell in love with someone, both started doubting our ambitions, and you did the thing that I was supposed to do?"

"Yup, so in the end, I might have lost the presentation, sister. But I win at love."

"Oh my God, this is freaking unbelievable. So, last night…"

"I took the private jet, flew to Vegas, and married him. I don't care about the company, Alissa. My 4% stock in the company will be enough for me to launch that sneaker company I've been dreaming of."

"What sneaker company?"

"Ah…there's a lot about me that you don't know. I'm assuming you'll also be cashing out your 4%?"

"Haven't thought about it, but screw that! Congratulations,

you idiot!" I fall over Chris, pulling him into a bear hug.

"Alissa, but now that you've told me I can be the CEO, I'm having second thoughts," he whispers in my ear as I hug him.

"Chris, you can't—this is good for us. Finally standing up to Dad, choosing to live our lives on our own terms. Don't backtrack into that prison. Live your life and—"

"Oh my God, I was just joking. Look at you, morphing into a life coach all of a sudden," Chris says, his smile revealing a set of perfect pearly whites.

"Taking acting lessons from Sophia? Getting into charades with her little entourage, are we?"

"Are you jealous?" Chris arches an eyebrow, his eyes twinkling with mischief.

"Yes. And speaking of Sophia, don't spill the beans to her. I want to handle this my way."

"Does 'your way' involve a wedding ring? Because mine did," Chris retorts, flaunting his newly-acquired wedding band.

I roll my eyes. "We don't have to turn everything into a competition, you know. My way may not involve a wedding ring—at least not yet—but it will hopefully involve a lot of makeup sex," I say, crossing my fingers for good measure.

"That's more information than I ever wanted, sis. So, what do you think Dad's next move will be? A billion-dollar empire, two gay children, and a clan of Andersons who'd probably prefer a Nazi parade over a Pride parade."

"Look, we can't just abandon ship. We've both been integral to major Anderson Corp deals. As long as he doesn't give us the boot immediately, I'm all for staying and helping him through this transition."

"Henry Anderson transitioning...the mental image that just popped into my head is something else," Chris chuckles.

"Anyway, I still have to drop my own bombshell on him. So, wish me luck."

"All the best, Robin to my Batman. Go live your life, while I work on winning back the love of mine."

∞∞∞

The rhythmic cadence of hooves against the earth fills the air as I guide my horse through the sprawling Texan ranch. Up ahead, Sophia's silhouette dances in the morning light, a vision of grace and beauty. She's wearing a summer dress that flutters in the wind, its floral pattern a vivid contrast to the earthy tones of the landscape. Her hair, a cascade of dark waves, flows freely behind her, mirroring the untamed spirit of Buttercup beneath her. I marvel at how she's learned to maneuver the animal so expertly, her posture confident, her hands gentle yet firm on the reins.

As I close the distance between us, the morning sun casts its golden glow on the fields, turning the blades of grass into a sea of shimmering emeralds. The ranch stretches out in all directions, a testament to the Anderson legacy, but in this moment, it's just a backdrop to the woman who's captured my heart.

I spur my horse to a canter, catching up to Sophia. As I pull alongside her, her eyes widen in surprise, as if she's just realized she's not alone in this idyllic setting.

"Morning," I say, my voice tinged with a warmth that the Texan sun can't rival.

"Morning," she replies, as we ride together at an idyllic pace.

"You're getting pretty good at this," I say, nodding toward her horse. "Been practicing?"

Sophia chuckles. "Well, when you're pretending to be a Texan's girlfriend, you've got to learn to ride. It's like learning to make pasta if you're pretending to be Italian."

I laugh, appreciating her humor. "You look stunning, by the way. That summer dress really suits you. And those legs..."

Sophia grins, her eyes twinkling. "Thank you. I could say the same about your hair today. It's more wavy and curly than usual. And those white denim shorts? You're killing it."

We share a moment, our eyes locking as we ride side by side. The tension is palpable, but neither of us breaks the silence. Finally, I speak up.

"You know, there's an abandoned barn around here," I begin, my voice tinged with nostalgia. "It's a relic from the early 1900s, built by my great-grandfather. It's perched on this green mound, right where the lake broadens to its maximum breadth. The view is breathtaking."

Sophia listens intently, her eyes searching mine. "Why are you telling me this?"

"How about I take you there? We can have one final talk. As closure."

Sophia hesitates, her eyes clouded with a mix of emotions. Finally, she nods. "Alright, lead the way."

I guide my horse onto a narrow, dusty trail, Sophia following closely behind. The path is lined with wildflowers, their vibrant hues a stark contrast to the earthy tones of the landscape. Overhead, the sky is a canvas of swirling clouds, their shapes ever-changing as if undecided on the day's mood. We pass through a thicket of mesquite trees, their twisted branches reaching out like ancient hands. The scent of dry earth and foliage fills the air, mingling with the subtle aroma of horse sweat and leather.

As we approach the barn, the green mound I spoke of

comes into view. It rises gently from the earth, crowned by the weathered timbers of the barn. The lake stretches out beyond, its surface shimmering in the sunlight, as if winking at us from a distance.

We dismount, our horses grazing lazily as we make our way to the barn.

Our bare feet crumple grass blades as we ascend the mound, each step a quiet punctuation in the comfortable silence that envelops us. The barn ahead stands like an old sentinel, its timbers weathered but still sturdy, a testament to the craftsmanship of generations past. The air around us is thick with the scent of damp earth and wildflowers, a heady aroma that fills the space between words left unspoken.

As we reach the top, I glance over at Sophia. Her eyes are fixed on the horizon, where a bank of stormy clouds has begun to gather. Their dark, billowing forms contrast sharply with the otherwise clear sky, as if nature itself can't decide on the day's mood.

"Looks like we might get caught in a storm," I joke, breaking the silence.

Sophia laughs, a sound that seems to echo in the open space around us. "Well, it wouldn't be the first storm we've weathered together, would it?"

We sit side by side near the entrance of the barn, our shoulders almost touching but not quite. The atmosphere is charged, like the calm before a storm, both of us aware that the words we choose next could change everything.

"So," Sophia finally says, turning to face me. "What did you want to talk about?"

"Closure," I say.

"Okay, what closure?"

"I want to say goodbye."

"You brought me all the way here to say goodbye to me?"

"Not to you." Sophia looks puzzled, and I revel in the cuteness that takes over her beautiful face.

"Alissa, there's a storm coming…"

"Sophia… the storm has already passed. I want to say goodbye to my old life. To a life of nothingness. I want to say goodbye to being scared. I brought you here to embrace my new life, with you."

The wind picks up, and Sophia's hair starts flapping around her face. A strand gets stuck to her face, and before she can do something about it, I reach over and tuck it behind her ear.

"What are you saying?" Sophia's eyes bore into me, and behind her, the clouds approach fast.

"I love you too. Couldn't say it last time. But here it comes, Sophia. I love you."

"But…"

I place a finger on her lips. "There are no buts. There is only us, now. I gave up the CEO position and told Dad I'm gay and in love with a woman named Sophia. And I hope you'll take me back and guide me through this new journey that I've started on because, I'm scared, Soph… I need you."

"Is this a joke?" Sophia whispers. "This is a very bad joke if it is, Alissa."

"It's not. I'm here, out of work, and probably out of my house very soon, hoping you'll take me back and become my new… home."

"I'll be your home, Alissa. If you'll be mine…"

Rain bellows down from above, droplets spattering all around us.

I grab Sophia by the back of her neck and pull her in for a

kiss that will be etched in my memory until the end of my days.

Our lips meet, and it's as if the heavens themselves have orchestrated this moment. The rain pours down, each droplet a symphony, each gust of wind a crescendo. My hands find the small of her back, pulling her closer, as if I could meld her into me. Her arms snake around my neck, her fingers threading through my wavy hair, grounding me in the electric charge of our connection.

Sophia's lips part, and a sigh escapes her, mingling with the rain and the wind. It's a surrender, a yielding to the magnetic force between us. I seize the invitation, deepening the kiss, our tongues meeting in a dance as old as time yet as fresh as the rain cleansing us.

The world falls away. The looming storm, the abandoned barn, the sprawling Texan landscape—they all become a blurred backdrop to the vivid clarity of her. It's just Sophia and me, two souls entangled in a moment of pure, unadulterated connection.

The rain intensifies, soaking through our clothes, but we're lost to it, lost to everything but each other. Sophia's hands move from my hair down to my shoulders, her touch leaving a trail of fire even as rain cools my skin. I reciprocate, my hands tracing the contours of her waist, feeling her shiver under my touch.

Finally, we break apart, gasping for air but not letting go, our foreheads resting against each other. Our eyes meet, and in her gaze, I see it—the raw, unspoken love that mirrors my own.

"I love you," I whisper, the words barely audible over the rain.

"And I love you," she whispers back, sealing it with another kiss, softer this time but no less meaningful.

Sophia's gossamer-like kisses along my neck and shoulder send shivers through my body as her hands move in slow, erotic circles down the curves of my body. I can hardly feel her fingertips on my skin, yet their light caressing is driving me wild.

As I move against Sophia delicately, letting out small moans to encourage her further, I feel myself relax into the pleasure. All I can do is meet each touch with an arch of my back and gasp for breath between softer kisses.

I tug gently at the straps of Sophia's wet summer dress and let my fingers slide down to pull away its clinging fabric. With a passionate growl, I rip it off with one swift motion, exposing her pale skin in the dim light that shines through the rain-clouded sky.

We lock eyes as we fall downwards into the soft grass together, our supple bodies entwined in an embrace bound by love and desire amidst nature's chaos all around us.

I let out a desperate moan as Sophia's hands skillfully undo the button of my shorts and tug them down over my hips. My eyes widening in anticipation, I feel Sophia's deft fingers slip beneath the waistband onto my skin and go exploring.

I know I have to focus on something else before it becomes too much for me and all rational thought disappears in an overwhelming wave of pleasure. I lean up, pressing our bodies together again, and start gently suckling at her breasts, while Sophia moans and growls, her fingers finding the entrance to my throbbing pussy.

"Tell me you love me as you enter me," I whisper, my lips brushing against Sophia's nipples.

"I fucking love you," she hisses, and thrusts two fingers inside me.

I buck, gasp, and then let out a wild howl.

"Baby! Fuck!"

"I love you," she says again, and starts finger banging me with all she has.

I move my hands down her body, pressing and exploring with each stroke. She moans beneath me in delight as I find the folds of her pussy. My fingers eagerly delve deeper, discovering a new realm of pleasure for us both to explore.

Our bodies intertwine further as we get lost in our intimate exploration, wet, naked and screaming each other's name into the stormy skies.

The sky roars above us, but it is not loud enough to drown out our screams of pleasure, as we bring each other close to climax.

"Yes! Yes! Alissa! Yes, baby, don't stop. I've missed your fingers so much, baby! Take all of me! Oh fuck pleaseeee!"

I look into Sophia's eyes and go as deep as I physically can, making Sophia's eyes roll into the back of her skull.

Our hands work on each other, like machines, undisturbed and untroubled by the wave after wave of rain crashing down on us.

Just then, a bolt of lightning splits the sky, its electric charge mirroring our own crescendo of emotions. In that charged moment, we both reach an emotional peak and a physical peak, climaxing together, and sealing our love with a moment that none of us will forget in a long time to come.

Epilogue

5 Days Later

The evening air is warm and inviting as we all gather around a rustic wooden table, set under the vast Texas sky. The stars are out, and the atmosphere is buzzing with laughter and conversation.

"So, Bella actually called her lawyer on Henry Anderson?" Alissa asks, her eyes wide with disbelief but also a hint of admiration.

Ava, my mother, chuckles. "Oh, you have no idea. She told him, 'I've paid for this place, and I have every right to stay here as long as I want.' Then she called her lawyer just to make sure."

Alissa shakes her head, grinning. "I should've expected this from Dad, but I didn't think Bella would be such a warrior."

"Bella doesn't back down from a fight, especially when she's in the right," Mom adds, sipping her wine.

Across the table, Mark and Chris are engrossed in a whispered conversation, their faces close. Alissa catches my eye and rolls hers playfully.

"Look at those two, so lovey-dovey. It's like they're in their own world," she says, squeezing my hand under the table. I squeeze back, my heart swelling with love for her.

"Yeah, like we don't know what's going on between the two

of you under the table," Mark shoots back, his banter with Alissa still going strong.

"Mark, I would always be jealous of you when we were kids, you know. Chris and I used to be so close, and then you showed up, and stole him away from me. Had I known what games the two of you were playing…"

"What would you've done?" Chris asks.

"Would have made a beeline to Dad and ratted you out," Alissa laughs, "See? I wasn't as mature as I am today."

"I wonder why?" I say, cocking an eyebrow and tapping the table with my fingers.

"Yeah, babe, you are to thank for my enlightenment, and *I* am to thank for all those new moves you've been pulling off in bed."

"Alissa, my mom's at the table, and I *just* got her to stop PDAing all over the place with Bella. I *should* be setting an example!"

The table laughs, except Mark and Chris, who are once again living in a world of their own.

And so am I. A world where I am finally at peace.

I turn my attention to Nicole, who's sitting next to me. "So, the pole dancing studio—I hear LA can't get enough of it?"

"Yes! We are booked three months in advance. Emma is handling all of it on her own, and I just feel guilty about deserting her like this. But someone had to come here and check up on you. I knew you were hurting," Nicole says, and I give her a little hug, "I'll never forget what you did for me."

"And I won't let you! However, Alissa *has* been pestering me about that lap dance quite a lot. Just give her one already. She won't shut up about it. You know what," I continue, swallowing my pasta, "you should open one studio in Dallas as well."

"Yeah, we've been thinking of it. But it seems like you've set your eyes on Texas for a long term stay?"

I glance at Alissa, who meets my gaze with a warm smile. "Well, Alissa and I are thinking of renting another ranch for a long-term stay. After that, we'll figure out what to do."

"But until then..." Alissa chimes in, joining our conversation, "we'll be staying here, even after you all leave. Mom finally stood up to Dad. She told him she'd leave him if he kicked Chris and me out of the family. And that would be a bigger scandal than having a gay child."

"And he backed down?" Nicole asks, intrigued.

"Yeah, surprisingly fast. I think he really does love Mom. And, I'm not entirely sure, but I think he loves us too. Yesterday, he texted me, asking if I needed anything for the house—more staff, horses, a new stable. Today, he sent me an Excel sheet to review the financing for a new store we're planning in Florida. I think he misses Chris and me. I think he'll come around."

Nicole leans in, curious. "So, if he offers you the company a few months down the line, what would be your answer?"

Alissa glances at me before responding, "Chris and I have already discussed it. I don't want the job; I'm certain about that. If Dad ever comes to his senses, Chris will take the position, and he's asked me to serve as an advisor. I'll be involved from the sidelines while raising horses with this lovely woman." Alissa leans over and kisses me on the cheek, making my cheeks flush with warmth.

"And I'll be right there with her, continuing my influencer work but on my terms this time. More like a hobby than anything else," I add, leaning back into Alissa, who wraps her arms around me from behind.

Chris suddenly pipes up, mimicking a high-pitched voice, "Oh, look at those lovebirds...bla bla bla."

I point at him, chuckling. "A grown-ass man, ladies and gentlemen."

Bella laughs so hard she almost spits out her food, and the table erupts into laughter. In this moment, surrounded by love and acceptance, I realize that I've found my home, and it's not just a place—it's a person, and her name is Alissa.

And together, we've found a world of our own.

The End.

Did Ava and Bella's characters in this story intrigue you?

Would you like to know how they ended up together?

Click Here to read **'Fated To Love You'** , with Bella and Ava as lead heroines, taking you all the way to back to Brooklyn, for another steamy installment of this series.

Or

Read the first chapter from 'Fated To Love You' from the next page to get a taste of what you will be in for!

Free Lesbian Romance Novel by A Goswami

Hello Dear Readers,

Please don't forget to download your free **300-page** Lesbian Romance Novel by me that I would like to give to you as a thank you for reading and enjoying this book.

Download it right now by clicking here

For paperback readers, copy, and paste this link in your browser : mailchi.mp/8f0f411551ce/a-goswami

Fated To Love You (When Blunders Turn Beautiful)

"Read the hugely popular, top ten bestseller that tells the story of Bella, a young DJ in Brooklyn, as she falls for Ava, her best friend and roommate's mother. Ava, an astrophysicist, and Bella meet, make love, and later realize the blunder they have just committed!"

Start Reading From The Next Page or Click Here To Read Now!

Chapter One

(Bella)

A bevy of beautiful girls gyrate on the dance floor in front of me, and the usual, often depressing, but mostly routine question pops into my head.

Who should I fuck?

I scan the dance floor.

I spot the blondes that look like me, with cute, innocent faces, but there was nothing innocent about the way their hips were moving.

I had had my fill of blondes. Tonight, I wanted something exotic.

And as the word materialized in my head, so did she, in the corner of my eye.

Yes, she was exotic, but she was also so much more.

A purple beam of light moves through the dance floor and briefly illuminates her gorgeous face.

I only get a brief look at her face, but it is enough.

I know who I am fucking tonight.

She is standing alone, looking bored, looking like she

would rather be anywhere else in the world.

Me too, babe. Me too.

My fingers graze the many knobs and sliders on my Pioneer DJ mixer, finding the one I need.

I twist the knob, and the volume of the trance music that had been blasting through the speakers decreases, and a groan of disapproval flows towards me from the crowd.

I hold the mic close to my lips and lick them once.

I am not usually nervous, but suddenly, I realize I am sweating.

She is unbothered by the sudden decrease in volume.

In fact, the look on her face says she welcomes the unexpected quiet.

"Hello folks, this is your DJ, DJ Aphrodite in the house, can I get a 'hell yeah' if you are enjoying the party, and can you make sure you are loud enough to shake the fucking foundations of Burj Khalifa?"

I point the mic at the crowd.

They scream their approval, and I smile.

I like it when the crowd is responsive and alive, and when it comprises a beautiful, older lady, who I desperately want to see naked.

I flick my blonde hair out of my face.

My ocean-blue eyes are drawn to her once again, and I find her finally looking at me.

She has a glass of whiskey in her hand.

A woman who likes whiskey is a woman who likes danger.

"Those of you who know me, know I like to do this thing during my sets, where I shine the spotlight on someone I either find extremely beautiful, or someone… who looks like they would rather swim with sharks than be at my concert."

I signal with my hand, and suddenly, beams of white light from above, pierce the darkness of the club and start moving around amidst the crowd, like searchlights searching for escaped criminals.

The crowd howls and starts chasing after the spotlight, like children running after fireflies.

Ms. Exotic is rooted in her spot. She wants no part of this.

Little does she know, I am going to make her a part, whether she likes it or not.

I slowly start twisting the volume knob, gently increasing the volume.

The crowd starts jumping, as the music climbs, and nears crescendo.

"Are you guys ready to be 'spotlighted'?"

Yeah, I know, it's a cringe term, but it's stuck now, and my fans kinda know me for it.

A cocktail waitress climbs onto the little circular stage from where I had been DJing the party.

"Which one?" she whispers into my ear.

"Woman in black, wearing the strapless dress…curly

hair, with the glass of whiskey in her hand."

The waitress nods and leaves.

I am now blasting the music at full volume.

People in the crowd have begun dancing.

In a sea of people twisting, grinding, and throwing their bodies around to the beats of music, beats that I produced, Ms. Exotic is standing still, sipping her whiskey as if she is staring at art in an art gallery.

Am I the art?

I signal with my hand once again, and the music stops.

All the spotlights disappear, except one.

One shines down upon Ms. Exotic, illuminating her like a unicorn in a mystical forest.

And now, I can see her clearly.

I can make out her features, and after a few seconds of staring at her blankly, I realize I might have stumbled upon God's greatest creation.

"Hi, I guess the spotlight has chosen you," I say into the mic.

The corners of her mouth curl into a mischievous smile. She looks around, and then back at me.

"The spotlight…or you?"

Even without the mic, her voice carries to me.

"Guilty as charged!" I raise my hands in defense, "Would you like to know why the spotlight chose you?"

"No."

"Because you are both the most beautiful, and the most bored of all the people here tonight, and I have no idea why. Your looks should be enough to cause chaos around you."

"The eye of the storm is always calm."

The crowd cheers for her response and quick wit.

Her smile lengthens to a grin.

"Look at the mouth on this one, and by that I mean, gosh, your lips are pretty!"

The crowd now cheers for me.

"What's your name, honey?" I ask.

"Ava."

"Ava, the rules state that if the spotlight chooses you, then you gotta give a solo dance performance on a track of my choosing."

"What if I don't want to follow the rules?"

A few boos crop up from the crowd.

"Then you would leave this crowd, and me, very disappointed in you. You have a body that's made to dance. And all of us here, would like to see it move, am I right, people?"

The crowd cheers. They are so drunk, they would cheer for Nazis at that moment.

Ava presses her lips together.

I notice the fullness of her mouth, and how thick and juicy both her lower and upper lips are.

I lick my own lips in anticipation.

She is driving me crazy.

"So…Ava…will you dance?"

"I will," Ava takes a step closer to the dance floor, "but not on a song of your choosing, but mine."

"Accepted," I say, making an exception to my rule for the first time since the inception of my 'Spotlight Trick'.

"What kind of music would you like me to play?"

"Something that is out of this world, quite literally."

"What do you mean?"

"I am an astrophysicist, darling. I would like you to play something that brings me closer to the universe."

I laugh, "Can I play the Star Wars theme?"

"I would prefer that over the nonsense I have been hearing ever since I stepped into this club."

"Yo, the scientist coming in with that nuclear heat!" someone shouts from the crowd, eliciting a few chuckles, but I am not laughing.

She might be hot as fuck, but she can't get away with calling my music 'nonsense'.

"Maybe you are too old to understand it, Ava?"

Yes, I went there, although she hardly looks a day older than 35.

"Is it so easy to rile you up? Come on, Aphrodite, show me what you can do."

I suck in my cheeks and stare Ava down.

She glares back.

"Come forward, Ava. I want you on the dance floor."

Ava climbs the three steps, and steps onto the floating dance floor, hanging a few feet above the swimming pool.

No one is allowed here, except the person I want.

Ava affords me the best view of her body ever since I spotted her, and I stifle a gasp.

She is tall, statuesque, and curvaceous.

Elegance drips through her posture.

Her hair is the color of chestnut, and they fall in electrifying curls down to the small of her waist.

Her strapless dress hugs her frame, making me dizzy with desire, and her hands, resting on her waist, make her look like she is modeling for the biggest fashion brands in the world.

Scientists look like this? Well done, Neil Degrasse Tyson, on getting hot women to take up science, man!

"Where are you from, Ava?"

"I am from America. I am an Iranian-American."

A middle eastern beauty. That explains the flawless skin.

"Ava, from America, especially for you…this is my own produced track, 'No Time For Caution' from Interstellar."

I see Ava's mouth part in surprise.

"I want no lights, except the one on Ava. And I want us all to look at the stars outside, from the highest floor, in the tallest building in the world, as the music of 'Interstellar' takes us to a place beyond our imagination. And Ava, maybe after this, you'll think better of my music."

I open the folder titled 'private', on my Mac, and click on 'No Time For Caution'.

My eyes find Ava, who is still confused as to how a Trance DJ had remixed a song from 'Interstellar'.

"Ava…" I call out to the Middle Eastern, "No time for caution, baby."

The synth beats start flowing from the speakers, overlayed with the iconic piano piece from 'No Time For Caution'.

Ava closes her eyes the moment she identifies the track and starts to slowly move her body.

Like a ballerina, she starts to spin, waiting for the beat to drop.

Ava spins, and she spins with full control.

I look in awe, as she keeps spinning, and then she raises one leg in the air, and starts spinning on just one leg.

She *is* a ballerina!

She stretches her arms out, her body now a little blur of black.

And then the beat drops, and picks up again, with electric guitars ripping through the track, going crazy along with the pianos from Hans Zimmer, and it seems like something has caught hold of Ava.

A ripple runs through her body, and she does the wave with the flexibility of a gymnast.

The crowd stands still, and then erupts when the song

comes to a close.

Ava stands panting, clutching her sides.

All the spotlights are turned on, but I wish they weren't.

I was not done gawking at this beauty.

Ava bows, and the crowd goes berserk.

She turns around and walks to my DJ console.

She grabs my hand and raises it in the air, while taking the mic in her hand. "Never have I heard Hans Zimmer's work remixed such flawlessly. Your music *did* take me to a different world, DJ Aphrodite!"

"Bella," I whisper to her.

"What?"

"My name is Bella, and I would like to buy you a drink."

***

I am alone with Ava at the back of the club, as the party slowly draws to a close.

Another DJ is helming the music, while I lean against the bar counter, as the city of Dubai twinkles below and behind me.

"I think you are really hot." I do not waste time.

"I think you are very pretty yourself," Ava says with a subtle smile.

"Are you single?"

"Yes."

My heart leaps with joy, and my panties become a little wetter.

"I can't help but think of how flexible you are," I say, frantically trying to come up with one-liners that would get me in bed with the goddess in front of me.

"Why would you think of that?"

"Flexibility has its uses, especially in bed."

Take the hint, woman!

"Oh…umm…yeah." Ava takes a sip of her whiskey, and turns her gaze away from me.

She doesn't want me. Good thing I am on the 154th floor from where I can jump to my death!

"Do you like women?"

I guess it's time to be direct to save time.

Better rip the band-aid off as quickly as possible.

"Yes, but Bella, I am not interested in hooking up at the moment."

I nod.

"Am I not your type?"

"Yeah, hot, young blondes with the body of a gymnast are not my type," Ava says sarcastically.

"Then what's the problem?"

"I am here to support my friend, Samantha, and I wouldn't be a good friend if I abandoned her right after the party celebrating her becoming the head at Louis Vuitton."

"Samantha Brooks is your friend?"

"Yeah."

"How does an astrophysicist strike up a friendship with a fashion designer?"

"Long story. It will take time."

"But I won't, in making you…cum."

The missile is away.

Ava blushes and hides her face behind her glass.

The missile has locked onto the target.

"You really want this, don't you?"

"As much as I wanted you to dance."

"Well, blow my mind again, and I might just do…what you want."

Jackpot. Missile has demolished its target.

"Ava, you look like someone who likes being in control."

Ava frowns and looks at me with confusion.

"Why would you say that?"

"I have a hunch," I say, "and I know exactly…what would blow your mind."

I wait for a group of tipsy, staggering girls to pass, and then unzip my clutch.

"Give me your hand," I ask Ava, who extends her right arm, palm facing upwards.

I drop a cylindrical bullet shaped not much bigger than an actual bullet, in Ava's hand.

I look around to see if someone has seen me hand Ava a sex toy.

"What is this?"

"Power."

Ava looks at the pink bullet-shaped vibrator, her eyes studying the fascinating object like it was material from outer space.

"Ava, you gotta be subtle, babe. I don't want people to find out how desperate I am for you."

Ava smiles. "Who's gonna be using this, you…or me?"

"I am giving you the power," I say and take the vibrator back from Ava, "and I am keeping this."

I glance around, and when I am satisfied no one is watching me, I slip the vibrator inside my skirt, and with a gasp, I insert it inside my vagina.

Ava's eyes widen.

They look prettier than ever.

If only it was my mouth between her legs making her eyes go wide.

"This…is your power."

I search inside my clutch once more, take out a small, rectangular remote, shaped like a Wrigley's Doublemint chewing gum, and thrust it into Ava's hand.

"The controls are easy enough to understand, especially for an intelligent scientist like you. Just make sure you don't start off with max speed. Be…gentle with me." I graze Ava's arm with my fingers.

"I'll be in the washroom." I lean closer to Ava and touch my lips to her cheeks.

She withdraws, but out of the suddenness of my movements, and not because she did not like it.

Or I hoped so.

I make my way toward the washrooms and feel the vibrator start vibrating the moment I step into a stall.

She did not waste time.

She is eager.

I grab the sides of the stall with both my hands, as the vibrator starts humming intensely inside me.

I close my eyes and imagine Ava, leaning against the bar counter in her black, sparkling dress, her fingers playing with the buttons on the remote, controlling me like a puppet, wondering how soon she wants to burst into the washroom to see the consequences of her actions.

The vibrator speeds up, and I gasp, and then moan.

A knock on the door scares me.

Have I been caught?

"Yes? Just a minute!" I say in my most natural, not close-to-cumming voice.

"I don't think I can wait a minute," comes the voice from the other side of the door.

I unbolt the door and pull Ava in.

She crashes into me, like monstrous waves crashing ashore, like women crashing into a store with end-ofseason sale.

She is hungry, and I am ready to serve.

I am pushed against the wall, in the cramped little space, with Ava's body pressed tightly against me.

She searches for my lips with her own, and I offer her my mouth.

She pulls my lower lip with her teeth and moans when our tongues meet.

Her hands are already on the small of my back, her legs sliding between my thighs.

"What's your age?" she asks, nibbling along the sides of my neck.

"Old enough to show you the time of your life."

She holds me by my throat. "Tell me your age, Bella."

"20." I smirk, while Ava chokes me lightly.

"Fuck, you are too young."

"I am above 18."

"I am 19 years older than you."

"That's hot."

"That's inappropriate." She is slowly backing away from me.

I stop her by grabbing her waist, turning, and pushing her against the wall.

"It's 2023. We are consenting adults, and I don't think I can let you go now before feeling your fingers in me."

I nuzzle the sides of her neck and take a big whiff.

She smells of lust and seduction, mixed with notes of pear, tangerine, and bergamot.

Prada.

I see her battle with her thoughts.

She is deciding whether it would be morally justified to fuck a girl who is 19 years younger than her.

I pull the top of my jumpsuit down, to reveal my left tit, and to help her make a decision.

She lowers her eyes, and I see her lick her lips.

I grab the back of her head and direct her towards my swollen nipples.

She thrusts her tongue out, to taste it, while also coming to a decision.

"We need to go somewhere else." She is hardly able to speak with her mouth stuffed with my breast.

"I know just the place," I say.

∞∞∞

I have VIP access to the observation deck of the Burj Khalifa, which is empty as Ava and I enter it through gold, metallic doors.

The city glitters around us.

We are on top of the world, up in the clouds, and I am with an angel who can't keep her hands off me.

We stumble our way to the very edge of the observation deck, where only a chrome-finished railing separates us from massive glass panes affording 360-degree views of the city.

Ava has me pushed against the railing, which is biting me on the small of my back.

But I couldn't care less.

I am in a daze, numb to everything except pleasure.

Ava is gasping, her breasts rising and falling like musical notes in one of Beethoven's symphonies.

"I had no plans of doing this tonight," Ava mumbles against the skin of my neck, as she kisses upwards, and bites my ear lobe, "but you are so…fucking…hot."

I arch my back and lean backward over the railing. "I had no plans of making out with an astrophysicist, like ever," I say, running my hands through Ava's chestnut-colored hair, "but you are fucking hot as well…"

"I don't have much time. We'll have to be quick," Ava says, taking deep breaths and undoing the knots of my top.

In the few seconds that we stop making out, we look at each other.

Her fingers work frantically on the knots, while her eyes peer deep into my soul.

My knees suddenly falter, and I feel my heart filling up with emotion.

"Your eyes are kind," I say.

"No one has ever said that to me. People mostly think I

am a cold-hearted bitch."

"People don't know shit. I know my shit. I can read people."

"What else can you read?"

"That you wish I hadn't tied these knots so tightly." I smile as Ava unties the last knot.

Straps of my dress fall off my shoulders, now revealing both of my breasts.

"My…god," Ava mutters.

She stands and gives my breasts an eyeful, while I smile at her childlike excitement.

"You like them?"

Ava replies by stuffing her face between them.

Her tongue explores my under-boob, and I feel my nipples hardening to their max potential.

I want them inside her mouth.

Behind us, the sound of helicopter blades rotating disturb the silence surrounding us.

Ava stops feasting on my tits for a second and looks past my shoulder.

"We have company," she says, and before I know it, I am pulled down to the floor by my shoulders, behind the opaque part of the balcony running parallel to the glass panes.

"Shit." A searing pain on the back of my neck makes me wince.

"Fuck!" Ava pulls her hand back from my shoulders and reaches for the railing.

"I broke your necklace," she says somberly, holding up my broken 'Aphrodite' chain with the Greek symbol of Aphrodite as the pendant.

"It got stuck in the railing, and broke as I pulled you down. I am so sorry!" Ava hands me the necklace.

"It's okay. Forget it. It's not very expensive."

"Are you hurt?"

"Yes, I am in extreme pain, Ava…pain of not having your mouth and hands all over me! Stop torturing me and continue what you were doing."

"The helicopter is right on top of us," Ava warns.

"Good, let them enjoy a few minutes of excitement in their mostly boring job."

Ava smiles and pushes me flat against the cold, granite floor of the observation desk.

My head rests against the hardness of the floor, but I don't care.

I watch as Ava lowers her face on my tits and starts sucking one again, while palming and kneading the other.

My tits aren't very big, and I feel a little insecure as Ava tries to grab a handful with some difficulty.

But soon, Ava's mouth alternating between my tits makes me forget all about my tiny tits and makes me arch my body in sheer, unadulterated pleasure.

I part my legs and groan, "Fuck me, Ava. Please fuck

me!"

Ava sighs and, without leaving the assault on my nipples, pushes the hem of my skirt up my legs, and finds my soaking-wet panties.

She pulls them to the side.

I love it when a woman does that.

It tells me they are impatient.

That they don't have the time to undress me. They would rather make space for themselves, in the shortest time possible.

"Yes!" I moan, as Ava toys with my pussy lips, rubbing the edges of my opening, while swirling her tongue around my nipples.

"Don't…" I gasp.

"Don't what?"

"Don't make me beg for it."

"That's exactly what I want you to do."

"Power…you like power, don't you?"

"I like beautiful girls begging me to thrust my fingers in them."

"Then do it, baby. Stick them in. As far as they go. Please! Please!"

Ava succumbs to her own impatience and enters me.

I let out a muffled scream as I clasp my arm over my mouth.

I didn't want to be caught indulging in lesbian sex in an

Islamic country like Dubai.

Although, I hear prison isn't that bad for lesbians.

It took Ava one finger and a few thrusts to get me cumming all over her hand.

I was embarrassed.

I hadn't cum so soon in months, or maybe years.

"That was quick," Ava laughed, licking my juices off her fingers.

"Thanks for confirming what I was only assuming," I say, feeling my cheeks going red.

"It's okay, I have this effect on girls."

"An assertive woman scientist who is full of herself, do you *want* to make me fall for you hopelessly?"

"No, I want you to help me cum."

"How can I be of help?" I ask.

"By staring at me with your beautiful blue eyes and playing with your tits."

"What? That's it?"

"Yes, I don't need much."

Ava straddles me in a way that my thighs are pressed firm against her crotch.

She lifts her dress, and I feel her pussy on my thigh.

It is wet, leaking, and warm with desire.

Ava starts rubbing herself on my thigh.

"I am ready for round two." I hand Ava the vibrator,

who inserts it inside my pussy and presses a button on the remote.

The vibrator comes to life.

So does Ava's need to ravish my thigh.

She starts riding my leg, like a cowgirl on a mechanical bull.

Her expressions change from sophisticated ecstasy to ugly lust.

She is sucking her teeth, groaning wildly, and putting her all into feeling my skin rub against her clit.

"Play with your tits," she commands me.

I grab them hesitantly. I am still insecure about their size.

"They are perfect. They are heavenly. And they are the ones that convinced me to fuck you."

It's like Ava has read my mind, but I don't let my surprise boil to the surface.

Hearing her call my breasts heavenly gives me the boost of confidence I need, and I grab them and press them hard for Ava.

"Is this turning you on? Watching a 20-year-old manhandle her tits for you? Huh? Do you like fucking my leg? You like feeling my young skin?"

"Oh fuck yes!!!" Ava screams and cums.

It's all over.

She collapses on top of me, as the sound of the

helicopter fades into the distance.

Did we really put on a show for them?

Am I really focusing on that right now? What's wrong with you, Bella?

I hug Ava, and suddenly, she backs away.

I am confused.

"That was…amazing. You are really hot, Bella."

Ava stands up, and I am forced to stand as well.

"Are you leaving?"

"I have to meet Samantha at 11 in one of the restaurants in this building. We have planned our own little afterparty."

I look at my watch. It's 10:50 pm.

"But I didn't even get to see you naked?"

"Was it really required?"

I make a face that says 'duh'.

"Maybe next time?"

"Ava, you can't just leave like this."

I try to soften my tone, but I let slip in the frustration anyway.

"I am sorry. I wish I had more time. But I really don't. I…am thankful that your 'spotlight' chose me tonight. Otherwise, this party would have been torture for me. And thank you for the amazing time." Ava extends her hand for a handshake, and I look at it in disbelief.

"You are more Gen Z than me, an actual Gen Z! Are we really going to say bye with a handshake?"

"Why not? Do you want a goodbye kiss? I can give you one if you want."

"What? Not like this! I can't believe this is happening. Anyway, thanks for your time, Ms. Ava, I am glad my legs could be of service to you tonight."

Ava looks at me with pity.

I hate that.

"I'll see you around, Bella."

"How? We don't have each other's numbers."

"I'll reach out to you."

I scoff.

"No need."

I pick up my broken chain from the floor and stuff it inside my clutch, along with the vibrator and the remote, while Ava watches me curiously.

"What are you looking at?" I ask her.

"How beautiful you are."

"Then why are you leaving me?"

"Because I am 39, and you are 20, and I can read people too. You look like someone looking for love."

Is it that obvious?

"You are wrong," I say resolutely.

"Maybe. But I can't take the chance. Goodbye, Bella, or

should I say, Aphrodite?"

Ava turns around and leaves me with the sight of her perfectly shaped hips and the sound of her heels.

"What a night," I murmur and follow behind her.

∞∞∞

My phone wakes me up, and I grudgingly look at the screen to see who has dared to disturb me from my slumber.

"Yes," I say in a drowsy, raspy voice.

"I need you!" Sophia whispers urgently from the other end.

"I need sleep, bitch," I say lazily.

"I am at a cafe with my mom, and things are getting awkward at the rate of 36 'umms' per minute."

"Umm…so? How can I help?"

"You can bring your ass down here and help save me from this vortex of awkwardness."

"It's your mom, Sophia. How awkward can it be?"

"Don't you know what's it like between my mom and me?"

"No, because you never speak of it." I lift myself off the bed and sit cross-legged, staring out the window.

"There was a reason. Now, are you coming or not?"

"Do you know I landed at 2 am this morning from

a 14-hour flight from Dubai?" I stand up and stretch, admiring the shards of sunlight filtering through the netted window in my room.

"I know, and I also know you had sex with a lovely old lady while you were over there, so I am very sorry if I am not able to empathize with your labors. The Little Sweet Cafe. 77 Hoyt Street, Brooklyn. Be there in the next 15 minutes."

Sophia hangs up on me, leaving me with no option but to visit her and her mother.

I decide to throw on a hoodie and gym leggings, anticipating the cold October weather of New York.

I look at myself in the mirror before stepping out and wonder if the 'old lady' that Sophia had mentioned would still appreciate my beauty if she saw me looking like a homeless teenager, with frizzy bed hair and sunken, sleep-deprived eyes.

Click Here To Continue Reading

Author's Note

Hi Readers,

I hope you enjoyed the romance between Sophia and Alissa, and had fun getting to know their story through this book. If you did, then it would be very helful to me if you could give this book a posive rating or review.

If you did not like something about book, please mail me at **agoswamibooks@gmail.com** , and I will make sure I give heed to your constructive feedback, or you can just mail me to say Hi, i would love to interact with you!

Join my newsletter for new release updates, discounts and free books by clicking here or going to this link : mailchi.mp/8f0f411551ce/a-goswami

Happy Reading!

A. Goswami

Books By This Author

A Royal Runaway Roadtrip

The Queen Of My Heart

The Fire Between Us

Beyond Boundaries

Stumbling Into Happiness